"With seven Cooperman mysteries behind him, Howard Engel is in danger of becoming a national treasure."

The Gazette (Montreal)

"*Dead and Buried* is first-rate mystery."

Toronto Sun

"Engel's string of Cooperman novels have been consistently excellent."

The Hamilton Spectator

"Bound to delight . . ."

Star-Phoenix (Saskatoon)

"A riveting read . . ."

St. John's Sunday Express

"In *Dead and Buried*, Engel again delivers a quality mystery with a distinctly Canadian flavour."

Quill & Quire

D1311191

PENGUIN BOOKS

Dead and Buried

Howard Engel was born in Toronto but raised in
St. Catharines, Ontario. He later lived in Nicosia,
London and Paris, where he worked as a journalist
and broadcaster. Back in Canada he became a distinguished producer of programs at the CBC,
where he stayed for many years. *Dead and Buried* is
his seventh novel in a series that includes *The
Suicide Murders, The Ransom Game, Murder on
Location, Murder Sees the Light, A City Called July*
and *A Victim Must Be Found*. His endearing private
eye, Benny Cooperman, has been described as a
cherished national institution. He is also rapidly
becoming known internationally through the
many foreign editions of his adventures. Both *The
Suicide Murders* and *Murder Sees the Light* were
made into TV films. Engel is a member of the
Mystery Writers of America, the British Crime
Writers' Association and a founding member of
the Crime Writers' Association of Canada. He was
1984 winner of the Arthur Ellis Award for crime
fiction. He lives with his wife, the writer Janet
Hamilton, his son, Jacob and his two cats in
Toronto.

Dead
and
Buried

A Benny Cooperman Mystery

Howard Engel

Penguin Books

PENGUIN BOOKS
Published by the Penguin Group
Penguin Books Canada Ltd, 10 Alcorn Avenue, Toronto, Ontario,
Canada M4V 3B2
Penguin Books Ltd, 27 Wrights Lane, London W8 5TZ, England
Penguin Books USA Inc., 375 Hudson Street, New York, New York 10014, U.S.A.
Penguin Books Australia Ltd, Ringwood, Victoria, Australia
Penguin Books (NZ) Ltd, 182-190 Wairau Road, Auckland 10, New Zealand

Penguin Books Ltd, Registered Offices: Harmondsworth, Middlesex, England

First published in Viking by Penguin Books Canada Limited, 1990

Published in Penguin Books, 1991

1 3 5 7 9 10 8 6 4 2

Manufactured in Canada

Canadian Cataloguing in Publication Data
Engel, Howard, 1931-
Dead and buried

ISBN 0-14-012920-0

I. Title.

PS8559.N44D4 1991   C813'.54   C90-094015-8
PR9199.3.E54D4 1991

*For my friend
David Berger,
1936–1989*

I would like to express thanks to my friend Doug Monk for his help in getting the business, corporate and taxation details as nearly correct as they appear. Any errors, of course, are mine, not his. I would also like to thank my friend Gary Thaler for putting me in touch with Hesperis matronalis, *upon which so much depends.*

Dead
and
Buried

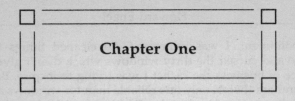

Chapter One

I rma Dowden looked over my office. She took in the convenient downtown location, the active business files scattered in front of me and the framed licence behind my desk. Furtively she gave the cotton-draped mannequins in the corner a rapid scrutiny. Their breasts were peeking out from under the cloth again. I cleared my throat before she formed a question. "My father closed out his ladies' ready-to-wear business downstairs," I explained. "I'm temporarily minding some of his things. You may speak quite freely in front of them."

She nodded like she knew already. Come to think of it, the mannequins had been around for a few years now. Even without their wigs and wearing a dusty remnant of factory cotton, the trio had become indispensable for second to fourth opinions. As company, they still made me nervous. But Mrs Dowden didn't want to know about that. She sat there, cheeks daubed with half-hearted rouge, straight as a post, with her black purse in her lap.

"How can I help you, Mrs Dowden?" I pushed the files to one side. I didn't want to discourage her by suggesting that I had other business on hold while we shot the unprofitable breeze. I sat there, giving her all my attention and trying to look affordable. That little black purse could buy my time for a few days at least.

Irma Dowden hadn't just walked in my door that Tuesday in early October; she'd phoned first for an

1

appointment. I was impressed. I'd cleaned things up a little and cursed the dirty windows which didn't give my place of business the cachet I was trying to inspire. But in Grantham there's only one reliable man for windows and I hadn't seen him in months. Waiting for Mrs Dowden to keep her three o'clock appointment had made me nervous. I had even thought of getting up and opening the door for her, but the last time I did that it was a patient of Frank Bushmill's, the chiropodist who shares the running toilet, the rent and the second floor overlooking St Andrew Street with me. I realized I was rambling in my thoughts, so I asked my question a second time.

"Did you read in the paper about Jack?" she asked, her eyes like two black currants rolling in my direction. I told her I'd not read anything about Jack, whoever Jack might be, but I was prepared to be sympathetic. She pulled a clipping from her purse and handed it to me. A pencil scrawl in the white space on one side of a heading said: 16 July. That was nearly three months ago. I recognized the type as belonging to the local paper, the *Beacon*. It was a small item, insignificant enough so that I was now no longer guilt-ridden for missing it in the first place. The heading read: LOCAL MAN CRUSHED BY TRUCK. The story described the death of Jack Dowden on the 13th at the yard of Kinross Disposals. The truck had apparently slipped off the brake and pinned Dowden against a cement brick wall. I read the details and handed the clipping back to Irma, who was now looking like she was Jack's widow.

"I'm sorry," I said. She nodded her head in sympathy with mine. She looked small and insubstantial sitting there. The falseness of the rouge was standing out on her velveteen cheeks in the greying light coming in through my venetian blinds. I went back to my opening question for the third time: "How can I help you, Mrs Dowden?"

She leaned closer to my desk and tried to find the words that would convince me to take her case. "Mr Cooperman, I want you to look into Jack's death. I think they murdered him, the bastards, I do!" That made me blink and I smiled to encourage her to go on. At the same time, my heart was joining the *Titanic* on the bottom of the North Atlantic. Rule number one for private investigators: you'll never make a nickel competing with the cops. I asked Mrs Dowden to continue. She moistened her narrow lips and tried to find the place where she'd left off.

"Jack wasn't the sort to get himself killed in an accident like that," she said. "I've lived with the man these eighteen years and I know the things he'll do and the things he won't. If they told me he'd run off with the payroll, I wouldn't have liked it, but it would have been like him. Jack could do a daft thing like spending his wages on a pine cupboard, anything made of wood, but walk in front of his truck, no sir. When it comes to machines, Jack was as careful as an airline pilot. You see, his friend Charlie Bowman was killed that way ten years ago."

"Was there an inquest into your husband's death, Mrs Dowden?"

"Oh, yes. They held one of those. Company doctor told how he came on the scene and there was nothing he could do. A company director told how there were signs posted everywhere warning the drivers to be careful. Another driver said that Jack hadn't been keeping his mind on the work the last few weeks. Well, that's a plain lie and Brian O'Mara knows that, Mr Cooperman."

"O'Mara's the other driver, right?" She nodded. "Who's the company doctor?"

"Name's Carswell. Imagine him just happening to be there!" I wrote down the names on a pad of paper that so far only held the name of my client.

"Why do you say O'Mara lied at the inquest?"

"I don't know why he lied, unless he was paid off, but I know for a fact that Jack was talking about the job all the time. He never shut up about it. He was more involved in his work than before, not less."

"I see," I said, drumming my ballpoint pen on the desk and trying to look intelligent. "What do you think was on Jack's mind?"

"He was worried about the stuff he was hauling, that's what. I'll admit he was worried, but he wasn't ever careless with his truck."

"And you think they murdered him? Who exactly is *they*, Mrs Dowden?"

"Why, Kinross, of course. All of them. They just roll over little people like us!" She looked at her knuckles for a minute before going on. They looked cold. "I want you to see if Jack was killed to hush up something he found out about. I know he was murdered. I'm not looking for another whitewashing inquest. I want you to find out what Kinross wanted covered up."

"You don't want much, do you?" She looked back at me with a set jaw and steady eyes.

"I want you to get the goods on Kinross. You'll do us all a favour if you put them out of business."

"Look, Mrs Dowden, that's not really my sort of thing. You know I used to do mostly divorce work. I look into small fraud cases and some family law. I don't usually get involved with outfits as big as Kinross. And I don't dig up dirt just to make things look bad, not even to please a lady." She was looking over my shoulder to the wall where my licence was hanging in its Woolworth's frame. She didn't rush her answer.

"Mr Cooperman, I'm not asking for you to be making things up about Kinross. I didn't say it right. I *know* the dirt's there. But I don't expect you to be convinced just because I say so. I tried speaking to the police about Jack's death. They don't want to get involved."

"They didn't say that, Mrs Dowden."

"No, but they thought the inquest was very convincing. It was tidy, all tied up at the end like a movie. If Jack wasn't my husband, I'd have been taken in by it too. But he is—was—so I could see through it. They appeared to be so concerned for my welfare, so broken up about their spoiled safety record, so solemn about everything. They sent me a big cheque. If it had been smaller, I would have been less suspicious. It seemed to say 'keep your mouth shut and nobody'll get into trouble.'" By now she was daubing at her eyes with a small piece of blue tissue. I pushed the box of Kleenex across to her side of the desk.

"What else have you got for me besides this? You have to admit that the cheque could be seen as the very opposite of what you're saying just as well. What else is there?"

"Another cheque! I phoned Brian O'Mara—the other driver?—just to talk, you know? And I got another cheque a week later."

"These things might not be related."

"When they sent back Jack's things, there was another cheque, Mr Cooperman. There's a fishy smell to it. I watch TV. This has cover-up written all over it."

I tried to explain to her about the differences between real life and television. She wasn't listening. "Businesses do a lot of crazy things, Mrs Dowden, but not all of them are illegal. Have you been threatened in any way? Have you been warned off?"

"I went up to the yard where it happened."

"On the Scrampton Road?"

"Oh, you know the place?"

"A divorce case once took me up there." It was a dusty road I wanted to forget. The memory of that case was still green and unpleasant.

"I took a taxi one day when I couldn't stand it any more. Jack was the driver in our family, I never learned. I wanted to see the scene of the crime."

"I hope you didn't call it that."

"Give me credit for some sense, Mr Cooperman. I went in the gate at about noon and I was back on the road in less than ten minutes. Everybody I talked to was so polite and understanding and helpful that it made my head spin. Everybody was so kind, it made me sick. You know what I mean? I felt like I'd been handled, manipulated like a puppet. I still haven't seen the place where it happened."

"What do you think I can do?"

She looked at me like I'd been missing the point for the last half-hour. "You can go up there, can't you? Say you're taking a survey of some kind. A man can go places a woman can't. You can get the other drivers talking. Don't expect me to teach you your trade, Mr Cooperman. Will you help out a poor widow woman?" She tried to look as pathetic as she sounded, but the phrase "widow woman" was overplaying her hand. Without a grey hair in her head and with a jaw that strutted its independence, she looked a lot of things, but helpless wasn't one of them. I tried to imagine Irma Dowden in her prime: tiny, animated and cheeky. The late Jack Dowden had a formidable champion in his widow.

"What do you say to this?" I said. "Supposing I go up there to Kinross's yard, supposing I dig around for a couple of days and come up with nothing more than a case of ptomaine poisoning from those fast-food outlets on the Scrampton Road. What then?"

"I can try somebody else. There are three other private investigators in the book, Mr Cooperman."

"Wherever you go, it's going to cost you." Irma moved the corners of her mouth. It wasn't a smile, but maybe the ghost of one. "Mrs Dowden, hiring a private investigator can run you into money. I hope you know that."

"I've got his insurance money. I thought I could die of old age waiting, judging from the stories I've heard, but the company saw to it that the insurance was paid in record time." I made a note of that on my pad. Something for the record books. "You know, Mr Cooperman, Jack wouldn't want me blowing his money on a big headstone. Whatever way I look, this is the best way to use all that money. Somebody killed Jack, you see. If you won't help me find out who did it, I'll find a detective who will. I'll do it myself, if I have to."

"My rates are three hundred and twenty-five a day plus expenses." The hard numbers sometimes sober clients who are really playing around or looking for sympathy. Irma Dowden kept her steely eyes on mine. Never a wobble escaped her out-thrust chin. She reached into her black leather purse and left a flush of pink fifty-dollar bills on my desk. I felt guilty just looking at them. I didn't have the nerve to pick them up and feel them in my fingers.

"I'll want to ask you some more questions, Mrs Dowden, after I've had a chance to think about the case as it is shaping up. How can I get in touch with you?" She gave me an address on Glen Avenue, off Hamilton Street, over on Western Hill, and a phone number. I was thinking how much bigger fifty-dollar bills look than twenties, when Mrs Dowden got up. On the way to the door, she told me that she hoped I wouldn't get hurt. I smiled confidently at her as she headed for the stairs. As she went down them, I started feeling the pain in my nose where I'd been hit the last time I went through the gate that guarded the Kinross yard on the Scrampton Road.

Chapter Two

D r Gary Carswell was not answering his telephone. I got a worn-out recorded message on his answering machine that was no asset to his practice. Even the beep at the end sounded like a badly administered hypodermic needle surprising a tenor in the rear. I left a message.

When Irma Dowden had left my office, I started wondering how badly I needed her money. There was something about what she'd told me that didn't ring like my mother's crystal wine glasses. I couldn't put my finger on it, and hiked down James Street to the library. In the reference section, I looked up Kinross Disposals in a directory of Canadian businesses. The first news was good; there was no sign of Ross Forbes. He had been Chief Executive Officer at Kinross when I was acting for his estranged wife. The honcho of the moment was Norman Caine, who was new to my files, I was glad to note. That made me feel a little better about things. In the newspaper-and-periodical section, I went to the stack of old newspapers. My friend Ella Beames, who used to run the special collections department, and who had always been a big help to me in the past, before she retired to Newburyport, Massachusetts, told me that if you dug down deep enough in the stack of local papers, you could come up with the first in the series. They used to have a man on staff who pasted stiff paper on the insides of the covers of magazines and then carted them off unread to a vault somewhere, but they'd got rid of him. Here at the Grantham Library, library science was tempered by local need. Having the old papers on microfilm or in a warehouse on the bank of the Eleven Mile Creek met no local need, so, when you wanted to find an obituary, as I did, all you had to do was dig in. I dug in.

The date on Irma Dowden's clipping had been July 16. I found the 12th, 13th and then the 14th and 15th, but no 16th. What was going on? I looked closer. The 15th was a Saturday. Of course, there was no *Beacon* on the 16th; it was a Sunday and there is no Sunday *Beacon*. That set me back, but I ploughed through the papers around my date and hoped for the best. Nothing. Not only couldn't I find an obituary, or a notice of death, but I couldn't even find the clipping I'd just read in my office. Things were moving in the direction of peculiar, and peculiar gives me gas.

After about ten minutes, I gave up the search. I knew it had something to do with the uneasy feeling I had about my client. I had to go along with the facts in the library: either the death of Jack Dowden hadn't rated a word in the papers or it hadn't occurred. If Jack's death was phoney, why did the money his widow gave me look so real?

From one of the pay-phones in the lobby, where school kids were drinking pop from the refreshment stand, I made a call to Chet Bryant, the crown prosecutor. I identified myself to him, and he saw no reason why I shouldn't be able to have a look at a copy of the Jack Dowden inquest transcript. After checking with his secretary to see if there was a copy in the files, he told me to come right over.

Shortly after that, I was sitting in Bryant's outer office, staring at the date on the transcript, while his secretary prepared to leave the office for the day. I watched her clear her desk of every scrap of paper and rubber bands and turn the key in the drawer. I looked down on the open file on the death of John Edward Dowden.

"Shit!"

"I beg your pardon?"

"Damn, damn, damn!"

"Mr Cooperman, are you all right?"

"No! I've been had! Jack Dowden didn't die three months ago, he died a *year* and three months ago! No wonder I couldn't find it in the papers!"

"That still doesn't account for your language, Mr Cooperman."

"How do I get sucked into these things?" Bryant's secretary looked like she had an answer. Some people don't know how to deal with rhetorical questions. Others have problems with clients with beady black eyes and black leather handbags to match.

Bryant's secretary snapped closed the buttons along a line of filing cabinets. I hoped the keys were inside one of them. It was with little enthusiasm that I glanced at the transcript.

The medical evidence presented at the inquest showed that Jack Dowden had died of injuries consistent with being leaned on by a ten-ton truck. Three men on the site saw the truck roll from a parked position and catch Dowden by surprise against a wall of concrete blocks. I noted the names of the witnesses, recognizing, in passing, the name I already knew: Brian O'Mara. The other two were Tadeuss Puisans and Luigi Pegoraro. They gave the alarm, and that brought the doctor, Gary Carswell, to the scene. He examined Dowden and declared that in his opinion the man had suffered a crushed ribcage and possibly a broken spine. Dowden had lost consciousness immediately and died almost at once. The medical examination dressed up the doctor's guess in finer words, but the diagnosis at the scene of the accident was upheld.

The inquest added details to the clipping that Irma Dowden, my fibbing client, had shown me, but the facts remained about the same. The false date was the only lie I had caught her in so far. And Dowden was still just as dead.

I was curious about the company doctor. What was Carswell doing at the yard on the day of the accident? It was just a little too neat. I was beginning to think like my client. I looked deeper into the transcript to find out.

Q. Dr Carswell, how did it happen that you were at the yard that morning?

A. I had arranged to see Norm Caine. We were going to have a bite of breakfast together. But he wasn't there.

Q. Do you have a regular association with Kinross?

A. Primarily I'm in private practice here in the city, but I also have a part-time association with Kinross, where I act as a trouble-shooter for the company in the whole area of ecological concerns. I'm gravely involved in the issue of the disposal of toxic wastes. I've been called an expert in the field, although I make no such claim myself. Some say I'm an apologist for the company. That is nonsense, of course. I also attend to the full range of medical matters involving the workmen during my visits to the yard.

Q. When did this association begin?

A. Early April of this year . . .

Walking back to my office, I got to thinking about the sort of mess I was getting myself into. Dowden had been hauling hazardous toxic wastes in his truck. How close did I want to get to that? Toxic wastes make me nervous. I can take all the areas of family law and never lose a night's sleep, but the moment I get involved in our polluted environment I begin tossing and turning all night. It's a bit like all those requests for charity I get in the mail. They are

all worthy causes, but I can't afford to support them all, so
how can I choose? Maybe I am getting too old to be
involved in a subject that affects the future of the planet. I
remembered a series of articles in the *Beacon* last year.
They were calculated to keep me awake all night. The
writer told how toxic wastes were being mixed with fuel
and moved across the U.S./Canadian border. That was
when a provincial investigation started to probe the behaviour of the firms involved. Dr Carswell joined Kinross
in April? Yeah, the timing was about right.

I recognized that any illegal activity involving the disposal of hazardous chemical wastes was a worthy subject
for investigation, but with the full resources of the province of Ontario on the trail of wrongdoers, what did they
need me for? I was just a little guy trying to make a living.
Wasn't Environment Front the organization that blew the
whistle on all aspects of pollution? Weren't they commit-
ted to saving the planet? They are the guys who should be
getting Kinross to clean up their act. How can I make them
ozone-friendly overnight? I'm a one-man operation. Another thing worried me. It was a question of mental health.
I had to protect myself from knowing chapter and verse on
the dumping of toxic industrial wastes. Too much knowledge is a dangerous thing, especially when the facts can be
detected in so many parts per million in my drinking
water.

At the corner of James and St Andrew, I ran into Chet
Bryant on his way back to his office. There was a sweet
smell of a friendly drink on his breath. Since he towered
above me by a full foot, I wasn't about to mention the old-
fashioned boozy way Grantham still carried on business.
The wheels of Grantham had always been set in motion in
a back room at the Grantham Club and it looked like
things weren't about to change. I reminded him that I'd
just left his office.

"That's right. Why the hell are you getting into that old case?"

"Just a little research I'm doing. Nothing to get excited about." Chet nodded without believing me and kept his eye on the changing stoplights over my shoulder.

"Sure, sure," he said. "For an old file, that one's been getting a lot of action lately."

"What do you mean?"

"Oh, Thelma—that's my secretary—said that one of those Environment Front people was in to see it a couple of days ago." The light must have changed, because Chet beamed down a big smile and challenged me to have a good day. Since it was already getting dark, I couldn't see how I could improve on what I'd already had. He was half-way across the street before I decided that no answer was expected. That's when I climbed up the twenty-eight stairs to my second-floor office and made my call to Dr Carswell.

I made two other calls while waiting for Dr Carswell to catch up to his accumulated messages. The first failed to find my client at the number she'd given me; the second failed to find anybody at Secord University's History Department where Anna Abraham worked. No answer got me off the hook as far as dinner was concerned, but it did nothing for that part of me that wanted to hear her voice. Anna was becoming an important part of my life, and I hadn't heard from her since Saturday night. I didn't like calling her father's place up on the escarpment above the city, because I didn't want to imagine the expression on Jonah Abraham's face if he took the call. Abraham and I weren't in the same tax bracket for a start. He'd been a client of mine, which didn't make things any easier. The fact that I knew the father before I met the daughter confused things. I didn't like to mix business with pleasure. I'm sure he felt the same way, and I don't think he liked the idea of his only daughter being my idea of pleasure. I resolved to try her later in the evening, in spite of my reservations.

I was on the point of going out for cigarettes, when I caught Dr Carswell calling back. I jumped in before my answering service could take the message and garble it. I wonder whether they have a scrambler specialist on the payroll, somebody who can make Henry Gibson into Henrik Ibsen without even trying. I explained to Carswell who I was, and that I was looking for information and checking some facts. He agreed to see me after his last patient at six-thirty that night. Good, I thought, at least I'll be able to talk to him before I make a call on Irma Dowden. At least I'll have been able to add something to the facts in the clipping. That would show I'd been working.

There was over an hour, nearly two hours to kill before setting out to see Carswell. I spent the first half-hour paying bills to the various oil companies that fuelled my car. I began feeling guilty about tapping limited fossil fuels and helping to wipe out the remaining Indians along the Amazon. Was I aiding and abetting in the destruction of rain forests somewhere, or perhaps killing North Sea seal pups? Once you dip into the question of pollution, you soon discover that it's all around you and that you are the chief villain. I needed to confess to having stuck gum under my desk at Edith Cavell School, to not bundling and salvaging my collected newspapers and to using leaded gas in the car. I was a mass of vices calculated to destroy the ozone layer and speed along the disastrous results of the greenhouse effect. I looked at the yellow patch of ceiling above my desk, my own area of peak pollution. I resolved to put a piece of time away to begin thinking about cutting down on my tar intake. I made an appointment with myself to consider a plan to bite the bullet. I frightened myself out into the street and lighted up a

Player's until all was right with the world again.

There was still time enough to pay a fast visit to my friend Martin Lyster, who was a patient in the Grantham General. He was a book dealer around town and I heard that he was in a bad way. I'd been putting off this trip for over a week.

After getting the room number from Admitting, I took the elevator to the fifth floor, where I walked past the nursing station to Room 509. My hands were sweating already. I poked my head through the half-open door. Martin was in neither of the beds in this semi-private room. The first was occupied by a man with a bright orange face, partly covered by an oxygen mask. His open eyes were wide and staring, his breathing was frantic. The second bed, by the window, was empty. I was about to turn and check the door number again when a familiar voice called my name.

"Benny! Are you looking for me?" I followed the sound of the voice to a corner partly obscured by the open bathroom door. Martin, dressed in a striped terry-cloth robe, was sitting in a chair reading the *New York Times*. He was incredibly thin.

"Hello. I heard you were in here," I said, and added stupidly, "How are you?"

"Much better, Benny. I think they've got a pretty good idea about this thing now. It's taken them long enough, I'll tell you. They won't let me smoke or drink. I think they want to quarantine my liver. They've got a lien on my lungs." Martin still sounded like Martin, although he looked terrible. He was wearing half-moon glasses. There is something indestructible-looking about people in half-moon glasses. Martin was still speaking, but my day-dreaming had partially tuned him out. What was he saying?

". . . I found a Brian Moore you might be interested in."

"Who?"

"He wrote it under a pseudonym. Early on, you know. It's a detective story. That's right up your street, isn't it? I told Anna all about it when she came to see me."

"Anna? Oh, sure, she told me she'd been in."

"Would you like to take a walk down to the end of the corridor with me?"

"Sure." I helped him to his feet. I could hardly find an arm inside the sleeve of his robe. He was as light as cream, and it frightened me as we moved past the IV stands and folded wheelchairs to and beyond the nursing station. Nobody looked up as we went by.

"You've got a wonderful woman in Anna, you know, Benny. She's read just about everything. What a girl! I think I'm going to get serious about finding somebody. We Irish always marry late. It's time. I can see that."

"Anna's great, Martin, but the knot isn't tied yet. We're not a number yet. It's early days. Her old man's suspicion may be the only thing that's holding us together. But you're right. I think she's great too."

"I told her about the Moore and she knew the title. How do you like that?" Martin leaned into the window alcove at the end of the passage. For a minute or two we watched the eddying circles of fallen leaves down in the street below. They blew in and out of pools of light around the streetlights. It was all rather theatrical.

"Are you still fighting your fate, Benny?"

"If I read you right, I guess I can say that I'm still resisting a call to manpower about a *real* job? Is that what you meant?"

"Look, Benny, you and I are alike. We're a dying breed. We're nearly extinct. What is it the French call it? We're the *fin de race*, the end of the line. We're the last individuals left in town. Nobody rates independence any more. It doesn't count. Everybody's into life-styles and sitting pretty. I'll tell you, Benny, we are witnessing the Yuppification of North America. The bottom line has replaced what we used to call ethics. It's a terrible, terrible thing, Benny. You understand me?"

"Everything has its price but nothing has any value? Something like that?" He turned to rest his behind on the window ledge. He was breathing hard.

"Now Anna, Benny, she's a great woman, but even the good ones slow you down. She'll put fancy doilies on all of your rolling stones. I know what I'm talking about."

"I thought you wanted to settle down?"

"I do, I do." He was smiling. "But I haven't got the rhetoric down yet. It's slow work, Benny. Let's go back to the room, okay?"

"Sure. I have a hard time picturing you inside a picket fence, Martin."

"Just keep watching. But, before I settle down, I'm going to go south when spring training comes around. I want to cover the Blue Jays for the *Beacon* the way I did a year ago."

"Is that Sarasota?"

"That's circuses. I go to Dunedin. Ah, don't get me started about it. Baseball, Benny, baseball is the metaphor of our time. I want to explore that."

"You could do a book."

"I could indeed. And it would be *some* book. But first, I have to wait until they let me out of here. My doctor said this morning that I might be out by next weekend." His expression suddenly changed from a bright, many-lined grin to one of pain. "Oops, I think it's Demerol time."

Back in Room 509, Martin got into bed, still wearing the terry-cloth robe to help hide his wasted arms and legs. We talked for another few minutes. From the corner of my eye I could see that the man with the orange face, hidden from Martin by the curtains around that part of the bed, had stopped breathing. I was surprised, but I didn't say anything. It was so ordinary. He had been breathing when we came back to the room, but now he had stopped. There was a tear running down from the eye closest to me to the bright earlobe below it. I couldn't understand why I wasn't shouting, calling for help, raising the alarm. I simply said good-night to Martin, and mentioned what I had seen to a nurse at the nursing station on my way out.

"It was expected," she said with a sad smile, as though that would make me feel better.

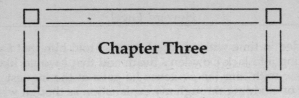
A t six-thirty I presented myself in the waiting room
of Dr Gary Carswell. He had a fine collection of old
magazines. For five minutes I read about the ban-
ning of mussels from Prince Edward Island and the arrival
of the Olympic torch in Calgary.

"Mr Cooperman?" I dropped the magazine and tried to
reorganize the pile I had taken it from, while getting to my
feet. Before me stood a huge bearded man of perhaps
thirty-five, no more. He was wearing an English-tailored
suit with a vest to cover his impressive belly. His sandy
hair was parted on the right; a lock of hair nearly covered
one of his eyebrows. The eyes themselves were wide-set
and squinting at me. A muscle in his cheek twitched and
his mouth moved. It resembled a pained smile. He repeated my name while we shook hands, and I followed the
doctor's retreating back into his inner sanctum.

It was an interior decorator's idea of what a doctor's
office should look like. The books on the dark wood
shelves looked unread. The plaques and citations on one
panelled wall were calculated to impress the visitor, to
create a welcome full of warmth and trust. On his broad
desk were picture frames with their backs turned towards
me. A family man no less. "Well, now," he said, placing
his palms flat on his desk top. "What can I do for you?"
For an educated man, he had a short memory. I repeated
the information about me and my profession. The doctor

19

nodded in time with my disclosures. I told him that I was looking into Jack Dowden's death and that I would like to review with him the evidence he gave at the inquest. He kept on nodding through my explanation as though what I was asking was as reasonable as seat belts and Christmas. Jack Dowden might have died yesterday; Carswell's interest couldn't be improved upon. He sat back in his chair, letting his bulk carry him hard against the spring, tilting towards the curtains, away from me. "Now, let's see," he said, placing a pair of chubby hands behind his head. "You would be representing somebody in this, Mr Cooperman. May I ask you who that might be?"

"Dr Carswell, that comes under the head of privileged information. You wouldn't tell me what's ailing Mrs Brown, if Mrs Brown was one of your patients. It's the same thing in my business. Now, Jack Dowden wasn't one of your patients; you just happened to be there when he died. You gave testimony at the inquest. I'd just like you to expand on what's already on the public record." I made a gesture to show that I wasn't asking for the crown jewels.

The doctor thought about that for a second, nodding over the width of his desk and bringing his brows together to add the necessary accoutrements to deep thought. He was generalling this interview very well so far. I was prepared for bad news. He was going to stonewall me with that smile on his face. "I see," he said. "Mr Cooperman, I don't quite know what to say. You see, in a way, Mr Dowden *was* my patient. I am retained by the company to deal with medical problems that arise from the dangerous substances that the Kinross people come in contact with. They routinely handle some very nasty things, you see, and I have to deal with things like skin eruptions and generally give advice about the results of contamination from these toxic wastes." He took a deep breath and he was off again, this time it sounded like part of a prepared text.

"You know, everybody's excited about what's happening to the environment these days, and the Environment Front people aren't above using scare tactics, exaggerations and half-truths. That's why you see my face on television so often. I'm just trying to keep things in perspective."

"Excuse me, Doctor, but what has this got to do with Dowden's death?"

"The point is, Mr Cooperman, that I've been turned into a busy man by all this. I have to watch my time. I don't want to insist on that, but since I've already said everything about the incident at the inquest . . . You see what I mean? It's all on public record. Besides, I don't think I have anything more to add that would be helpful. You see the spot you put me in? And, remember, it was well over a year ago."

Now it was my turn to nod and look sage. It's easier to do sitting behind a desk. Carswell wasn't going to give me much time. He was already shifting papers off his desk and into an attaché case. "I think I understand your position, Doctor," I said. "I'd just like to be sure that the account of the injuries sustained in the accident square with the circumstances described in the inquest transcript."

"Well, I can put your mind at rest there, Mr Cooperman. I was one of the first on the scene, and I saw the man just after it happened."

"But you didn't actually see the accident?"

"No. I thought you said you'd read the coroner's report?" He was getting angry now, but keeping his hands on the arms of his chair helped to modulate his voice. I tried grinning to ease the situation.

"I'm just trying to get it clear in my head."

"I understand your problem, Mr Cooperman, but I don't see how I can help you. I don't think that Norman Caine would appreciate me speaking to you without you going through him first. I'm sure that that would be his view and I'm sure that Ross Forbes would back him up in that."

"What does Ross Forbes have to do with this?" I thought I had put that name behind me for all time. "He's no longer top man at Kinross, is he?" I hoped that my agitation wasn't showing. I wanted nothing further to do with Ross Forbes.

"Of course not," Carswell said, pitying my ignorance, "but he is still CEO at Phidias Manufacturing. Kinross, Mr Cooperman, is a subsidiary of Phidias. Ross Forbes would support Mr Caine in this, I think."

"You've changed a speculation into a certainty, Doctor." Carswell got up, terminating our conversation.

"Look," Carswell said, elongating the word so that it sounded like sweet reason, "I'd like to go on talking to you, Mr Cooperman, but I'm due to appear on a panel at the television station in less than an hour. As a matter of fact I'm going to debate some of the things we've been talking about." He moved around to my side of his desk. "It seems to me that you have just started your work on this. Am I right?" He didn't wait for an answer. He went right on talking as though I'd smiled, nodded or mimed assent. "After you get your feet wet, give me another call and I'll see what I can do for you. Your questions about Kinross and Phidias are all basic research. There are answers you can get from other sources. I think there is somebody up at the university researching a history of Kinross. It goes back to the beginning of the last century, you know."

I didn't know, so I hiked up one of my eyebrows to show surprise. I was impressed. In 1800 there can't have been much industry around Grantham. For a minute I thought I'd awakened the born teacher in him, but he quickly regretted the impulse and took early retirement.

When he beat me to the door, we shook hands and parted
on friendly terms. Only he wasn't feeling about as stupid
as moss. I was burning mad at the way things had happened today. At three o'clock I'd never heard of Jack
Dowden. Now the doctor was expecting me to be an
expert in everything he touched. Sure, I was out for
learning. My ignorance was almost total. Why not? Dr
Carswell watched me go through the waiting room to the
front door, judging by the sensation between my shoulder-
blades.

I walked up Ontario Street, feeling a cold wind blowing
off the park. Winter was coming, I thought, as a few rusty
leaves blew across my path. I remembered the smell of
burning leaves from years ago. The environment was now
safe from the smoke of burning leaves. It got plastic
garbage bags instead.

Back in my office, I tried Irma Dowden's number again.
She was still out on the town. Maybe she was bending the
ear of another investigator about her year-old loss. I tried
to imagine her jockeying three or more cards in a church
basement bingo game on Pelham Road. I made a mental
note to call her later.

The chief ingredient adding to the acid in my stomach
was the fact that Ross Forbes's name was back in the case.
My memory of picking myself out of his petunia bed in
front of his office at Kinross was still fresh, in spite of the
time that had gone by. It was a lucky punch, of course. He
was as surprised by it as I was. I remembered that I bled a
lot. Some of it got on his suit, I think. I hope he had to
scrap it.

That was ten years ago. I'd been hired by his estranged
wife to keep an eye on him. I played a small part in a long
and well-publicized divorce proceeding. My client, Teddie
Forbes, made a lot of money in the settlement. In spite of
this, it took me nearly a year and a half to collect the eleven

hundred dollars she owed me for getting to know her old ball and chain. That included my trip to the General to have my nose cauterized.

I checked my city directory and found the name of a friend of Teddie's. She put me on her trail and I had her on the other end of the phone in less time than it takes to smoke three Player's cigarettes. I tried not to look at my stained ceiling. Teddie had been a dressage rider when I first met her, and she still haunted horse shows all over the country and down into the States. She told me that she was staying in town temporarily, getting ready to leave again for Flagstaff, Arizona, but she agreed to have a drink with me. I didn't tell her what prompted the invitation, but it wouldn't be hard for her to guess. The end of my nose twitched at even the thought of the man that pulled us together. Passion is a wonderful thing. It was enough for Teddie to cancel her plans for the evening or to postpone a quiet hour or two bringing her scrapbook up to date. Better to sit across from me discussing her old *bête noire*. That punch in the nose could almost make me forget that I was working for a woman I couldn't trust. If I was in my right mind, I'd stop dieselling on about the past. The ignition had been turned off too long ago.

Chapter Four

"It's been sooo long, Benny. It's years since we did our little number on poor Ross," Teddie said, sending a broad smile across the table. "You're lucky to catch me in, you know. I'm only here for the wedding. Then I'm off to Arizona for the winter."

"It's only the beginning of October."

"Well, between you and me, Benny, I hate to stay cooped up in this town. I don't know how you handle it. Really I don't. I mean you're not so old, you've got a portable profession. I don't see the attraction, frankly."

Teddie Forbes had pressed my hand with something of the ancient warmth when she'd arrived in the Snug. She was looking at me so intently that I had to let my eyes wander away to the velvet and leather decor of the room. It was full of overtones of Ireland, from the piped-in music to the foolish leprechauns on the coasters under the drinks. She'd been her usual ten minutes late, just for old times, and I'd had plenty of time to take in the throng of trendy business people unwinding or wheeling and dealing over martinis and imported beer. Teddie was reminding me that a decade ago I had let the PI/client relationship get a little sloppy.

"My parents are still here, Teddie. I'm the apple that didn't fall far from the tree." She sent an intimate look at me over the rim of her martini glass and I lifted my rye and ginger ale to meet it.

Teddie Forbes had got prettier in the decade she'd been out of my sight. The puffy, dissipated face I'd been holding onto over the years had been replaced by sharply sculpted features with cheekbones and everything. The crowsfeet in the corners of her eyes made them look wiser than her years. I figured that she must be crowding forty by now. She was in the pink and had all the confidence that comes from knowing it. Her figure was still full, but now seemed as though she'd grown into it. She'd also learned a thing or two about clothes since I saw her last. She used to dress like a medicine-show wagon. Across from me, she sat in a tidy grey tweed that brought out the blue in her enormous eyes.

". . . Now a week after I get to Flagstaff, I'll start getting homesick for this looney-bin of home and friends and memories. I know it. I'm a sucker for nostalgia, Benny." She took a deep sip and then gave me a smile that said we had come to the business part of our meeting. I was glad of that. She'd had me worried for a minute. "Well?" she asked.

"Teddie, something is going on at Kinross Disposals. My client thinks a family member may have been killed because he stumbled on what's going on up there."

"Wow!" Teddie said, putting down her drink without taking her blue headlamps off my face. "Do you think Ross is behind it?"

"Teddie, I know what you're hoping. No, I don't know anything except that I can't see how I can get into the Kinross yard without being spotted. I'm not Dick Tracy and I'm not Sherlock Holmes. I can't drive a big truck. I don't even speak their lingo. It could take me a couple of weeks before I could arrange phoney ID, and that can run into money. If I go as myself, the phonebook unmasks me as a private investigator. Besides, in a place this size, I'm bound to run into somebody—somebody, hell! I'm sure to meet a dozen people who know me the first day on the job. That's assuming they'll hire me. I've never been in a spot like this."

"Poor bunny," she said, enjoying my discomfort.

"There's no way I can go undercover. No way into this puzzle. I'm going to have to do a crabdance around it until my client runs out of money. It's going to be two steps back, three steps sideways for every half-step forward."

"What are you going to do then? I can't help you get through the gate at Kinross, Benny. I'm on the board of the holding company, but that doesn't mean much, I can tell you."

"I thought that you could help me to get Kinross and Phidias straight in my head. Ross has nothing to do with Kinross any more, right?"

"Right. That's Norman Caine's responsibility now. Ross has been kicked upstairs to run the parent organization. That's Phidias."

"Good. Now we're getting somewhere. It's the human side I'm short on. I need the facts on what's going on behind the scenes."

"That's a tall order. I haven't seen those people in a long time."

"I know that. I know that. But I'm just trying to get a handle on this thing. I'm looking for a place to begin, that's all. I thought you could tell me something about Norman Caine and what's been going on."

"Caine's new. He hasn't been around more than a couple of years. I've seen him a few times with Sherry, of course. But that's only natural, considering —"

"Sherry?"

"Ross's daughter. I mean *our* daughter. Remember? She and Caine are engaged. They're getting married —"

"Great, Teddie! This is terrific stuff. It's just the sort of information I need!"

"You're a great talker, Benny. You come on like a real womanizer."

"Me?"

"Sure. I can always spot a womanizer."

"How?"

"When you tell them that you come from Grantham, Ontario, they lean across at you and say, 'So you come from *Grantham*! That's *very interesting*!'"

"And am I like that?"

"Aw, Benny, I know you too well." Teddie gave me one of those warm smiles that had Special Delivery written on it. She knew how to make a man feel totally alone with her and the sole focus of her interest. She probably didn't even know she was doing it, but I intended to relax and enjoy it all the same.

"Norman Caine is marrying Sherry. Is that like Kinross marrying Phidias, or France marrying Portugal?"

"It's a bit like that, but Caine isn't quite up there with the Forbeses yet. He's trying hard, but he hasn't quite made it."

"He has a free hand with Kinross, does he?"

"As far as I know, he has. But, Benny, they are both family companies. The Forbeses change the rules to suit themselves. I can't swear that Ross hasn't kept out of Kinross's affairs, honest."

"What's happened to Ross since you left him? Is he still with that travel agent?"

Teddie smiled and tilted her head at my ignorance. After scolding me for not holding my ear to the ground, she answered the question. "Ross left Marie Gladwell flat when he met Caroline Grier, back in 1982, I think. He and Marie had been keeping house without benefit of clergy for seven years. While he was still legally married to me, he kept up appearances, but that was it."

"It's beginning to come back to me. The last time I saw you, you told me I wouldn't have to testify after all."

"Ross sweetened the settlement when he found out what we had on him." She was trying to get the waiter's eye and wasn't doing any better than I was. Her martini had disappeared with impressive speed, and she was gnawing on the olive stone, prettily. She went on speaking, although her eyes were no longer on mine. "I got out of town for a year after that. Even now, I stay as far away from Ross as I can. Ross is the perfect bully, you know, aggressive when the light's on, but in the dark he goes to pieces. I should have seen him for a weakling from the beginning. He's not a patch on the Commander."

"The Commander? Ah, yes. His father. Has he been collected to his ancestors or does he still give Ross a hard time?"

"He's still alive, but I don't think he goes into the business any more. He must be pushing eighty! But, I'll bet he still gives Ross a mark to shoot at. Murdo Forbes! Gosh, he was formidable in his day. I remember him firing six executives on Christmas Eve without batting an eye. All friends of his, people he played golf with."

"Never had the pleasure," I said. "Who runs things now? Ross?"

"He's still CEO, but Norm Caine is breathing down his neck from one side, and the old man can't stay retired one hundred percent. The Commander's chairman of the board, naturally; Caine has the ambition, and Ross has the stock."

"I can almost feel sorry for him. He's the kid who can't escape the shade of his old man, and at the same time he's getting beaten by a poor newcomer. I'm glad I'm not Ross Forbes."

"That makes two of us. He always was a man whose grasp exceeds his reach. But he could be sweet when he was away from the Commander and not trying to wheedle something."

"Wheedling, yeah. That's what stays with me abou
him. He never came straight out of his corner at you. He
was always ducking to the right or left, always sneaking
around and backing away."

"Bicycle Ross I used to call him. It wasn't his fault when
you come right down to it. The Commander was always
paying people off to let him get out of one scrape after
another. He got expelled from one private school because
the Commander tried to bribe the headmaster. The Commander thought he could buy anything."

"There wasn't much he couldn't buy."

"But those were the things he wanted most. Ross adored
him but could never please him. You wouldn't believe the
things Ross did to make the old man respect him, love
him. It always ended with Ross and a bottle of Chivas in a
corner somewhere where I couldn't reach him." The
waiter's eye had been caught by one of Teddie's finely
arched eyebrows. A few moments later he brought her a
second martini. He left me and my nearly full rye and
ginger ale to wait out this round. Teddie went on:

"I think Marie was good for him. She was able to put
some sense into him. She was a smart woman, except
where her own interests were at stake. What did she get
out of it? A few presents, a few trips and a 'Dear Marie'
letter when it was all over. No! I take that back. Ross
wouldn't put it in writing."

"Is she still around? Marie?"

"Could be. I haven't seen her in a donkey's age. But then
we were never close, Benny. Christ, I was the wronged
wife!"

"One thing you can help me straighten out, Teddie, is
the relationship between Phidias and Kinross. Phidias
owns Kinross, is that it?"

"Let me see if I can remember all this. I have a seat on
the board at Phidias, but I never sit, if you know what I
mean. Kinross has been around for a long time, years and

years. I think it got started at the time of the first or second Welland Canal. The original Kinross was a contractor for a stretch of the 'Deep Cut.'"

"The what?"

"The Deep Cut was the hardest part of the canal to dig. They had to cut through a hump of land to avoid building a lock up to a new level and then another down to where they started. It was a major engineering —"

"Teddie, let's cut out the ancient history and get down to the present day. Who owns and runs it today? Kinross, I mean."

"It was owned by the Kinross family down to the 1950s. It was bought up by Phidias in the seventies. From excavating and haulage, they were specializing in trucking waste from industrial and municipal sites. For the last ten years, they've specialized further: poisonous waste is their main business."

"What about Phidias?"

"Well, first of all, it isn't as old as Kinross."

"Thank God for small mercies!"

"But, it's a lot bigger, Benny. It's a holding company with control of a lot of smaller firms like Kinross. Don't let the manufacturing in the name fool you. Phidias hasn't manufactured anything but profits for many years. It was started by a man named MacCallum, Sandy MacCallum, a one-eyed veteran of the First World War. He tried to start an airline with one plane. When it crashed, he turned his machine shop first to making bicycles, and then to buckets and other hardware items. MacCallum was a bright fellow, from all I heard at the time I was married to his grandson. He saw, so I was told, that with electricity available anywhere, it was no longer necessary to make a factory in a style designed for water-power. Most of the heavy industry in town used to be located along the canal. Sandy saw that he could locate a factory anywhere that was served by electricity.

"By the time Murdo married Sandy's daughter, Biddy, MacCallum was one of the biggest manufacturers of sharp-edged tools in this part of the world. And when the Second World War came along, they went into war production with government contracts for bayonets, helmets and mess kits."

"So Murdo Forbes was Sandy MacCallum's son-in-law?"

"He came with nothing but the bare buttocks sticking out of a worn-out pair of dungarees. He started as a clock-punching labourer and then gravitated into the office. They say he took night-school courses at the Collegiate. Old Sandy took a shine to Murdo before Biddy did. Thought he might fill the gap left by the son who'd died of diphtheria."

"The Commander became the Commander in World War Two? Is that right?"

"Murdo got a commission in the Navy. I think Sandy may have had to pull a few strings. We didn't have rules about political influence and the buying and selling of it in those days. The party in power got paid off and Murdo set sail into the North Atlantic. And another illustrious page of Canadian history was written. This second martini is getting to me." Teddie put down the empty glass and began looking for the waiter again. While she was waiting, I went on with questions that led with the precision of a blast from a cheap shotgun all around the area of interest. Teddie smiled over my shoulder when contact with the waiter had been made. Then she examined her empty glass, turning it around in her hand between the red-tipped fingers.

"How did he do in the Navy?"

"Oh, he came out of it alive, and a hero. He was torpedoed once and spent a week with a dozen men on a life raft. It was in all the papers at the time. He came home a big celebrity. That's why he's always been the

Commander. Every other officer has gone back to mister, but the Commander is still the Commander."

"What happened after the war?"

"Diversification. Phidias set up another company to take over the retooling of the old plant for peacetime work, leaving Phidias to dabble in real-estate speculation, building subdivisions, bridge-building, highway construction and I don't know what all. Each business was set up so that it was controlled by Phidias but had its own structure and a great deal of autonomy. From there Phidias got into distilling, trucking—that's when it picked up Kinross—and building apartments and office towers."

"They've got a lot to answer for. Especially if they did their building locally."

"Today, they're all over. You can't blame the look of James Street on Phidias completely. You have to share the blame around. It's the modern style, Benny."

"Yeah, pull down something worth saving, and put up something you've already seen enough of." Teddie was well into her third martini by now. I was still working away at the edges of drink number one. "Teddie, somebody at Kinross—I say it's somebody, maybe it's *everybody*; I don't know—may be up to dirty tricks. It could be overweight trucking on Sundays, it could be the illegal dumping of toxic wastes. It could be smuggling or dope or—I don't know exactly what, but I'm sure that it's being kept quiet. A year ago, according to what I've learned, a trucker was killed. Maybe it was an accident, maybe it wasn't. I'm keeping an open mind. It could be that this guy knew too much. Maybe he threatened to blow the whistle on the whole shebang, whatever it was." Teddie was watching me closely while I tried to put one word in front of the next. I lost my place. It was Teddie's interest that did it. She was leaning towards me across the table, her eyes on mine and reacting to all the turns in my story. It was just her interest, but I got it confused with her abundantly female presence. You'd think, with Anna in my life, things like Teddie's perfumed nearness would melt into the background so that I could get on with business, but no, I had to try looking not into those blue eyes of hers but at the bridge of her nose. That was safe, and I tried to get the story back on the rails. Teddie could see me struggling. She helped me to get started again.

"You think Ross is at the bottom of whatever it is?"

"I don't know. Either he knows all about it and ordered what happened, or he has been compromised by the people working under him. This Caine fellow, most likely. You know anything about him? Anything at all?"

"Well, I told you about the wedding. That's the big news. It's a week Saturday. That's why I'm in town."

"And the Commander's all for it, I'll bet. The wedding, I mean."

"Sure. And Biddy's giving silent support in the rear. Biddy's the tall, silent type. Clark Gable in skirts. She keeps out of the spotlight, but nobody makes a move she doesn't know about."

An old school friend came into the Snug and grinned at me over Teddie's shoulder. It was a nasty, conspiratorial grin that made me want to get up and set him straight, but before I could, he'd been claimed by three men our age at the bar, who made more noise than absolutely necessary. Teddie had been thinking meanwhile and finally let me know what it was. "All his life, Ross has known that control of Phidias—and that means control of a big industrial empire, Benny—was coming to him. When the Commander stepped down, Ross stepped in with the support of the board. But after the provincial inquiry was set up, he's been in a lot of trouble about environmental matters. The board isn't happy. Ross hasn't handled things the way the Commander would have."

"Caine, coming up fast on the outside, is looking better and better," I suggested.

"Sure, and after next Saturday, well, then it's the clash of dynasties, isn't it?"

"But, when all bets are on the table, the old man will have to back his own son, won't he?"

"We aren't talking about the same Murdo Forbes, Benny. Sherry's his granddaughter, after all. He got where he is by marrying the boss's daughter. I'd say he'll back his granddaughter's husband against her father. Don't you wish this were on television so you could watch it happen?"

I shifted myself in my seat. I felt like I wasn't asking the best questions again. It was an occupational bugbear and I was usually able to ignore it. "Teddie," I asked, trying to rescue the last minutes of our conversation, "is there any legal way that you can think of for me to walk through the front doors of Phidias's head office on James Street and not get kicked out on my ear?" Teddie smiled at what I imagined was a picture of me picking myself out of the gutter. She folded the corner of the scalloped placemat under her glass. I was about to tell her not to worry about it, when she came back at me with a vague but optimistic suggestion:

"I can't think of anything right now, Benny, but let me sleep on it. I get all my really good ideas in the morning." She set down her glass with a note of finality. She played with the stem. I wondered whether it would be her last drink of the day. Maybe these three martinis were just for old times' sake. Her appearance didn't hint at any problems with alcohol. I was glad of that. I'd always liked Teddie. Even at the worst of our dealings with Ross, I'd always felt that she was holding me back, holding her lawyer back, too, for that matter. She was always softening the blow.

"Well, Teddie, I appreciate your giving me all this." I put some money where the waiter could see it near the nearly empty saucer of salted peanuts. She watched me

return my wallet to my pocket. Was she holding on to me?
I could feel it as surely as if she had me by the sleeve. She
fiddled in her purse, looking for a photograph of her
Flagstaff home to show me. She found several of a pale
ranch-style place with a mountain view. Behind the last of
these I found a creased photo of a man in riding boots. I
smiled as I turned it around: my old sparring partner. She
took it from me and examined it as though for the first
time.

"I still have a tender spot for him, when I'm in the
mood." She laughed suddenly. "I know what you're thinking! I'm a mass of contradictions, right? Don't tell me. Two
analysts have got there before you. I'm not looking forward to seeing him again, but I can't throw his picture
away. I don't trust the guy, I don't even like him, but I
wouldn't want to see him dead. He's a son of a bitch, but
he can charm the pants off me if I'm not careful. Benny,
you try to be careful."

"Teddie, I'm planning to stay as far away from him as
the job allows. And I don't imagine for a minute that I'll
ever see the charming side of his character. I'm ready for
the worst."

I gave Teddie the two numbers where she could reach
me and we left the Snug. I was only half-prepared for the
good-night kiss she planted on me. By the time I recov-
ered, she was getting into her white Corvette. She was
gone when I reached my battered Olds.

Chapter Five

Before calling it a day, I thought I'd drop around to see my client again. She wouldn't be expecting me at this hour and I didn't mind, under the circumstances, giving her a moment's anxiety. A scare, even. By me it was still early, but by Irma Dowden it might be getting close to the middle of the night. Irma lived on Glen Avenue, just across the tracks from the street where I was born. This was a part of town described on maps as West Grantham, but everybody still called it Western Hill, an expression that went back to a time in the last century when this was a canal town. In those days a winding road curved down to a canal bridge and up the hill on the other side. Nowadays a high-level bridge joined both parts of town a hundred feet above the water of the abandoned canal.

The house wearing the number Mrs Dowden had given me was a bungalow going back to the 1950s, sandwiched between two older houses with the 1930s written all over them. I parked the car a little beyond my target, more out of habit than because I was worried about being watched. The sidewalk looked treacherous under the streetlight's slanted glow, as I walked up the length of my shadow to the aluminum screen door. I knocked and waited.

"Oh! Mr Cooperman! I didn't expect to see you again so soon. Don't you ever sleep?" A dog shoved its nose into the four- or five-inch gap Irma Dowden had made between the door and the jamb. It started barking at me. In that quiet part of town it sounded like an explosion. "Get back, Ralph! Get back!" Ralph was a small poodle, who found something fascinating about my right pantleg. That was better than big dogs; their interest is higher up. "Come in, Mr Cooperman. Get down, Ralph! Let him be!"

She opened the door the rest of the way and I followed her past a tiny telephone nook into the living-room, where the TV was flashing the image of a familiar face reading the news. The pick of Woolworth's art department decorated the walls. Mrs Dowden motioned me to sit on a long venerable couch, and she joined me on the companion over-stuffed chair. Ralph watched me from the floor, then jumped up on the couch, where he settled after walking around in a tight circle. I think he curled his lip at me as he tucked his snout between his short legs.

I tried to find any signs of Jack Dowden in the room, but apart from a photograph that I took to be him, standing on the mantel above an artificial fireplace, the male touch was totally missing from the decor. The picture looked fairly recent. It showed a man of forty-five or so, who might pass for younger. He had a square-cut solid jaw and even, white teeth. He was seen opening the door of an enormous truck with the word "Irma" written on the door.

The picture was useful to me: it gave me an idea about the man whose death I was looking into. He looked bright and alert, but not somebody who could be pushed around. The appearance of "Irma" on the truck told me that he owned it, a detail, but maybe an important one. A truck-owner was a broker, a man in business, not just a hireling, not casual labour.

"I'll put on the kettle," Irma Dowden said, watching me as I assessed her late husband. When I turned back to face her, she had made no move in the direction of the kitchen. She was playing with the ring on her third finger, left hand. "It won't take a minute," she said. "It was on the boil not ten minutes ago."

"Mrs Dowden," I said, probably more gravely than I intended, "I didn't come for tea or coffee."

"Oh," she said, as though she'd been stung or bitten.

"No, I came to talk to you about the things you forgot to tell me this afternoon."

"This afternoon." She repeated the phrase as though the meaning was beyond her; she hadn't taken it in. I could see panic in her little gimlet eyes. She was trying to think of what she was going to say.

"You know what I mean. You must have known that I'd find out."

"I don't understand, Mr Cooperman."

"Sure you do. I'm talking about a matter of time, Mrs Dowden. Three hundred and sixty-five days that slipped your memory."

"Oh, *that*."

"Yes, *that*."

"Well, if you figured out that much, you must have a good idea why I didn't tell you straight out. I figured you for smart."

"Save the soft-soap, Mrs Dowden. From now on, I want from you nothing but the truth. Is that clear? Otherwise you can take your troubles to Howard Dover or one of the other investigators."

"I've already been to them, Mr Cooperman. You're all I've got!"

"Well, stop abusing me. Go, make some coffee. That's a start."

"The kettle's just off the boil."

"You said that five minutes ago! That's not just off the boil in my book!" I surprised both of us with my outburst. Both of us knew that it had nothing to do with the cooling kettle.

In a moment she got up and left the room. Ralph jumped from the couch to the wine-dark carpet and followed her to the kitchen. In another minute, I followed Ralph.

"You're going to have to settle for tea. I'm out of coffee. As a matter of fact," she said, in an expression of purest candour, "I haven't had coffee in the house since Jack died."

"And how long ago was that?" I asked unkindly.

"A year and three months ago. There! I've said it. I won't tell you any more lies, Mr Cooperman. I've always been a truthful woman. Honest."

"I'm going to drop the case the next time you aren't being straight with me. I don't want to hear any more exaggerations or fibs. You understand?"

"Thank you, Mr Cooperman."

On her own ground, Irma Dowden didn't look so ferret-like, not so small and not so apparently determined to get her own way. She looked serious and I took that to be an humble and a contrite heart. She was used to feeling mistress in her own kitchen, but she gave me lots of room as she fussed with the cups.

"Mrs Dowden—"

"Oh, please, call me Irma. Goodness!" I nodded and started over.

"Irma, you said that Kinross had sent back Jack's things—the clothes he was wearing, his wallet, keys. Is that right?"

"At first they said I wouldn't want to see them, but in the end they sent them. Of course, except for digging out his wallet, I haven't looked at the rest. They were right about that."

"Where are they now? The clothes, I mean?"

"Jack's glory hole is in the cellar. Everything of his is still down there. I haven't had the heart to touch anything." She made a gesture suggesting her loss, and I sighed and shrugged to show sympathy. "You can have a look while I finish making the tea," she said. "His work clothes are in a shopping bag near the workbench, if you want to see them."

"It all ends up in a shopping bag, somebody once said." I don't think she got it, so I turned to the cellar door.

The steps leading to the basement were covered in linoleum, probably rescued from the most recent redoing of the kitchen floor. At the bottom, I found an ancient coal furnace adapted to natural gas. A pile of stored furniture rested against one wall. Some of it looked in bad shape, but I recognized a few pieces of Canadian pine—some chests of drawers and a hutch—that, with a little work, might pass for Early American. Besides the washtubs, a fruit-cellar, former coalbin, I discovered the workbench, a lathe and a few pieces of his handiwork: an arrow-back chair with one rung about to be replaced by a fine match for the broken pieces. Jack had been doing excellent work down here. He had left things so tidy, I wondered whether he'd had a premonition about his approaching fate.

And there was the shopping bag. I took a breath and dug in. There was less dried blood than I expected. I left the underwear unexamined in a separate plastic bag, through which I could see more than I wanted to. I found a green flannel workshirt made in Taiwan. The pockets held nothing but tobacco crumbs and lint. The trousers, heavy-duty denim that had never heard of Calvin Klein, held a soiled handkerchief, a comb that indicated a need for a dandruff remover, and thirty-seven cents. For some reason, maybe it was some scrap of my formal training showing, I looked in the trouser cuffs. Nothing but dried weeds in there. But I took a second look at them. There were a few stems, fragmented leaves and a long, silvery tissue with tiny dark seeds embedded along the length of the four-inch-long stalk. It looked a little beanlike, except that the pods were flaking off. The seeds were stuck in a delicate tissue that ran between the pods.

I slipped the dead contents of Jack's cuffs into the envelope with my electric bill and folded it closed. I had a friend up at Secord University who could tell me what the weeds had to say about Jack's death, apart from the fact that he may have had a ramble in the woods some time before the fatal day. There was nothing here that told me that the accident was murder. I still had only Irma's hunch about that. The chalky dirt on the back of the shirt told me nothing about why he was now numbered among the dead.

Irma was just pouring the tea when I went back upstairs. "Did you find anything interesting, Mr Cooperman?"

"Look, Irma, if you're going to be Irma and not Mrs Dowden, then you'd better start calling me Benny."

"Here's your tea." She put two blue-and-white mugs on the green table. She pulled out a wooden chair and slid into it. "This is a piece of early Canadiana, Jack told me," she said, tapping the table top with her teaspoon. "He was always going to strip it down to the wood, but we never could spare it long enough for the whole treatment. Jack always wanted to settle down and get out of driving for a living. He was always talking about setting up in the antique business. Jack loved wood."

We sipped our tea, while Irma told me about their life together. She dabbed her eyes a couple of times with the handkerchief I lent her. I tried to take in what she said, but the details of the children they never had or the uncles who could never leave them alone didn't really change anything. Even on the subject of Jack's relations to Kinross, I could find nothing sinister. Before I left, I asked to see Jack's papers. Irma shook her head. "Jack didn't leave anything in writing," she said, "unless you count the three love-letters he wrote to me, but I'll show you what I've got." She led the way into the bedroom, where in a corner a shoebox full of credit-card flimsies was produced. I asked if I could borrow these. As I was about to leave, I saw a few books in a pile.

"Are the books yours or Jack's?"

"Oh, Jack's. I'm not much of a reader. Television's too easy. I guess my brain's been softened, Benny." I tuned out Irma's prattle and checked the titles. There was a Robert Ludlum in paperback, two Stephen Kings and then the surprise: *Chemical Nightmare: The Unnecessary Legacy of Toxic Wastes* by John Jackson, Phil Weller and the Waterloo Public Interest Group. I opened the book and found that it was well thumbed. It wasn't much, but just what I needed for bedtime reading. Irma made no objection when I asked to borrow it. She saw me to the door and down the walk before she shut the front door to the night.

After a wash, I took the book under the covers with me and read myself silly for about an hour. When I woke up, the light was still burning and the clock told me that I would have to begin a new day in under two hours. I turned off the light and got rid of my bed-partner. *Chemical Nightmare* could hang around the apartment all day when it got light. It didn't have to make ends meet.

Chapter Six

The drive up to Secord University was one I always liked. It took me over the course my father used when he taught me how to drive. The curves of the road leading up the escarpment were recorded in my elbows and feet like they'd been programmed. The escarpment was heavily wooded, but the trees were beginning to lose their leaves. There were still plenty of maples strutting their stuff in reds and gold. The sumachs were scarlet at the edge of the quarry, where I caught a glimpse through the trees of the shack where Garth Gardenia and I'd spent a teenage afternoon with a Mrs Stagg. Mrs Stagg lived alone with a collection of photograph albums full of turn-of-the-century showgirl beauties. She might have been in the theatre herself, but we never asked. We'd heard that one of her legs was wooden, but it was hard to tell under her long skirts. During the spring and summer, her cabin is invisible from the road. Maybe that's why I never think of her except when I drive up the escarpment in the autumn and winter.

I'd phoned Eric Mailer, an old friend of mine, who'd once been a cut-up in grade ten science with Miss Red Scott at the helm. Now he was a lecturer in botany. I wonder whether Red Scott ever knew that Eric used to circulate drawings of flowers showing the reproductive parts in unmistakable human forms. And I remember a verse that accompanied one of them, something with the rhyme "saturnalia" and "genitalia" in it.

I found Eric by following a colour-coded stripe painted along the corridors. All of the departments were colour-coded for the illiterate. History was dark blue, biology was green. Eric's office was a large, dim room on the tenth floor.

"Benny! How are you?" Eric's grin took me right back to Red Scott's lab tables. "You son of a gun! I haven't seen you in five years. What have you been doing with yourself that you can say in a room that may be bugged by the Mounties?"

"I keep seeing your name in the paper, Eric. Didn't you get some honour a few months back? I'm sorry, I should keep up on these things."

"Yeah, I agreed to suppress some startling facts about the procreation of trilliums so that the province wouldn't have to find another official emblem for its logos. So they gave me a gong. I used it to crack nuts with, like Tom Canty in *The Prince and the Pauper*."

For a minute or two we chatted away, recalling old friends and trying to reconcile our present faces with the younger versions in our memories. "It's a nice place you've got here, Eric," I said at last, as an exit ramp from memory lane. Nothing very bright as an observation, but it did deal with the here and now.

"This, Benny, is not a place, it's a herbarium. Come in and roll up in an old newspaper." I followed Eric through rows of cabinets taller than both of us. The dark, institutional green killed much of the light coming into the room from the generous windows along one wall. Between the back-to-back cabinets, a few wooden desks were scattered, all of them stacked high with drying plants between layers of newspaper showing various tints of yellow. "This department should double as a periodical archives, you

know, Benny. Look at this." He picked up a folded copy o
a Toronto paper and read the headline: "JOHNSON REFUSES
TO SEEK ANOTHER TERM. I'm sure I've got one with Roosevel
going for a fourth term around here somewhere." Eric
found his desk. Like the others, it was cluttered and dusty
It must be the last desk on earth with a well in it for hiding
a typewriter. I was amazed that the university would
allow such ancient equipment into the science departments. It didn't seem so odd that I might find it in the
humanities departments.

"I'm working on a case, Eric," I began, trying to remember that my time was being paid for. Eric nodded as he
took off his tinted glasses and began cleaning them with a
tissue from his pocket. His strawlike hair, which made him
a wonderful Sir Andrew Aguecheek in *Twelfth Night* at the
Collegiate when we were in grade twelve, was looking
pale and thin. It was that sort of blond that goes grey
without anybody noticing. I took the envelope with my
electric bill and poured out the contents into a small pile
on a clear spot on Eric's desk. I hoped I wasn't going to
ruin years of research by bringing the pods and leaves
from Jack's cuffs to the herbarium. For all I knew, this
might have been a closed environment. Eric's mouth
frowned slightly as he examined the mess I'd made on his
desk. He poked about at the pods with a yellow pencil
with a pink Ruby Tip eraser on the end.

"*Hesperis*," he said.

"What?"

"*Hesperis matronalis* to be exact."

"And once again in English, Eric. What do you know
about it, and where is it found?" Eric smiled over the seed
pods, prodded them again and lifted up a silvery membrane with tiny brown seeds caught in the fine fabric of the
centre section of the beanlike pods.

"That's the septum," he said, "as in your nose and
mine." He touched the membrane gently. "*Hesperis* is also

known as Dame's Rocket. It's a member of the mustard family. The septum's the give-away; no native Ontario plant has one."

"Where does it come from, if it's not from here?"

"Oh, it's been here for a long time. Like starlings, Benny, they arrive here and multiply."

"Are you saying it's a weed, Eric?"

"Not usually. It's usually an ornamental plant found in gardens, but it sometimes escapes, and if it finds an agreeable habitat, Dame's Rocket does very well." Eric pushed the rubber-tipped end of his pencil into his ear and turned it absent-mindedly. "I've seen them at building sites and by streams. Never heard a wild one complain. Now, judging from this other stuff in here, the things that aren't from *Hesperis*, I'd say that this one was wild and not cultivated."

"How can you tell?" With Eric, I could never be sure when he was pulling my leg.

"Trust me, Benny. Here are wild-grass fragments, a bit of burdock, hummm, goldenrod, ragweed. No, these pods came from a wild, somewhat moist area, maybe by a river or bridge, or—"

"Eric, stop shovelling it! You can't tell that much from an envelope of dead seed pods! Who do you think you are, Basil Rathbone?"

"I said 'trust me.' Look, Benny, *Hesperis* is usually found cultivated as I told you. But when it's found rough, it's got to be near some explanation of how it got there. Now this could have come from a building site, where the original cultivated plants had been allowed to go back to nature. Or you could make just as good a case for a stream or river."

"Yes, but where'd you get the bridge?"

"Elementary, my dear Benny. The seeds had to come from some contact with civilization. I see them falling off on moist soil where a highway crosses a river or even a culvert. These plants came with garbage that was dumped or fill thrown over a guardrail. Something like that."

"And now you're going to tell me that in all of the Niagara Peninsula there is only one place where all of these conditions are met. Right?"

"Wrong. There are thousands of places. Well, at least hundreds. I can't do all of your work for you, kid." He gave me his big innocent grin and invited me for coffee. Before I got my hopes up, he took an electric kettle from under his desk and two unwashed cups with chipped rims from a bottom drawer. The coffee, when it came, was superior. I shouldn't judge by appearances so much. While we were sipping the brew, lightened with canned milk, Eric told me more about Dame's Rocket than I think the world is ready to hear. He told me about its spike of showy flowers, showed me pictures in several books and even found a specimen in a drawer in one of his smelly cabinets. His carefully preserved specimens had about as much colour and life as the samples from Jack Dowden's cuffs. Eric taught me not to confuse *Hesperis* with phlox.

"How silly," he said, giving his head a superior twist. "Phlox has five fused petals, while *Hesperis,* like all mustards, has four petals, arranged like a cross—cruciform as we botanists say—which has resulted in the family *Cruciferae,* which has world-wide about twenty-three thousand species in many genera . . ." He looked up just before I'd achieved the door. "Benny, you didn't finish your coffee!" I turned and made a helpless gesture.

"Eric, I thought mustards were either mild or hot. I'll have to come back for the rest of this some other time. Right now Anna Abraham is expecting me to drop into her office in the History Department," I lied. "Thanks a lot for the stuff on *Hesperis.* You never let me down."

"Benny," he said crossing towards me, "do you want to see a newspaper from 1942 about Japanese advances in New Guinea? I've got one here about the death of the

Duke of Kent in Australia. It's right here somewhere. It was in a plane crash; I think it has rosehips in it. I had one with the disappearance of Leslie Howard, but that got used up when I spilled coffee on the term paper of a B student." I backed out the door. "Hey, Benny, I thought you wanted to learn something about this stuff!"

A few minutes later, I knocked on Anna Abraham's door in the History Department. For several reasons, I thought it would be nice to see her. The very least of them was that it would correct the lie I'd told Eric while I was trying to get away from his tidal wave of information. I'd just given up knocking on her door when she walked into the corridor from the other end, struggling with an over-stuffed briefcase.

"Don't I know you from somewhere?" she asked.

"Cooperman's the name," I said, continuing in the same vein. "I've come to speak to you on a matter of some delicacy."

"Serious as that, eh? We better go down to the cafeteria, then. I've got some time before my next class," she said. I let Anna lead the way to the elevator. "Nearly called you last night," I said, "but I was staying up late with a fibbing client."

"At least she has some imagination. That's something."

In the cafeteria, Anna brought a tray of coffee and I cleaned off one of the cluttered white tables. She sat across from me and carefully set down two brimming cups. She caught me looking at her and smiled. I could never get enough of the way Anna looked. There were so many of her, all the different Annas I'd learned to recognize, like the school-marmish one with her dark hair pulled back away from her face, like the spoiled teenager who walked into my office a year ago looking like she'd just fallen off a motorcycle. She now brought me down to earth by giving me a demented cross-eyed grin, then let her eyes and mouth droop like an old bloodhound. That brought me

around and I lifted my cup. "What brings you up the
mountain, Benny? And so early!"

"I've come to check up on that Lord Macaulay you're
always quoting. I think you have a weak spot for British
aristocracy."

"Thomas Babington is it? Well, I've been nuts about him
since I was twelve. You're too late, too late. You'll have to
settle for the dregs he is pleased to leave behind."

"I'll settle."

"Why *are* you up here?"

"I've just been to see Eric Mailer, upstairs. He was
looking at some seeds I found." I told her about Irma
Dowden and the death of her husband and the trail I'd
been following all day yesterday.

"Was Eric much help?"

"Eric is a born teacher. He wanted me to learn all about
the mustard family. I nearly didn't get away from there. In
another minute he'd have had me rolled up in one of his
ancient newspapers and gasping out my last breath in one
of his foul-smelling cabinets."

"Poor baby."

"This is terrible coffee."

"It's not so bad when you have a degree. With a PhD
you can hardly taste the difference between this and the
real thing."

"Sorry I introduced the subject. You know education's
my weak spot. I want you to tell me why we can't go out
Friday night."

"Friday night's fine. It's *next* Friday night that I'm busy.
I told you that I'm the maid of honour at my friend
Sherry's wedding. That's on Saturday. Friday night's the
rehearsal. You can come if you want."

"Wait a minute. This Sherry, which Sherry is it?"

"The bride's an old school friend. I can't let her down."

"Last name. That's all I want. Save your excuses."

"Sherry Forbes."

"Ha! I thought so! In Grantham, coincidence doesn't have to have a long arm. Anna, I love you!" I leaned over the table and nearly spilled both of our cups.

"Hey! There goes the last of my dignity, Cooperman!"

"On you, it looks wonderful."

"Wait until you see it in pink organdy, kid. We'll look like a page from *Vogue* of maybe ten years ago. That's high fashion around here." Anna checked her watch and wolfed down the first two-thirds of her coffee. "Gotta go, Cooperman. See you on Friday night unless you get a better offer. And I'm serious about the rehearsal next week. Come and see the Forbeses at play."

"I wouldn't miss it. All that and pink organdy too! I've died and gone to heaven."

"No organdy or orange blossoms at the rehearsal. Control yourself."

I'd met Anna last year when I ended up working on a case for her father, who could buy and sell half of Grantham and not worry about having an overdraft. His family had made their money in the liquor business, but Jonah, Anna's father, was more interested in collecting art than in making more money. Anna thought I was trying to rip off her old man. When she decided I wasn't, she let me take her to a movie. That had blossomed into a relationship of sorts. I knew that I only knew about a quarter of what was going on in Anna's life. She finished off her coffee in one gulp.

"You don't have to work eighteen hours a day, you know."

"Yeah, it's not like marking papers."

"That's different. It's not dangerous for one thing."

"Neither is reading up on environmental concerns, unless I nod off with a lighted cigarette in my mouth."

"Well, I'm glad to see you're finally paying attention. If we don't start taking the environment seriously, we'll have to start scouting for a new planet to spoil. Everybody knows that the waste-disposal companies all get away with murder around here."

Anna's eyes were alive with what she was saying. She'd dropped the kidding manner she put on with me. I let her argument sink in, but I wasn't blind to the contrast of her light skin against her dark hair.

Before I left, I asked Anna to see if she could find out who in the History Department was researching the past of Kinross Disposals. She said she'd try. She was looking terrific this morning. I went back out into the world feeling like a very lucky private investigator.

Chapter Seven

Anna once tried to explain to me that there is an important thread in American literature that has to do with "the fixer" coming into the community from outside and then moving off into the sunset after the work is done, leaving nothing but an echo behind him: "Who was that masked man?" Maybe Sam Spade and the Lone Ranger are brothers under the skin, but I don't see how that affects me trying to make an honest buck up here north of the world's longest undefended frontier. We don't have that strain of vigilantism in Canada. Dirty Harry's looking for work in Toronto, putting in time until the streets get meaner. He may not have to wait long, but in the interval, the traditions aren't the same. Canadians are bigger consumers of law and order for one thing. Not spitting on the sidewalk or shooting the pigeons in the park is a sensible way to behave, a small enough price to pay for being allowed to stand aside from the mainstream of North American life. Maybe Anna thought I was part of the great American tradition. Maybe she saw a Canadian tradition with me in it. Most likely I was all that was left of her teenage crush on Nancy Drew.

When I got downtown again, I looked up Brian O'Mara's number in the phonebook. His wife, or the woman answering his phone, told me that he was at work and wouldn't be home until just after four o'clock. She asked me who was speaking, but I pretended I didn't hear her and continued to thank her before hanging up. I noted down the address on a scrap of paper torn from a bank-machine receipt and planned to call on him later in the day.

With a styrofoam cup of coffee in hand, I climbed the stairs to my office, shucked my jacket and then the lid from the coffee. My mind was drifting towards Friday night and Anna. I put a stop to that by getting out the phonebook. That kind of distraction I could do without. No wonder I kept nothing sharper than an electric razor in my bottom drawer.

The number I was looking for was for Environment Front. I dialled it. Every town has its media-conscious, pollution-sensitive activist who is always hard to get to. I talked to three people before I got to Alexander Pastor, who had written the newspaper articles about illegal dumping and bringing in toxic-tainted fuel oil from the United States. I remembered how these pieces kept turning up, keeping me away from my crossword puzzle.

"Yeah?" he said into my ear when I finally got to him.

"Is this Alexander Pastor?"

"You got him," he said. "You also got Sandor Pásztory. Take your pick." I didn't quiz him about that. The fashion for Canadianizing foreign-sounding names is dying out. Even the business pages of the *Beacon* showing back-lit photographs of newly appointed directors to important companies was a harvest of non-Anglo-Saxon names. In the old days, whatever the origin of the executive, the name was suitably North American. Even actors were sticking to their own names nowadays, and the world hadn't come to an end.

I explained to Pastor-Pásztory about my interest in the death of Jack Dowden at Kinross a year ago. I didn't even

have to remind him of the case; he was up on the details
and agreed to meet me at Gosselin's Turkey Roost up on
the Scrampton Road in half an hour.

"Why that place?" I asked. "It's right across from the
Kinross yard. I'm not looking to walk into trouble," I said
with emphasis.

"There's something I want to show you," Pastor-
Pásztory said and left it at that. It was a take-it-or-leave-it
situation. I took it.

That left me travelling time and not much else to get
there.

Gosselin's Turkey Roost was one of the fast-food outlets
on an industrial strip that took advantage of the workers at
two quarries, a gravel pit and several trucking firms
located along a concentrated three miles of chain-link
fences, corrugated steel Quonset huts and aluminum-sided
sheds. To me the eateries all looked alike. I was glad it was
the pollution expert who chose our rendezvous.

The customers sitting at the counter of Gosselin's Turkey Roost were mostly workers from the area: men working odd shifts, drivers of the rigs parked out front or in the
lot to one side of the one-storey brick-and-cinder-block
structure. Men in nylon bomber jackets with the names of
their basketball teams on the front and back, or in heavy
faded checkered shirts, contemplated the nuggets of turkey or their fresh French fries before putting them into
their mouths. At one table, a Hydro crew nodded hard
hats of yellow plastic over mugs of hot coffee. The corrugated broadside of a tractor-trailer obstructed my view
across the road through big picture windows. Occasionally, as someone came in the door, the waitress or the
short-order cook would look up. None of the customers
showed much interest. On the wall near me, a sign, framed
and covered in glass with a ketchup smear on it, read:

TEENAGERS & YOUNG FOLK
EFFECTIVE immediately
there will be a time-
limit of 15 minutes
imposed on all the
above!—*Management*

As far as I could see, there were no teenagers or young folk counting off the allotted time. The notice was a complete success, unless the faded ketchup smear could be interpreted as a sign of youthful protest. The music, which held sway over the din of talk in the room, came from a coin-operated, plastic-wrapped, inwardly illuminated juke-box. It played old-fashioned country-and-western songs by Johnny Cash, Ferlin Husky, Merle Haggard and Hank Snow. This wasn't a camp re-creation of an era; it was the real thing still happening, without even a sideways glance at fashion. I was trying to imagine what the place might look like after dark, when the man who couldn't have been anybody else but Alex Pastor-Pásztory came in. He had the look of a low-level bureaucrat crossed with a trailer-camp operator. There was some camp counsellor, graduate student and trail guide in there too. He didn't have trouble picking me out of the line-up either. He shambled over towards me from the door, removing a tweed jacket with leather patches on the elbows as he came. Under it was an old sweater, either moth-eaten in places or burned. He moved into the other side of the booth I'd taken and produced a pack of cigarettes at once. As he fished one out, I found matches and struck one. He leaned into the flame, nodding at my Player's dozing in the ashtray.

"We're a dying breed," he said. "In more ways than one. But I can't fight battles along a broad front. Can't arm-wrestle the world out there and me at the same time. Oh, well, there's next year. What's your excuse?"

"Me? I never thought of quitting. I like my vice. It's a poor thing, but mine own. I can't stand the self-righteous propaganda of the anti-smoking lobby either. They're right, I guess, but I wish they'd find a less self-satisfied way to make their points. I suppose I'll have to give it up one of these days, like I gave up jellybeans and licorice allsorts." Pásztory got up and waved for the waitress. When she didn't see him, he called out. I admired his direct approach. It brought two cups of coffee within a minute.

Pásztory had a friendly, lopsided grin that sat on a face that must have been dour in repose. Brown eyes came magnified through his thick, steel-rimmed glasses. He was going bald in front and wore the remaining fringe rather long over his neck and ears. He gave me the same sort of appraisal as we talked.

"You wrote those pieces in the *Beacon* about the toxic-fuel scam last spring, didn't you?"

"Yeah, I used my uptown name on those: Alexander Pastor. Did you see that the *Globe* took them too? They were in a lot of papers."

"Didn't you win some kind of award with them?"

"That's right, the Rushton Cup. I keep pennies in it." He was still trying to place me and not getting anywhere. "This environment stuff, this is not your usual beat, is it?"

"Right. I'm normally a family-law man. Reading about toxic waste steals my sleep. Your articles made me feel the ozone layer being peeled away. Ugh! I have to limit my exposure if I want to survive. No offence. I'm just being honest. Like it's not that I don't agree with you. That's not the point. I just have to control my intake, or it's like living through an earthquake all the time."

"That's a good description. We have to make this planet last at least until we have the technology to move to another one when this one won't support us any more."

"Yeah, 'Beam me back to Saturn, Scotty!' Right?"

"And what if we don't have the technology for that?"

"Then, we're out of luck." Pásztory added both cream and sugar to his coffee. Rather a lot of both.

"Sorry to sound off at you, Mr Cooperman. I get carried away sometimes. What can I do for you? What do you want to know about?"

"I'm interested in Kinross and the kinds of games they've been playing."

"What's your first name again?"

"Benny."

"Okay. Call me Sandy or Alex. I get both. I changed my name just when it was becoming popular to have a fine old Hunky name like Pásztory. A name like Pastor comes out of Saran Wrap."

Pásztory's fingers were stained with nicotine. He was a messy smoker. I could see where the holes in his sweater came from.

"I can tell you a lot about Kinross and about the parent company, Phidias Manufacturing. Hell, I can tell you something about almost every company working in the peninsula. Some are small independent operations; some have the mob playing a quiet role, like in Sangallo Restorations in Niagara-on-the-Lake. That's Tony Pritchett's little game. He launders some of his dirty money building driving sheds and sand-blasting old brick houses along Queen Street. Have you heard of him?"

"In Grantham, it's hard not to have heard about Anthony Horne Pritchett and his boys. But I haven't had the pleasure of meeting him."

"He likes to keep a certain distance from his dirty companies, even the ones he only puts money into quietly. But saying this is one thing, the difficulty comes in proving the allegations. Even when I get in trouble with libel, I have to prove my way out or pay up. I've had to do that twice now. It's like putting your head in a noose."

"Do you let that stop you?"

"Hell, no! But I'm trying to tell you that you need more than Boy Scout instincts in this racket. Tony Pritchett doesn't fool around. And even the companies with no links to organized crime can play tough. Does Kinross know that you are snooping around?"

"I talked to a Dr Gary Carswell who—"

"Yeah, I know him. You might as well have sent your picture to Norm Caine, Benny. You won't get through the gate pretending to be a salesman or in some sort of disguise."

"Hell, I thought I'd slip quietly in dressed like Captain Hook in *Peter Pan*."

"Don't joke about things like that. I've known guys who tried to do things that dim. One got his arm broken."

"Are you telling me that there's no way to prove what they are doing with their wastes?"

"I've been on their tail for three years at least. They have CBs—you know, radio-equipped trucks. If they spot you following them, they send an SOS and your goose is cooked. Without a relay team of cars, you'll never be able to get close to them. And, believe me, Benny, they play rough."

"What tricks are they up to?"

"You want the whole catalogue? They'll run a rig, say, to Boston and back and open up a tap on the Massachusetts Turnpike. You can get rid of a lot of PCBs that way. Or, they'll stick a hose in a storm sewer or a stream running into the Niagara River at night. There's so much crap going into the Niagara from both sides of the border that you can't make book on who's doing it more, the Americans or us."

"Are they dumping PCBs into the Niagara?"

"I don't think so. Not Kinross. They go more for plating sludges, you know, cyanide baths either organic or inorganic."

"You just lost me."

"Organic are things with carbon-related products. You know about the carbon rings?" I shook my head. Pásztory shrugged. He wasn't responsible for the quality of the detective asking questions. He didn't have time to worry about that too. He kept on going. "It doesn't matter. The inorganic stuff is solutions with heavy metals in them. Things like lead and zinc. They sometimes will sell oil with PCBs in it to township rubes for laying the dust on back roads. It lays the dust all right. Ha!" His cheeks got quite red when he laughed; the capillaries on his high cheek-bones stood out on his tough, tanned face. "But to be fair," he added, nearly choking on his sip of coffee, "even that's harder to get away with now. The province has just plugged this loophole on paper. You can't legally lay the dust as in days of yore."

"How do you know Kinross is doing these things?"

"I know and I don't know. I know because I've had a few spies out looking, but I don't know well enough to take Kinross or any of the others to court. I mean, short of having a photograph of a truck putting a hose into a sewer at midnight, you're talking about tough proof to collect. Okay, say you've got them red-handed, staring into the camera flash with their beady pink eyes. They up and say, 'We were pumping water from the river *into* the truck to mix with the waste.' Or they say, 'We were only dumping water from clean tanks.' What are you going to say to guys like that? They got you coming and going."

"At the time Dowden died, he was reading up on the subject. He must have been getting scared." Pásztory nodded and worked his mouth from side to side, as though there was a bit of tobacco stuck between his teeth.

"The post-mortem didn't show any organic disease that could be related to driving hot stuff," Pásztory said.

"Oh, so you've seen that too. I *know* you've seen the coroner's report. Have there been any other deaths at

Kinross since Dowden?" At the mention of the coroner's report, Pásztory sat up straighter in his seat. I think he appreciated the homework I'd been doing.

"I haven't heard of anything at Kinross. But accidents like what happened to Jack Dowden are rare. They look out for their drivers because there's so much riding on their goodwill. They get good wages for keeping their mouths shut, and there's always a medical man around in time of crisis."

"Like Dr Gary Carswell?"

"That's the one. Yeah, like him. On one side of the fence he deals with all medical needs. On the other he tells the world what the firm is doing to clean up the environment. He can make me cry when he talks about the evils of pollution in the Great Lakes. Have you ever heard him? He does the Chamber of Commerce and Rotary a couple of times a year," Pásztory said, lighting another cigarette.

"We know that Dowden was worried about the toxic substances he was carrying a year ago. He wasn't an activist long, before he died."

"I know what you're thinking, but you won't ever be able to prove a word of that. You weren't there and there are respectable witnesses who were, including your Dr Carswell."

"I'm meeting Dowden's friend Brian O'Mara this afternoon," I said. "Maybe he has done some thinking since the accident. Maybe he'd be willing to talk."

"'Accident,'" he sneered. "I guess we'll have to go on calling it that. I love the expression."

"Maybe there *have* been other Dowdens and we haven't recognized the signs," I said, thinking out loud. "They didn't all have to walk in front of their trucks."

"I'll keep on reading up old coroner's reports, but I don't think they'll give us anything we can use. Remember," he added, "I've been in this business longer than you have. I know more about the dirty tricks they play."

"So, your bunch isn't ready to take Kinross to court on a dumping of toxic chemicals charge, I take it?"

"We are closer to getting the goods on another company. Kinross isn't the only heavy around, Benny. But as I said, building up a case takes months of careful work. We were just about to act when we walked into a brick wall. That was about two weeks ago. You want to hear about it?"

"Sure. I've got time."

"Okay. There's an outfit named Millgate-Falkner down by Papertown South. The head man's Lloyd Barlow. M-F's a smaller outfit than Kinross, but they go through a fair amount of stuff. I had a number of the pollution people that hang around Environment Front keep an eye on M-F over a three-week period. We were on the brink of taking them into court when, somehow, they knew we were waiting for them. There'd been a tip-off and we were dead."

"You still had the evidence?"

"Sure, and they knew exactly what evidence we had against them. They had three lawyers working around the clock on our people. They nailed one for being an American draft-dodger who never applied for landed-immigrant status, another for having a marijuana conviction ten years in his past and a few more intimate tricks like that. We had a mole inside M-F. He suddenly moved to Prince Rupert, B.C. Do you want me to go on?"

"I get the picture. The security of your organization has been breached."

"Look, Benny. I don't believe in security. It can't be breached because I don't trust anybody. No, this went up in smoke after it left us and went to our lawyer."

"And your lawyer had to disclose to the Crown, is that it?" Pásztory lit another cigarette from the butt of its predecessor.

"All I know for sure is that we walked into court with

no surprises. I can still hear the horse-laugh we got as every one of our witnesses failed to appear."

"Sounds like a nightmare."

"I'm just telling you this to warn you so you won't have a nightmare of your own." Pásztory had been lowering his voice steadily as we talked, as though the listening walls were moving closer. Half the time I could hardly hear him from across the table. It was his way of making sure I knew that this was inside information. I had to piece together the sense of what he said from the general flow. "These guys," he went on, "are playing with big bucks. With little or no yelling from the public, they're making huge profits and not taking responsibility for getting rid of the garbage reasonably."

"Are you saying that nobody cares?"

"The only issue the average Joe Citizen gets excited about is when somebody plans to dump waste near him. Then he yells his head off. The papers pick up the echo and the idea dies. Now Kinross and M-F, they don't make the average Joe Citizen mad because they don't build dump sites. They dump at midnight or while Joe Citizen is watching the news on TV after the hockey game."

"So they stay clear of controversy."

"Completely. Their PR is great, their image is dust-free and untarnished. It makes me sick."

"So, what are you going to do about it?" I asked.

Pásztory grinned as though my question was a good one. "I'll tell you one thing," he said, lowering his voice a notch or two, "when I leave you, I'm going off to meet the AV. I've been looking forward to this for a long time." The AV, I wondered. What was an AV when it was at home? I'd have to look that up. I'm not up to date on all of the fancy initials they use in modern business. I didn't have the training. Then I remembered something.

"You told me that there was something in the Kinross yard you wanted me to see," I reminded him.

"I didn't say it was in the Kinross yard, but you're right. That's where it is all right."

"We can't just walk in there."

"When you leave here, take a peek through the fence beside the first of the Quonset huts. It's so unusual, you'll spot it in a—" He stopped talking suddenly. He held his coffee cup where it was, near his lips, but had stopped sipping between sentences. "I gotta go," he said, looking over his shoulder. He replaced the cup in the saucer, spilling and slopping some of the coffee on the table. "You were right about this place after all," he said. He threw a two-dollar bill on the table's vinyl top and got up to go. "Talk to yuh," he said and walked straight to the door and through it.

I turned around in my seat to see what had touched Pásztory off like that. The only thing odd I could see was a group of three men wearing yellow hard hats standing around a table and choosing who was going to sit across from whom. I was about to pass from them for another source of bother. Then I looked at the hard hats again. Two of them were strangers to me, but the one who finally sat looking in my direction was far from a stranger. Under the plastic helmet I recognized the features of Dr Gary Carswell.

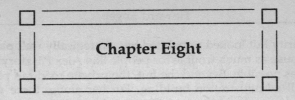

Chapter Eight

I'd be a bad witness on whether Dr Carswell recognized either Alex Pásztory or me. At least he didn't knock the dishes off the table and get suddenly to his feet with the whites of his eyes enlarged like Don Webster in the Grantham Player's Guild production of *Macbeth*. When Don, as Macbeth, saw Banquo's ghost, he let everybody in on it. At least Carswell was keeping it to himself if he spotted us. The yellow hard hats remained on the heads of the doctor and his friends. Coffee came for them and occasionally I heard a loud laugh from their booth. While I tried to think what to do next, I paid my check, adding another dollar to the two Alex Pásztory had left behind. The waitress swept the money away without a word; I'd had my fifteen minutes and it was time to move on.

After leaving the restaurant, I walked in front of the truck that had been blocking the view across the road. At least here I couldn't be observed by Carswell. Once again I was face to face with the Kinross yard. It hadn't changed much. The same chain-link fence surrounded the enclosure. Three strands of barbed wire formed the icing on the cake. An illegal entry would have to be premeditated. Something with a ladder, I thought, and a mattress. The gate, in its open position, swung back and stood twice as high as the wire fence. The crossbar at the top was as high as the very largest of trucks. Inside the gate, a small security hut looked unpainted but strategically well placed to cause as much trouble for people like Alex Pásztory and me as possible. Beyond the hut, the private road ran past a small administration building. Further along, there were warehouses, garages and Quonset huts. A line of heavy trucks stood guard on one side of a wide tarmac like they were armoured tanks. There was little human activity as far as I could see. I walked along the road, on my side, until I was across from the first of the Quonset huts. By now I was far enough along the Scrampton Road so that I didn't have to worry about being seen from the Turkey Roost. I crossed to the other side and approached the fence.

I wasn't sure what I was supposed to be looking for. Alex hadn't had time to give me any hints. There was nothing on the metal sides of the hut itself except the texture that weathered aluminum runs to. Along the narrow passage between the hut and the fence, there was a pile of discarded junk: pine boards, rusty metal stakes, a roll of snow-fencing, another of rusty wire fence, an oil drum with more garbage in it. Then I spotted something odd. A large seven was leaning against the drum. The numeral seven! On the ground near it were two metal arms, one larger than the other. Although they were face down, I could see that they were the arms or hands of a large clock. Made just like the hands on an old-fashioned watch, they would need a clock face of at least fifteen feet across to operate. A large seven and two hands of a giant clock! What the hell was I supposed to make of that?

Brian O'Mara's car was still warm in the driveway when I touched the hood on my way up to the porch of the small one-storey house about half-way up Junkin Street. The house was stucco with a pebble-dashed finish common to houses built during the Depression. An overweight woman with her hair under a net came and opened the door, giving me a glimpse into a living-room with a flight of plaster ducks hanging on the wall I could see best. The television was blaring unseen in another corner.

"Yes?" she said. I could tell she was not going to be helpful. I told her who I was. "He's not back from work yet," she said, trying not to look at the car in the driveway. "I don't know what time he's coming home tonight."

"You told me he gets off at four," I reminded her.

"Well, yes, that's true. But tonight, I don't know what's happened to him."

"I hope it isn't anything serious. Nothing as bad as what happened to Jack Dowden, for instance." She took that as though I'd hit her low in the midsection when the referee was turned away. She let her mouth sag open.

"Well he ain't here. That's all."

"May I wait?" I said, speaking correctly after her "ain't."

"I don't know when he'll be back," she protested, trying to end the conversation with the door. I held it from slamming with my foot. "He ain't here and I don't know when he'll be back!" she repeated.

"I just want to see him for a few minutes, Mrs O'Mara. I know he's in there!"

"I swear to God he ain't!" she said. Almost at the same moment a short, burly silhouette moved in behind her. He was wearing an open plaid shirt over a T-shirt and carrying the sport section of the *Beacon*.

"Are you Cooperman?" he asked, paying no attention to his wife's blasphemy. "I was talkin' to Irma about you. You know, Irma . . ."

"I know which Irma you mean," I said. "She told me you were a good friend of Jack Dowden's."

"That's right. She told you straight."

"Brian, I thought we talked about this," the woman in the hairnet interrupted, still testing my foot with the door.

"Dora, let me handle this. Okay?" He pulled Dora away from the door, making a space for me to push through. I moved through the vestibule and followed Brian O'Mara into the living-room. "Dora, be a sweetheart and go get us both a beer. I got a few chilling in the freezer. You drink beer, don'tcha, Mr Cooperman?"

"Sure. Thanks." He sat down on the low-slung couch and indicated that I should make myself comfortable as well. I sank deeply into a broad-beamed occasional chair facing the TV. Brian touched a remote-control box and the set went black. From the kitchen we could hear sounds of Dora taking out her fury on the freezer door and the opener.

"Don't mind Dora. She's just trying to look after me. It's just her way." I nodded my complete sympathy and understanding. He shoved along the couch so that we were nearly knee to knee. Next to us lay a coffee-table with a checkerboard pattern worked in two colours of inlaid wood. There were more plaster game birds in full flight behind me, as well as a genuine oil painting of the Toronto skyline with the whole thing reflected in a black velvet lake. I recognized the CN Tower both right-side-up and upside-down.

"You're still a driver at Kinross?"

"Sure. Seven years come next April. Jack got me in. I used to haul for Sunderland. Kinross is closer to home."

"You told the inquest a year ago that you thought that Jack had not been keeping his mind on the job. Did he tell you what was bothering him?"

Brian O'Mara thought about that before answering. He had been giving me the once-over as I sat there leaning back in the chair to increase the distance between us. "Jack was a real careful driver," he said. "Nobody ever had any trouble with him. He could go twenty-four, thirty hours at a shot without sleep when I first met him. He never gave nobody any Mickey Mouse nonsense, if you get what I mean."

"But he was worried just before his death?"

"Not worried exactly, but not keeping his head straight. He was, what do you call it?—muzzy the last couple of weeks."

"That's what you said at the inquest, but Irma didn't believe you."

Here Dora came in with the beer. She dropped the bottles and recently rinsed glasses on the coffee-table for the men to sort out. She gave O'Mara a look that aspired to be meaningful and left us alone again. I poured a very cold bottle into a damp glass, watching the beads of moisture form on the sides as I waited for the head to settle. O'Mara waved his glass at me without saying anything, but I think he intended it to be a toast of some kind; mute, cautious, good wishes. He sipped at his beer, then held it out to look at and made a comment about the first beer after a day's work that didn't add to my investigation.

"We were talking about Irma," I reminded him.

"Yeah, I know. Irma don't believe that it was an accident. She thinks that us witnesses just cooked up a story and got the coroner to rubber-stamp what we said."

"That's about the size of it. Where were you at the time of the accident?"

"I was just coming out of the locker hut with Pegoraro. I heard Jack yell and saw the truck roll into him. He went right under the Freightliner. Just like I said at the inquest. It was pretty gruesome, I'll tell you."

"Is Pegoraro still working for Kinross?"

"No. Last I heard he was out in Alberta somewhere, Hinton, I think. He liked long runs, Luigi did."

"And the other fellow? The other witness?"

"Teddy Puisans? He went back to the old country. Somewhere in eastern Europe. Latvia, maybe. He'd made a pile, never got married. He had it made, and then his mother writes him from behind the Iron Curtain somewhere that she's sick and can't feed the geese no more. Just Teddy's luck. He cut out about four months ago."

"So, that makes you the only witness to the accident still on the scene," I said.

O'Mara grinned like I'd just told him that he was the oldest living inhabitant, that he occupied a place of honour, but one that no one would attempt to deprive him of.

"Wasn't Jack crushed against a cement-block wall, Brian?

"Yeah. There was a wall there. But by the time I got there, he was under the truck. Look, Mr Cooperman, we're talking a whole year ago, right? More than a year. I try to put such things out of my head. The doctor up at the yard told me that it wasn't good to let my mind linger, you know what I mean?"

"Sure. It isn't healthy, right?"

"Hey, I didn't mean that! I meant—"

"I know. I know. How wide is the bumper on a Freight-liner truck?"

"Huh? Look, ah, they make a few models."

"You know the one I mean. The one that ran into your pal, Jack Dowden."

"Yeah, oh, yeah. That one. Well, the bumper runs right across the front, about a foot wide, I guess." O'Mara was nearing the bottom of his glass of beer. It didn't appear that it had had a cooling effect on him. His neck stood out red against his plaid shirt, which was hard to do. "Look, Mr Cooperman, I can't remember that long ago. I been over it so often, I don't remember what I saw any more. Honest."

"Okay, I'll change the subject for now. But I might come back to it some day. Tell me about the kind of things Jack was talking about around the yard just before he was killed."

"I told you. Just stuff he shouldn't have worried about."

"You mean the waste he was carting?"

"Not only that, Mr Cooperman. He was talking about

how we were killing the Great Lakes and poisoning the rivers and all that stuff you see on the CBC. He was getting to be a broken record every time I seen him. He wasn't paying attention to his work. And him once the most careful driver around. One time nobody had a better sheet than Jack. No major traffic convictions, no pile-ups, no subpoenas, nothin'." O'Mara leaned over into my airspace and pushed his empty glass into my chest for emphasis. "I'll tell you somethin', Mr Cooperman," he said, "I always modelled myself on Jack Dowden. I'll tell you that for nothin'. There were lots of young guys around the yard, guys that look like they know it all, but they watched Jack like a hawk, let me tell you. If Jack wore a leather jacket, all these young kids would start wearing them too. It was a laugh to see it, but, hey, what a tribute, right?"

"Did you and Jack talk about his environmental worries?"

"I don't get paid for talkin'! I just go in the office, pull my work order, the waybills and I'm off. I might see Jack for a second hauling his tractor over to a trailer, but more than wave at each other, we didn't talk."

"But you told the inquest that he'd been less attentive to his work."

"Yeah, well. You don't have to have a conversation to see that he was getting careless."

"In what way?"

"Well . . . Hey, you're forgettin' this was some fifteen months ago!"

"I'm not asking what he had for lunch; I'm asking what he told you."

"The talk around the yard was that he was bending everybody's ears with all that pollution stuff."

"But he didn't talk to you about it? Not just before the accident?"

"Naw, the last time we shot the shit was over coffee a few days after he was a finalist in the National Roadeo

Championships in Toronto. Jack could haul a rig through the eye of a needle. Then we talked again. Where was it now? Must have been that truck-stop called The Fifth Wheel near the Hydro Canal fill. About two miles from Niagara Falls." I made a mental note to look the place up on a map. O'Mara went on. "He told me about the books he'd been looking at and explained about the chemicals we were hauling. We never asked questions about that kind of thing. We're paid to drive, not ask for information we won't understand anyway. Besides, it's an old story in this business: the less you know, the safer you sleep. You know what I mean?"

"Were you dumping in sewers at night?"

"I'm not saying a thing about that."

"I'm not asking for the record; I just want to get a handle on things. I'm not working for the cops, you know. Just Irma. Just trying to find out if there was something fishy about Jack's death."

"Christ, Cooperman, I don't know you and I don't owe you! Hell, you could be wearing a wire for all I know. I think we're getting close to the end of this."

"Okay, I'm nearly through. Wasn't it very convenient that there should be a doctor on hand at the time of the accident?"

"Dr Carswell comes in maybe once a week. Nothin' strange about that. Mr Caine wasn't there, just Webster, the yard manager."

"Funny he wasn't called as a witness."

"If you say it's funny, then I guess it's funny."

"Okay, what about the dumping? Off the record."

"We haul all kinds of stuff to local dumps. That's it."

"What about the stuff that doesn't get to the dumps."

"Okay, you better finish your beer," he said. And I knew I wasn't going to get any more out of him just then. He wasn't visibly sweating, but he wiped his forehead with a neat white handkerchief just the same. I thought truckers carried red bandanas. I was obviously out of date about a lot of things.

I thanked him for his help. Even knowing that there was more where that came from, I could see he was scared. I didn't blame him. In his place, I'd be scared to death. O'Mara watched me move closer to the bottom of my glass in silence. I'm a slow drinker, so the silence was considerable. At last, as I hoped, he filled it. A witness who is trying to say nothing is often undone by a long pause in the conversation. "Look, Mr Cooperman, I'm not a hard guy to get along with. I'm just lookin' out for my end."

"I understand, Brian. Don't give it a thought. We won't be able to bring Jack back from the dead, will we?"

"There's a lot of money tied up in that business over at Kinross," he said. "It's a sweet line of work from their point of view: all profit and no risks."

"What do you mean 'no risks'?"

"Well, for one thing, who'd believe somebody like Jack or me when there's Mr Caine and Dr Carswell on the other side. And for another thing," he said, taking the last of his beer down an open throat, "and for another thing, Kinross and the city are in bed together on this waste-disposal business."

"What?"

"You heard me. It's no secret. Kinross gets rid of the city's unwanted waste the same as it does for industry. If the city calls the cops on Kinross, it'll be calling the cops on itself. And you and me know the people downtown aren't that stupid."

What O'Mara said enlarged the picture I'd been working on. If City Hall was involved, I was creeping into a bigger rats' nest than I'd imagined. I tried not to let O'Mara see how worried he'd made me. Why can't cases get simpler instead of always getting more complicated?

There was a slight commotion in the kitchen after a door slammed. For a minute, I thought Dora had stepped out for a walk, but I heard her voice alternating with a deeper one.

"That'll be Rory," O'Mara said. "He's my boy, just home from practice." I looked up, and, in a second or two, Rory came into the living-room. He was a tall, skinny kid with dark hair dyed darker. Black was his theme colour. It was in his tight trousers, his shirt and his windbreaker. All of this was set off against his pale, unlined face. He saw me as an obstacle sitting in the chair opposite the TV set, frowned and sent a glance in his father's direction, but it didn't land anywhere.

"What's all this?" he said with another look at me. His voice had a slight Mersey twang in it. Were the Beatles still a major influence today? "Dad, is it your birthday or something?"

"It's a friend of Jack Dowden, Rory. This here is Mr Cooperman. We'll be finished in a minute."

"Glad to meet you, Rory," I said, holding out my hand, half-getting out of my seat. Rory didn't see it.

"It's getting on time for 'People's Court,' Dad."

"You got a set upstairs."

"Ah, come on! I like it in colour. Give us a break!" I moved from half-way out of the chair to fully upright. Rory was bigger than me by three inches. I thought, maybe he'll have back trouble in middle age. I made my way to the front door, thanking O'Mara for his help. Dora came to see me off the property too. Rory turned the TV set on and I heard the familiar theme music.

"Mr Cooperman," O'Mara called after me, "don't get me in shit with the company, you hear? I got responsibilities?"

"You didn't tell me anything. You never said a thing."

I heard the door close behind me, and I made my way along the sidewalk to the driveway and down to the car. I wondered what it was that Rory was practising. I couldn't come up with an image that was foul enough.

Chapter Nine

The information I'd just heard from Brian O'Mara had nearly knocked me over onto the checkerboard coffee-table, scattering the artificial flowers. I had built a career on staying well away from City Hall. City Hall was nothing but bad news to me ever since the time I found the deputy mayor in the undignified position of filling his pockets from the public purse. You can bet that the city was full of thanks to Benny Cooperman for pointing out the guilty party. City council never did get around to voting the money for a monument to be erected to my memory, although there were a few aldermen who wished the occasion for a wreath at least would come quick. They say that the ancient Greeks used to kill the messenger who brought bad news. The elected officials of Grantham were still in favour of that treatment where I was concerned. My mother says I'm just sensitive to criticism.

The idea of walking into City Hall asking questions of the appropriate party about the disposal of the city's waste and the politics that guided the designated contractor, namely Kinross Disposals, filled me with cowardice. I just wanted to go back to Irma Dowden and tell her to forget the whole thing. Maybe I should have done that, but I didn't. I called Martha Tracy instead.

"M'yes? Who is this?"

"Martha, it's me."

"Cooperman, is that you?"

"At your service."

"Listen, Cooperman, whenever you say you're at my service, you are trying to get some service out of me. Don't argue, I know you too well."

"Martha—"

"I've billeted friends of yours—friends who up and leave without saying thanks or even goodbye. You spent a few nights here when the posse was out looking for you and I've been called at all hours of the day and night to get you out of trouble. What is it this time?"

"Martha, you are my one true friend in all the world."

"Sounds serious. You want me to put up a whole hockey team this time? Benny, one day you'll go too far!"

"Martha! Please!"

"Oh, God, I hate to hear you whine, Cooperman. You are one of the great whiners. You should get a medal."

"I only want information tonight. Honest, Martha. No billets, no meetings with distinguished forwards or defencemen. Just my undying gratitude."

"Cooperman, your gratitude will last the night. Your needs will die when you do and your habits don't lead me to think you're going to outlive the flower of your generation."

"I'll take my thanks beyond the grave, Martha. There's a crown on high with your name on it."

"In pawn, I'll bet and you've got the ticket. What is it this time?" She was beginning to unwind. Martha really knew how to use the telephone. With her, it was an art.

"Who is it down at City Hall," I asked, "who is in charge of handling the city's waste? You know, garbage, stuff like that?"

"Cooperman, you're transparent and manipulative. Why don't you pick up some beer and a pizza—hold the anchovies—and get your little bottom over here? We can settle all this under my roof," she said, and added archly, "unless the girlfriend has a prior claim."

"Anna's not the girlfriend, Martha. Wishes still aren't horses. I'm on the prowl on my own."

"Whoopee for us! See you in half an hour. For you, I'll even put some clothes on."

"Don't break the habit of a lifetime for an old pal."

"Maybe I was in the mood anyway. Bring some real beer, not that play-beer they sell on television."

"I'll see what I can find. See you."

"M'yeah, I guess." And she was gone.

An hour later three pieces of uneaten pizza lay congealing in their carton and four of the bottles of ale had been returned empty to their case. Martha had put on slacks and a pink sweater topped off with a round medallion on a chain. She'd even done something new to her hair since I saw her last, but I couldn't figure out what. Part of the effect of the transformation was spoiled by the fact that she was still wearing bedroom slippers that had probably been around when William Lyon Mackenzie roused the province to rebellion in 1837. With her Churchillian chin, Martha could have outfaced a battalion of rebels or the same number of Tories if it suited her.

I'd met Martha Tracy about ten years ago when I did that investigation into wrongdoing at City Hall. Martha worked in a real-estate firm that was mixed up in the story. She'd been keeping her eyes open around the powers that moved and shook Grantham for many years. Nobody knew Grantham like Martha. She once hinted that the firm she worked for, Scarp Enterprises, kept her on because they couldn't afford to let what she knew fall into other hands. She didn't do much around the office any more, but she answered the phone and watered the plants in a way that gave peace of mind to the partners. Her telephone manner was gruff; she tended to discourage triflers.

"There's nothing more burnt-out looking than a cold pizza, is there?"

"Reminds me of lonely birthdays in strange towns. Not mine, but I get that feeling. Another beer?"

"Moved and seconded. Why do you want to know about what the city does with its garbage, Benny?"

"I'm not sure I know yet myself. But if the city's up to some funny business, I won't find out by asking questions without knowing the background. If I'm going to stir up a local bees' nest, I want to know when I'm doing it. It's easier to stick handle the traffic that way and stay alive. I'm not interested in all of the garbage, just the toxic stuff: PCBs, dioxins and heavy-metal waste."

"Hey, Benny, you're pretty good! You must have been reading up on the stuff."

"Bedtime reading since I got involved," I said. Martha shook her head in sympathy. But she was right, I was getting better at talking about toxic garbage. But it was still more abstract than real to me. I couldn't really imagine that stuff leaking from a truck could send me to hospital. In fact, I was dreading my encounter with reality. What form was it going to take? For Martha I tried to look innocent. Maybe I achieved the look of a kid caught cramming before an easy exam.

I opened a beer for Martha, and she poured most of it into the glass in front of her. My own glass was still full. What with my visit to the O'Maras', I was seeing a lot of beer suddenly. I got back to questioning Martha. First, though, I decided not to light a new cigarette. It was a peculiar feeling.

"Who is in charge of the toxic waste that comes out of the city, Martha?"

"The head man is Paul Renner, director of sanitation.

"Is he elected?"

"Not on your life. It's a paying job and Paul's been in it for four or five years. As director he sits as a commissioner along with other non-elected heads of standing departments: roads, parks, finance."

"Does the city deal with its own waste?"

"No, it does what you and I do: it passes it on to somebody else. In this case it's a contractor. Kinross, I think. Why are you grinning like the Cheshire cat? You know I can't stand secrets. Benny!"

"Okay. Okay. Kinross has been doing a lot of dumping, legal and illegal. Some of that is for the city. How much does Paul Renner know about what Kinross does with the toxic stuff it collects?"

"How come you give a damn? What's in it for you?"

"Three hundred and twenty-five dollars a day, expenses and maybe a broken kneecap if I make the wrong moves. So far I haven't been moving at all, just asking fool questions. Who controls the money and the hiring of an outfit like Kinross, Martha?"

"The purse-strings of city council are held by the inner circle called the executive committee. The committee picks the contractors to do all sorts of jobs. It's the old tender process. You know, justice must not only be done but be seen to be done. The director of sanitation has a job to do, he gets a description of the job circulated and contractors put in their bids. The winning bid is often, but not always, the lowest bidder. That's the way business is done by governments. Doesn't matter whether you're a hamlet out in the township or a big outfit like Toronto or the province. Everything has to be seen while the deals are being made. No secret deals."

"Really?"

"We're talking theory here, Cooperman. Sure there are small jobs that are below the tender minimum. Sometimes big jobs get chopped up into smaller bites so that they'll avoid the whole process. But in the case of Kinross . . ."

"Uh-huh? What's the scoop on Kinross?"

"As far as the city's concerned, there isn't another outfit big enough to take on the city business. Whenever the contract comes up for renewal, there's not a competent rival putting in a bid. Kinross has Grantham's business sewn up."

"What responsibility does Renner take for what Kinross does with its toxic waste? We'll assume that the sweet-smelling stuff goes into land-fills and regular dumps. What about checking up on Kinross? Is there an inspection setup?"

"As far as I know, the only inspection system is what we get from the media and that Environment Front outfit. Anybody can lodge a complaint."

"Can you find out when Kinross is coming up for renewal?"

"Shouldn't be too hard. I do have friends in high places, you know."

"You're an amazing woman, Martha."

"Keep it coming, Cooperman. You know I eat it up."

"All I want to know is what you left out. What's the keystone to what you've told me?"

"Oh, that's easy. You know Paul Renner I was telling you about?"

"Yeah."

"Well, he's married to the former Adelaide Grier."

"Give that man a chocolate mouse."

"You haven't been doing your research. You're slacking, Cooperman. Not up to the mark. Adelaide is the older sister of one Caroline Grier Forbes. She's Ross Forbes's sister-in-law!"

I knew I lived in a small town. I knew that in the nature of things there were lots of shortcuts. I knew Pete Staziak from school. Now Pete's a staff sergeant at Niagara Regional. I never walk up St Andrew Street without seeing dozens of people I go way back with. So, why was I getting so excited? The Griers, Forbeses and Renners moved in the same exalted circles, that's all. I couldn't bring Renner and Forbes to book because of a little nepotism. And which came first, anyway? I'd have to get better information than just a family connection. I can't remember ever reading about a local story dealing with a conflict of interests. Conflicts of interest were items for national or provincial stories. We all loved them but, of course, nothing like that ever happens around home. We keep our integrity all locked up in a blind trust. That way it won't spring out and shoot you between the eyes. Nepotism, like charity and incest, begins at home.

I gave her a warm hug before I left and she saw me out onto the porch in her slippers. I looked back along the street and returned her wave.

Before calling it a day, I dropped by my office to see whether anybody was looking for me. The answering service disappointed me as usual. I consoled myself by going through the box of papers I'd borrowed from Irma. It was an old shoebox, held together with three elastic bands. Two of them snapped as I tried to wiggle them free. What is the life-expectancy of a rubber band? About fifteen months, I guess.

Whoever did Jack Dowden's last tax return had forgotten about or never knew about this box of credit-card receipts. Most of them were from oil companies. Following a paper trail was like old times again. I must have followed hundreds of them when I was in the divorce business. I started putting the flimsies in piles according to oil companies and locations to see what kind of pattern would show through. There were a few fill-ups in distant places like Tarrytown, New York, and Springfield, Massachusetts. There were a couple from as far west as Dryden and Kenora, Ontario. I inspected the bunch from places in Grantham. Nothing odd about them. I used some of the same service stations myself. What surprised me were the receipts from Niagara-on-the-Lake. Niagara-on-the-Lake isn't on the road to anywhere except Niagara-on-the-Lake. Unless Dowden was meeting a boat, and I doubted that, Niagara was the end of the line. What was the attraction, I wondered.

I was still dreaming over Jack Dowden's shoebox, when the phone rang. It was too late for business, so I answered hoping for personal. It was Anna, the particular personal caller I was hoping to hear from.

"Hi, Benny. You really work for your money in your racket. It's late!"

"I've been busier. I just got back from Martha Tracy's." I filled Anna in on the beer, pizza and conversation. I added: "Martha's a fan of yours. She thinks I could learn about fish forks from you. What's to know about fish forks?"

"She still looks out for you, doesn't she?" Anna said. "As for fish forks, I'm sure Martha knows as much about them as I do. I eat mussels with my fingers," she said, making slurping sounds. "Hey, Benny, when do you let your operatives make their reports?"

"What do you have, H21? I'll take it down in invisible ink. No, I'll have to settle for invisible crayon."

"I found out that the person looking into the history of Kinross Disposals is the guy who writes about the environment in the *Beacon*, Alexander Pastor. He's with Environment Front."

"I should have guessed."

"Thanks a lot! Next time you can do your own digging."

"Sorry, Anna. It's just that I saw him today for a few minutes. It makes sense that it should have been Alex."

"What's my next assignment?"

"Get some sleep. That's what I'm going to do. All play and no work, you know. We should go to the movies again soon, okay?"

"There's the weekend."

"You've got that wedding."

"That's *next* weekend! Benny, you never listen. How do you stay in business?"

"That's part of the secret. Good-night, Anna."

I hung up and reached for my map of the area. Unfolding it over the desk blotter, I found the village. There was Niagara-on-the-Lake on the way to nowhere for a truck loaded with dioxins and PCBs. No bridge over the mouth of the Niagara River. Was the truck headed up the Niagara Parkway to a favourite dumping place? Was O'Mara going to speed up or retard the time on the floral clock with a watering of choice poisons? The map wasn't passing on any answers so I pulled out the dictionary instead. I flipped through to the end where the abbreviations were kept. I was worried about the term Alex Pásztory had used on me: AV it was. What was an AV anyway? The dictionary let me down like the map. Unless Alex was talking about paying a visit to the Authorized Version or the Artillery Volunteers. There were some Latin things too but they didn't fit either. I tried to recapture my former line of thought, but Anna's voice kept running through my head. After another minute, I put the still unlighted cigarette I'd been holding in my mouth back in the package again and turned out the lights.

On my way through the door, the light from the hall hit something white in my mail slot. Another handbill? I reached for it. It was a folded sheet of letter-size paper with a photocopied piece of fancy calligraphy. It was a familiar quotation, I'd seen it a dozen times. It may have been a final examination that calligraphers have to write in order to get their masters' papers. It began:

Desiderata

Go placidly amid the noise and haste and remember what peace there may be in silence . . .

The quotation went on and on. The part I've quoted had been underlined with red ballpoint. What was going on here? Was this somebody's idea of a warning for me to keep my mouth shut? Whatever happened to notes made out of letters clipped from newspapers and magazines? If I wasn't giving way to a persecution mania, I was standing in the way of a very classy type of goon. I shut the door behind me and reflected upon the virtues of silence as I went down the stairs.

Chapter Ten

I got up late. I'd been dreaming about Anna, Irma Dowden, Brian O'Mara and me going for a picnic to Niagara-on-the-Lake. We were being followed by an empty picnic hamper. In the end all we could find to eat was fudge. I tried to finish off the dream in the shower, give it a happy ending, but after the first minute of sweet-toothed joy, the dream became a glucose nightmare. The ringing of the telephone, as usual, ended the shower.

"Cooperman. Hello?"

"Benny! I only half-thought I'd find you there. But there was no answer at your office." It was Teddie Forbes.

"Morning, Teddie. What time is it?"

"I never wear a watch," she said. I don't know why I asked. "Benny, I'm sorry I didn't call yesterday, but I've been hung over since Tuesday when some guy got me loaded in the Snug." The reference went over my head. At first I didn't think her drinking had anything to do with me. Then I remembered her three martinis. I apologized to her.

"It was your fault. I'm not used to it any more. And there was somebody at the table I couldn't completely trust after I got started. I don't mean you, Benny."

"That's all very flattering, Teddie. What's it going to cost me?"

"Is that the thanks I get? I've been in conference with Jim Colling since sun-up, as we say down in Arizona, and you don't even want to hear what we came up with." Jim Colling was Teddie's lawyer, a smooth, intelligent man, with tiny corn-kernel teeth. He'd steered Teddie's divorce into the big numbers.

"Okay, astonish me. What did you two think up?"

"Meet us at the Di right away."

"Make it twenty minutes and you've got a deal. I have to put some clothes on."

"Right, you make yourself presentable, then hurry to the Di."

"What kind of lawyer is Colling anyway he can afford to put a hole in his morning? There aren't many Grantham lawyers who step out of their offices for under five hundred dollars."

"Jim has a score to settle with Ross, too."

"Hey, Teddie, I don't want to get in over my head! I try to keep things simple and as honest as I can afford to be." Teddie laughed into the phone.

"Just make it snappy," she said. "See you in twenty minutes."

"Yeah," I said, wondering if I had any clean socks.

There was an eddy of wind blowing dust and chewing-gum wrappers into a minor disturbance outside the apartment when I stepped out into the sunlight nearly half an hour later. I caught some of it in my left eye. It was still bothering me when I entered the Di, which is short for Diana Sweets. Gus, the counterman, paused with his chopping knife held above his sliced olives, and smiled as I walked past him looking for Teddie. I spotted them with my good eye, half-way down the aisle on the right side. They looked buoyant.

"Benny, what kept you? Aren't you excited to know—? What did you do to your eye?" Teddie went from being generally excited and friendly to instant motherly concern in less than a second. She caught me under the chin and tilted my head up towards the suspended globes of light. "That's dirt in there," she said with emphasis that didn't put me at ease. I handed her a wad of tissue from my pocket. She took it and dabbed at me with it, her long fingernails making a permanent impression in the back of my neck. "There!" she said at last, after scouring my cornea and holding up the tissue like a trophy of battle. "There, it's out!"

"Thanks," I said. "It was only a speck of dust."

"Horatio Nelson went nearly blind from dust in the eye," said Jim Colling, who had been watching Teddie's demonstration of first aid. Both Teddie and I looked at him and he backtracked. "Well, it was gravel. Much the same." Teddie released the vise on my neck. We both settled into the stained-maple seats of the booth, she beside Jim and me facing both of them. I think we expected to hear more from the lawyer about Horatio Nelson, but he seemed to have shot his bolt with the information already given. A waitress approached.

"Have youse decided what youse want yet?" she asked. She was balancing the edge of her empty tray on her hip, her weight unevenly distributed so that she looked more the coquette than she intended. We ordered coffee and she was off. Colling watched the ribbon that tied her apron on as it danced up the aisle to the service centre and the silexes of coffee. Teddie made a comment about "youse" and we all said something to make us feel superior. It felt good for a moment, like I'd joined the club. In the minutes that followed the arrival of the coffee Jim said "hopefully" and I got "lay" and "lie" twisted again. Grammatical purity is an elusive brass ring on the communication carousel. It's like a flag blowing in the Antarctic wastes, out of reach to all but the pure of heart. I thought of Scott and Amundsen for a moment, then remembered my mother saying, after watching the re-created drama of the

race to the pole on television, that she had always wanted
to be the first woman to get to the pole in heels. Jim and
Teddie exchanged looks as they sipped from their coffee
cups. Jim's saucer, like the cup in the Twenty-third Psalm,
ranneth over, and he mopped up the spillage with a paper
table napkin.

"Well," I said, still uneasy about what I might be getting
into, "what have you two come up with?"

"Jim has a lulu, Benny," Teddie said. She was leaning on
her elbows like a little girl about to tell a secret. She turned
to face each of us as she said our names, as though without
the glance we might get ourselves confused. "We considered a few schemes, but they all collapsed because Ross is
such a suspicious bastard." The waitress hovered again
with a silex and refilled our half-empty cups. She didn't
appear to have been offended by Teddie's language. She
didn't look as though she listened to conversations, not so
much as a matter of principle as from a desire to keep life
as simple as possible. Teddie unarched the raised eyebrow
and dug an elbow into Jim's well-hidden ribs. "Tell him,"
she said.

"You see, Benny," he began, "Teddie still has a legal
right to ask for favours from Phidias. She's still on the
board. She's well known and they value her connection
more than they otherwise might, considering the way
things between Ross and her turned out." Jim began to tell
me about how Teddie had come into the firm and how
many shares of what kinds of stock she was seized of. I
kept one ear on the monologue while I tried to remember
what I knew about James J. Colling. Jim was an educated
farmboy from out in the township. He'd done a law
degree in Toronto and had slowly built up a practice
centred on the real estate he'd wandered over as a boy. All
those vanished farms were now subdivisions under the
brow of the escarpment, and he was one of the best-known

lawyers in Grantham. I watched him talking at me, smiling with what looked like a mouthful of a hundred baby teeth. His fat cheeks were unlined, his nose, rather piggish but well centred. He had the shoulders of a wrestler and a collar that looked too tight. I tuned in again.

"The moment Teddie wants something, Ross would know that something was up. He knows she has rights, but he watches her like a hawk. As a director of Phidias she has more rights to see the company books than you or I." Teddie caught my eye with one of hers. I wonder when she began to get so sensitive to Jim's rough edges. "So, I thought of a scheme that might work *because* Ross has little regard left for Teddie." They exchanged a conspiratorial grin and faced me again. This time Teddie took up the plot.

"That's right! If you go to the office, Benny, saying that you are doing me a favour, Ross would stall and stall. But, if you go in saying that you're from the IRS in the States, you know, Internal Revenue, doing an audit on my status as a non-resident, or that you're from Revenue Canada auditing my return for, say, two years ago, Ross would lead you by the hand to the minute books of the corporation just hoping that you'll nail me good."

"Teddie, I can't go in there pretending to be a government officer!" I protested. "That comes under at least three criminal statutes that I can think of without even looking it up!"

"Cyrano to the life!" she said. I didn't catch her meaning. What did this have to do with the long-nosed guardsman in a play?

"I admit it's sailing close to the law," Jim said, pulling at a tightly knotted necktie thoughtfully. "What about this: suppose you are working as an agent for Teddie, hired by me to check the dividends owing to Teddie in the company books. You see, Teddie has an apartment here in

town and her place in Flagstaff. Teddie has chosen the
Grantham place as her permanent residence and pays
Canadian taxes. You follow me?"

"So far," I said, "but you could lose me in a second.
Why not get an accountant to examine the books?
Wouldn't that be more normal?"

"I thought you'd ask that. There are a few reasons. One,
you're cheaper; two, it's not very complicated; three, bringing in a bunch of chartered accountants is bad for business—it puts the wind up; four, if you need it, you are
known to have acted for Teddie in the past." I nodded that
I had heard him, but I was still just listening. I could still
not agree to any of this.

"You see, Benny, residency is a grey area in tax law. The
main thing is that Teddie has been paying Canadian taxes.
She has to pay here or there, and since her income comes
from here, there's no reason that she should have to pay
Canadian witholding tax." Colling was quickly losing me
as I had predicted.

"Benny," Teddie put in, "Ross put my American address into the Phidias records, so they take fifteen percent
of my dividends as witholding tax. That means that in
spite of my paying Canadian taxes, I'm also paying extra
as a non-resident."

"But you are a non-resident, Teddie. I don't see the
miscarriage of justice."

"As long as I maintain the apartment, I'm living here,
Benny. It's not a scam, honest."

"Look, for years I've tried to get Forbes to direct the
dividends to Teddie's Canadian address and stop the non-
residence witholding tax. But Ross isn't about to do Teddy
any favours."

Both of them were looking at me from across the table
like they were selling a new brand of drug. I still didn't
like it.

"Benny," Teddie said, "if the IRS is auditing me, and demanding that I file a U.S. return, I have a right to try to show that Phidias has exaggerated my dividends. We hire you, and that way you'll get to see the minute books of the corporation."

"Teddie's right," Colling said. "Phidias is a private corporation, so the minute books will show all share transfers and all leases, just the things that Teddie told me you wanted to have a look at."

"The beauty of the scheme, Benny, is that the IRS isn't going to put anybody wise. They never tell people what they are up to. They don't explain their actions to anybody."

"And you think that Ross would let me into Phidias just because it may put Teddie in wrong with the American tax people?"

"Exactly!" Colling resembled a happy convert to a new sect or schism.

"Why won't he stall us?" I wondered whether he was listening.

"Because it's in his interest to see that Teddie's life stays as complicated as possible." I believed him about the complicated part. "And as far as Section 319, et cetera, of the Criminal Code goes, you are not going to profit by any of this information financially. Not directly, anyway." Colling was still selling. Teddie was backing him up to the hilt.

"I only regret I won't be here to see the look on Ross's face when he finds out!" Teddie said. Colling shot her a quick look and my eyes must have given me away too. She quickly added, "Years from now, I mean, Benny. Years from now. After it's all over and done with."

"Thanks a lot, you two," I said, ripping open a plastic cream container I had no intention of using. "The best that can come of this is the lessons I'm going to get in how to stitch mail bags in Kingston pen. Haven't either of you any idea that I can't go around saying I'm an accountant when I'm not?"

"You don't have to say anything," Colling said, making a soothing gesture with both his chubby hands at once. "Supposing I set it all up from my office?" Jim suggested. "Without making any false claims, I can say things in an ambiguous way so that the treasurer of Phidias will expect you and then, once in, you can take it from there."

"Oh great!" I said, trying to think things through. "What happens when Ross recognizes me? What happens if he asks me a question I can't answer ambiguously? He knows I'm an investigator."

"Okay, you're an investigator. That's just as good."

"He'll see through it," I said, shaking my head.

"He hates me too much," Teddie said. "I'm his blind side, Benny. If he thinks I could get hurt, he'll show you the books himself. Trust me, Benny. I know him."

"My nose still itches where Ross Forbes flattened it."

"Benny, I said trust me. I *know* Ross. I was married to him for Christ's sake."

"You're all moving too fast for me. I have to think about the angles, Teddie. Remember, I don't have an Arizona bolt-hole to run back to."

"I thought you wanted to get inside Phidias, Benny. Were you just romancing me the other night or were you serious?" She was right. I had asked for help. It was just that I had an instinct to keep life simple. I was like the waitress. Simple is sometimes all I can take. As I watched the faces opposite me, I began to doubt my motives for getting inside the boardroom at Phidias. What was I expecting to find? An order to break the law and pollute the environment set out in black and white? Moved to snuff out one Jack Dowden for running off at the mouth. All those in favour? Carried.

Another two things bothered me. First, if Phidias knew what was going on at Kinross, then in the quiet offices of Phidias I'd be in as much trouble as I'd be walking into the Kinross yard asking questions. I could get myself killed and still not get any wiser.

The other thing was that I was in the dark about what Teddie and her lawyer were getting from all this. I didn't like to hold the hammer Teddie was hitting Ross with. It was like standing between two cars bent on ramming one another. While you couldn't tell how much damage they'd do to one another, it was pretty clear that I'd be a write-off.

And what about Colling? What was his interest? Is he just accommodating a lady or is there something in it for him? Teddie and Colling were watching me. I sat and sipped my cold coffee. Colling's twin rows of tiny teeth were smiling expectantly. Teddie tilted her head sympathetically as I ruminated. I tried to go through all of the possibilities again in my head. I sweated the idea for another minute, then accepted on the principle that I hadn't a clear alternative and what the hell.

Chapter Eleven

I t was going to take a few days for Colling to work his
magic on the treasurer at Phidias Manufacturing. In
the meantime, I gave Kinross another chance to settle
things before I had to run the risk of meeting Forbes again.
I drove up to the Scrampton Road and took a table at the
Turkey Roost where I could look out across the road at the
front gate. For half an hour I watched the way the guard-
house operated. There was a man inside who checked the
documents of all trucks leaving the yard and who kept
track on a clipboard of all the cars and trucks coming in. I
wondered about the page for the day of Dowden's death.
I'd like to see that.

The only trucks I recognized were Euclids and Macks. I
tried to concentrate on the rigs with closed containers and
the ones hauling storage drums. Most of these were huge,
lumbering things, with more wheels than the insides of a
ten-dollar watch. I paid my bill for the coffee I'd consumed
and the styrofoam cup I was taking back to my car with
me. Once in the car, I decided to follow one of the trucks,
just to see where it went. I didn't see the driver's face as he
climbed into the cab.

I trailed him, slow and steady, staying just far enough
behind him so that he wasn't tempted to use his CB and
send for help. He took the Queen Elizabeth Way towards
Niagara Falls. Ah, I thought, pay dirt on the first try. But
he turned off and stopped at the little park with the floral

clock in it just outside Niagara Falls. The clock was shut down, of course, waiting for spring like the eager student horticulturists who maintained it from April to Labour Day. I saw the driver retrieve a few large metal planters made in the shape of numerals, a three and a six, which he put into the back of his trailer before getting back on the road again. After less than three minutes, he'd pulled into a truck-stop called The Fifth Wheel, the restaurant O'Mara had mentioned. I could see that the lot at the side was full of loaded rigs from all over. I suppressed an urge to drop in. I didn't know which of the faces inside I was following. I made a U-turn and returned to the Scrampton Road again, thinking about the floral clock and the things I'd seen behind the Quonset hut.

After a toasted chopped-egg sandwich at the Turkey Roost, I tried again. This time it was a tanker, which headed straight for the City Yard on Louth Street. Here I was stopped at the gate, not by a guard, but by a failure of the imagination. I couldn't think what I would say to anyone challenging my right to be there. I used to be better at this, but now television has turned all parking-lot attendants and yard men into Perry Masons. There was a time when I could work for a year and never have to flash ID. Even phoney ID. Now you have to wave paper or plastic in front of everybody, even when all you want to do is use the toilet.

The tanker had disappeared around one of the two beehive-shaped storage sheds. From the street, as I turned off into the approach to the yard, they resembled two enormous breasts reminiscent of the busty pinups of the 1940s. The nearest intersection was notorious for the number of accidents that occurred within eyeshot of these mammoth mammaries. I wonder whether there is any connection. From my standing position at the gatehouse, I could see that the sheds had non-erotic functions as well as the fender-bending ones. I could see grey piles of road salt ready to attack the bottom of my car in the coming winter. The salt kept ice off the roads, but it exacted a random tax on the cars that used them: a muffler here, a tailpipe there and other bits of rusted underpinnings, mute testimony to the efficiency of the roads services of the Department of Works and Sanitation.

A big fellow in a nylon anorak of faded green had caught sight of me admiring his sheds. He stood looking at the car for a few seconds while a thought began forming under his yellow hard hat. When he was fully aware of its nature, he waved me off the property. Maybe he was reading my mind; I couldn't think of what I was doing there either. I turned the car around and came to a stop long enough to let a big, flat-bottomed, wide-bed truck with a medium-sized load under tarps out to Louth Street. It was a huge thing and I had to back up further to give it elbow room to pass me. I always have a lot of respect for anything that size. It would collect it, whether I was willing to give it or not.

My foot nearly froze on the brake when I saw that the man in the cab of the truck was Brian O'Mara. It took a second to react. Just like the guard, who was now closing the gate. I let the rig get ahead of me and I completed my turn and pulled out after him. I was fairly sure that he wouldn't beat me up even if he did catch sight of me in his rear-view mirror. But with all of his side mirrors he would have to be half asleep not to catch the shape of the Olds coming after him.

He moved north-east along Pelham Road and turned off into Glendale Avenue, where it crossed the Eleven Mile Creek, and followed it parallel to the base of the escarpment through the vanished farms and fields that are now subdivisions and shopping plazas until it crossed the Queen Elizabeth Way. This was major traffic, and for a moment I thought that I would lose my prey either to Toronto or Buffalo. But he didn't join the highway, he crossed over to the other side and picked the old road to St David's and Niagara-on-the-Lake.

O'Mara's apparent destination pricked up my ears. I took my eyes off the colouring trees, the blowing eddies of fallen leaves and the bright red of the sumachs and thought about Jack Dowden's shoebox of credit-card flimsies. Niagara-on-the-Lake was popular with Jack too. I was doing something right for a change.

I kept a pick-up truck with bushels of squash and turnips between me and O'Mara. The pick-up's suspension was dragging and raised a few sparks when the asphalt got rough. O'Mara had the road ahead of him clear; he didn't seem to be out to set a new speed record. Maybe he was looking at the changing leaves too.

Niagara-on-the-Lake has become a sand-blasted antique early-nineteenth-century town since the days when I first knew it. Then it was just a sleepy backwater with a jam factory. Now it was a tourist mecca because of the success of the Shaw Festival, an annual theatrical tribute to the bard of Ayot St Lawrence. Apart from the theatre, of course, there was the fudge. Places like Niagara revolve around fudge in the summer. Every other store sells it, tourists munch it as they stare through store windows at paper flowers, local history books and expensive soap smelling of sandalwood. People seem to be able to concentrate on fudge, which you could see being made through other store windows, long after interest in antiques, theatre and shopping has worn off. In August the stately brick homes of Niagara, the old Presbyterian church with its Greek columns, the sand-blasted façades along Queen Street dissolve into a mad rush of tourists with a need for a sweet fudge fix.

O'Mara stopped at the lights on the way into town, then headed straight up Mississauga Street to Queen. From here, over the fairways of the golf course, I could see the point where the Niagara River empties into Lake Ontario.

Across the water, on the American side, three flags flew from Fort Niagara. Three hundred years ago, Fort Niagara was the only man-made structure around here except for teepees and wigwams. On the Canadian side, the smaller of the two Canadian forts looked like an up-ended flower-pot or a child's one-scoop sand-castle in the middle of the golf course.

The truck turned east at Queen; then, after a block, it turned off the main drag into Simcoe and headed towards the river. I followed at a safe distance, catching a glimpse of the clocktower in the middle of Queen Street further down by the old town hall. With the golf course on our left, we both continued down Simcoe to the corner where it met Front Street. The houses along the other side of the street were big and old, going back well into the last century.

O'Mara took a left at the corner, where a temporary construction road headed off across the open terrain of the golf course in the direction of the fort. I turned the Olds in the opposite direction along Front and parked in the lot reserved for guests at the Oban Inn. I watched his rig bounce over the uneven ballast of the work road, seeing it grow smaller as it approached the Canadian Fort. I dismissed the idea of following it; out on the fairway, I'd be as conspicuous as a dead fly on a white sheet. That would have got O'Mara in trouble as well as yours truly. And I needed O'Mara. There were a lot of things he'd forgotten to tell me the other night.

I got out of the car and raised the hood, just to give me something to do in case there were eyes behind the window curtains of the Oban Inn. Across the warm motor, Fort Mississauga looked like it was painted by an amateur against a blue backdrop of lake and sky. It looked squatter from here than it did from Queen Street. There were no crenellated walls, no bastions, ravelins or parapets as far as

I could see, just a row of loopholes around the waist of a brick tower. For musket fire, I guess. The curved surface of the otherwise unadorned wall suffered from a skin disease; the plaster was peeling off to expose red brick underneath. For years the fort's thick hide had withstood the seasonal barrage of countless duffers from the second tee. I don't remember hearing whether it ever exchanged shots with Fort Niagara across the mouth of the river.

The truck disappeared behind a temporary enclosure that had been thrown up around the fort. It didn't look solid enough to protect it from tourists' golf balls, but it was a gesture in the right direction. A wind had come up, blowing eddies of dry leaves around in front of the Olds. There were whitecaps on the slate blue tops of the waves in Lake Ontario. It was hard to tell from where I was whether I was looking at the river or the lake. I wasn't expecting to see a dotted line separating the geographical features, but from ground level it was confusing.

There was no movement at the fort as far as I could see. O'Mara's truck had been swallowed up into what must be a depression in the ground close to the walls. I got the feeling that there was activity going on behind the fence, but I couldn't prove it until another truck emerged from the gateway. It had its headlights on and it headed over the bumpy construction road in my direction. By the time it reached the corner of Simcoe and Front to turn towards the highway, I was apparently lost in thought as I contemplated my distributor under the hood. The truck had a yellow panel on its door. It read: Sangallo Restorations, Niagara-on-the-Lake. It was a Euclid truck and the hopper in back was full of Ontario real estate. I was closing up the hood of the Olds when I remembered seeing the yellow Sangallo sign on a truck parked outside The Fifth Wheel less than half an hour ago. I knew I was going to see a lot of similar signs now that I was aware of Sangallo's existence. That's the way life works. Alex Pásztory had mentioned Sangallo. Something to do with Tony Pritchett and his mob.

I started the engine and slowly drove down Front Street, away from the golf course, and parked again not far from the corner of Front and King. King Street is the dividing line in Niagara. Streets crossing it change their names when they continue on the other side. Front becomes Ricardo, Prideaux becomes Byron, Queen becomes Picton and so on. It made the town seem bigger, I guess.

Through the car window I could see an athletic-looking man of middle age busily raking leaves from the lawn at the corner house. It was one of those picture-postcard houses that the town is famous for. This one wasn't given over to the fudge trade; its sign advertised Bed and Breakfast. The man with the rake paused to see what I wanted. With his pointed beard he looked a little satanic, but there was a twinkle in his eye.

"We've closed for the season," he said before I'd fully got out of the car.

"That's a shame," I said. No sense disillusioning the man whose enthusiasm causes him to rake leaves even in the off-season.

"Fellow in an antique Bentley parked outside yesterday and we had half a dozen people asking if we were open. You wouldn't consider parking right in front, would you?"

"Sure. Anything to help." I didn't know whether he was joking or not, so I moved the car just in case he was serious.

"I thought of renting a Rolls to park out front when we first opened, but business caught on. It just took time and word of mouth." He told me this when I joined him again on the sidewalk. I looked at the Olds. It wasn't in the first blush of youth, but it wasn't *that* bad.

"Do you know where I can rent a boat?" I asked.

"How big? What kind?"

I hadn't given the idea much thought. Vaguely I was wondering whether I might not be able to get closer to the fort from the lake than by trying to make out anything over the expanse of the golf course. "Something simple," I said. "It's just for me."

"How long will you need it?" he asked, taking another pass or two at the leaves. Maybe it warmed him up; he was standing in his shirt-sleeves.

"Oh, maybe an hour, an hour and a half. I just want to have a look at the famous fort from the water. Just to see what the enemy saw, if you follow me."

"I've got a small fibreglass rowboat, if that's any good to you," he said. "You won't be able to rent a boat at this time of year as far as I know. The Boat Works has been closed for a few years now."

"Oh, I wasn't looking for anything fancy. I'll be glad to rent yours, though."

"I can't rent it to you. It's just collecting dust and spider webs in the shed. If you'll help me down to the water, you can have it for as long as you want."

"Ed?" It was a striking woman in grey on the porch. Was she going to revoke the offer, I wondered. Such was my experience of life. But no, she had a good face, both wise and beautiful all at the same time. "Don't forget about the outside lights. They'll have to be covered before we get a frost."

Ed smiled up at the porch and signalled me to follow him to the shed, where he dug a small plastic rowboat out from under the rubble of rolled-up rugs, miles of green garden hose and a few spare bedsteads. We each took an end and walked across the street to Queen's Royal Park. Apart from the trees, which had seen a lot of history, the other object of note was a green-roofed gazebo with eight delicate arches. "They sure knew how to build for pleasure in those days," I observed out loud.

"You mean the gazebo? That was left by a film crew a year or so ago. Looks like it belongs, though," Ed allowed. I made no more observations until we had the boat in the water and the oars fixed in their oarlocks. I said thanks to Ed and told him not to report me missing until midnight.

"What name shall I give?" Ed asked.

"Cooperman. Ben Cooperman from Grantham."

He kept his eyes on me until I started along the shore. The postage-stamp park with the gazebo slid away, and I was treated to a look into a few backyards and a view behind the clubhouse of the golf course.

The boat was light and sat like a cork on top of the water, rather than settling into it. Every time my oars got out of phase, I turned dramatically either out into the lake or pointing to shore. The lake was calmer than when I'd first seen it that day. The whitecaps were gone this close to shore, and even out towards the middle it didn't look so formidable any more. As I began to get my second wind, I noticed that for a little boat, it handled very well. I knew that on the homeward journey I might wish for an outboard motor, but that was only natural. At the moment, I wasn't complaining about the boat. What troubled me was the fact that the shoreline was rising. The golf course was higher than I expected. My first glimpse of the fort was disappointing. I couldn't see the loopholes I'd seen from dry ground. Even though I was getting close enough to see individual bricks on the flanks of the partly plastered walls of the tower, I could see less of what was going on on the ground than before. I should have figured that.

But if I couldn't see anything, I could hear motors. There was the steady drone of a compressor and the irregular din of heavy, earth-moving equipment. Facing the water, I could see a fortified gate that had been cut in the shoulders of the surrounding earthworks. The fort was standing in a depression and it was circled by built-up berms or earthworks of some kind. The fence that hid the front of

Fort Mississauga from me did not hide the view from the water. The trouble was, the view was not very interesting. I should have asked my friend Ed at the Bed and Breakfast if he had a small plane for me to borrow. A low flight over the fort would have told me more about what was going on there and given me fewer blisters.

I decided to beach the boat and see what was to be learned by simply looking around. I ran it as far up the small patch of beach as I could, first moving to the stern in order to raise up the bow. I walked out without getting my feet wetter than they already were. In a moment or two I'd pulled the boat over large boulders to some bushes which marked the beginning of a short, steep bank of dark, slippery soil. I pretended not to see the "No Trespassing" signs that were posted with enough frequency to awaken curiosity in a radish as I scrambled up the slope. The noise of activity was more intense now. But since it was bounced around the earthworks and the single tower of the fort, the sound could have been coming from anywhere.

Through the grill of the gate facing the lake, I could clearly see a similar gate at the other end of a short tunnel that cut through the earthwork paralleling the lake. Obscuring most of the view beyond the second gate were a sheet of plywood and the handles of some tools that had been leaned against the bars. I saw two men in hard hats cross my field of vision and a puff or two of diesel smoke. From what must have been a deep excavation, I next caught sight of the jointed arm of a back-hoe as it lifted a scoop of earth past my sight-lines and then vanished.

I tried to open the gate on my side, but the ancient bars were held fast, not by the huge lock that had been built into the gate when it was made, but by a tough modern padlock joining together lengths of formidable un-rusted chain. I watched through the two gates for some time, but saw only a repetition of what I'd already observed. I was beginning to think that I'd picked a bad time, and that I would have to make a midnight run back in this direction after a good meal at the Prince of Wales, when I heard the sound of a motor dying. A short time later, this gesture was seconded by a cough as the generator cut out. We were suddenly surrounded by silence that almost hurt the ears. It was quickly getting dark. I checked my watch; a very respectable quitting time, nearly six o'clock.

I retreated down the bank to the shelter of some bushes to wait out the time until it would be safe to have another look. This was a fine place to be hungry. I tried my pockets. Nothing. I would have gladly settled for the crumbs from a bar of fudge. I began giving myself hell for damning the town's chief industry so roundly earlier. I checked the bushes for berries and nuts. Nothing doing. But what I did see took my mind off my stomach. I was sitting in a clump of bushes containing various sorts of leaves, but what I recognized were some pods. I'd seen them before. I recognized the dry pods peeling away from the shiny seed-carrying septum. I was sitting in a clump of Dame's Rocket. And there was still enough light available for me to see that there were other samples of it here at the bottom of the bank and at the top. I checked my cuffs. I still hadn't collected any *Hesperis matronalis* there. But the night was young.

Chapter Twelve

I watched the last of the sunset darken in the western sky. I wasn't situated so that I caught the best of it, but the north-western horizon did have a sideshow. My best view was of the sun hitting the American fort across the river to the east. Fort Niagara looked more like a big country house with a wall around it than it did a fort. I read somewhere that the French built it that way on purpose so as not to unsettle the Indians. The "French Castle" was once bombarded from close to where I was huddled against the gathering cold. The British set up a battery near here in 1759 and sent a cannon-ball over the river and down the chimney of the French commander. That, of course, was long before the fort I was interested in was built. Back in the 1750s there wasn't anything, not even fudge, on this side of the river. The earliest permanent settlers came after the American War of Independence, and Fort Mississauga didn't come along until after the war after that, the War of 1812. They say this fort was built from the brick from an old lighthouse that used to grace this point. Others say that it was constructed from the rubble of the village of Niagara which had been burned to the ground during the war. As a fort, it was a washout because peace broke out and hasn't been ruptured since. In the 1837 Rebellion in Upper Canada, Fort Mississauga was refurbished, and during the War between the States it was manned for the last time. If it is written in the cards that some forts should become conversation pieces on golf courses, then Fort Mississauga was a good candidate.

I climbed up the cold bank to the top again. This time there was no noise. Since I already knew there was no entrance to be had through the back door in the earthworks, I climbed to the top of the overgrown earthwork to the left of the gate. It was a short scramble; the berms that made up the outer defences of the fort were not high. On my way up I encountered more *Hesperis*. It was trying to tell me something, but I was too busy to read the message just then. From the top of the scarp or whatever military engineers call what I was catching my breath on, it could be a redoubt or a bastion or chopped liver for all I knew, I could see the rest of these defences as they zigzagged around the central keep of the fort, if that's what it's called. From here I could see the distant lights of the town which stopped just short of the edge of the golf course. It made me feel like a rather isolated private investigator. Lights meant life and warmth. Up here I could feel the cold settling in around my bones. Looking over my shoulder I could see that the lake was beginning to mist up for the night. Thanks a lot! Damn it, even an illegal operation such as what I suspected was going on here lets its workers off at a reasonable hour. Maybe the crookeder the scam, the better the help is treated. Private investigators have no union. I can't grieve to anybody. There's no joint standing-committee to see that I get as much time off as the men I saw working here an hour ago.

The front and sides of the fort had been surrounded by a low plastic mesh fence. I guess they hadn't expected trouble from the rear. They might have learned a lesson in history from the French commander of Fort Niagara. He hadn't anticipated trouble from this direction either. As I sat on the top of the earthwork, I kept my head and shoulders as low as possible. I didn't want to present a silhouette against the night sky. There might be a watchman out there beyond the fence, maybe taking shelter in the golf course clubhouse. In the back of my mind I could see him unchaining his half-starved Doberman pinschers. I could imagine them drooling for a taste of Cooperman flesh.

The fort's only roofed structure was the rough-cast flowerpot keep I've already described. It was circled by a flat grassy area, which was about the same height as or a bit lower than the golf fairways on the other side of the heaped earth defences. From where I was, it was hard to tell exactly. One thing, the area of the enclosure was a lot bigger than it appeared to be from the street. Most of it was the former second green before the excavations started. I could see some of these from my perch. There may have been others on the far side of the keep. The ones closest to me looked like small garden plots, with string running between wooden stakes in the ground and shallow depressions showing where limited digging had taken place. But over towards the berm next to mine, there were signs of serious digging. Here was a hole big enough to find three or four Troys in, a hole that a modern engineer could be proud of. I'd seen some of the digging equipment in action earlier. Now I could see it, a big yellow back-hoe at the bottom of the dark hole.

I scrambled down the inside slope of my earthwork and moved to the edge of the excavation. It was deep enough to support the underpinnings of a three-storey building. What were they up to, these archaeologists? Building a parking garage on the side? With the sod from the excavation neatly stacked against the base of the fort, the hole, which was roughly fifteen feet across and nearly seventy-five long, ran from beside the tower of the fort across the

old green and through the distant earthwork on the other
side of the back gate that looked out on the lake. I followed
the curved base of the earthwork towards this point. Just
where the hole reached the earthwork, I found a ladder set
into the wood-reinforced side of the excavation. My feet
found the rungs, although I was already thinking I'd been
there too long.

Here it was nearly impossible to see anything. What I
could make out was this: the excavation had sent branch
tunnels under the earthworks. I know nothing at all about
fortifications. Maybe these were the original defensive
tunnels being restored. The butt ends of stout timbers that
I could see disappearing into the dark supported this
notion, but then I caught sight of some very un-nineteenth-
century-looking corrugated galvanized iron arches. What
was going on here? I struck a match and lit my way to the
end of the tunnel. As far as I could tell, it followed the
circular curve of the existing earthworks. At the distant
wall of the cavelike space, I could see where recent work
had been going on. There were shovels and wheelbarrows
at the end, like the coalface in the illustration of a coal
mine in *The Book of Knowledge* I'd grown up with. I guess
the idea was to hollow out a tunnel deep down under the
earthworks right around the fort. I struck another match
and walked back towards the relative brightness of the
main excavation. Cupping my hand over the light I crossed
the open part and went into the other arm of the tunnel. I
didn't have far to walk. This end of the tunnel had either
not been dug yet or it had already been filled in. I picked
up a shovel and worked away at the sides. Here the clay
hadn't been moved since the last glacier passed through
here, maybe twelve thousand years ago. But in the middle,
the earth was less densely packed. Then I caught sight of
end-beams disappearing into the clay. Somebody's dug
out a cavern here and then filled it up again. What was the

point, I wondered. This wasn't part of the restoration of the fort as far as I could see. It didn't look like archaeology to me. But, what do I know about these things?

A sudden light nearly knocked me over. Two beams from flashlights crossed one another like searchlights looking for enemy bombers in a wartime newsreel. I moved as fast as I could into the deepest part of the shaft, near some oil drums and tools stacked to one side. Without making a noisy clatter, I turned a wheelbarrow over and climbed under it. By now the lights were getting brighter and I could hear voices.

"Crazy, I tell you."

"I'm not drunk like you're thinkin'. I seen a light!"

"St Elmo's fire is what you saw, Kirby."

"In October? I'm tellin' you it was a light!"

"Well, look for yourself." Without sticking my head out, I was all too well aware that the two beams of light were making sweeps into the excavation.

"You goin' down to look?" dared the one called Kirby.

"Christ, you're the one who saw the damned light. I got good pants on."

"Well, I'll go alone then. I've done it before."

"You see lights down here all the time, eh?"

"Ah, come on, Roy, get off my back!"

"You hear anything? Listen." The three of us listened to the night air and the distant sound of the lake for about a minute. To help, I suspended my breathing. I couldn't do much about my heart beating against the metal bottom of the wheelbarrow, though. The first minute was lengthened towards the end of my breath. Then:

"Shit, I'm not goin' down there again today. They don't pay enough, you know what I mean?"

"Yeah. You could break your neck on that ladder in the dark and you won't even see compensation 'cause we're casual. I say," said Roy (I think it was Roy), "since we're casual let's act casual and get back outta the cold before we get pneumonia."

"Right. It must of been Elmo's fire all right."

The voices continued out of hearing and the beams of light moved off in a new direction. I didn't try to move the wheelbarrow for nearly five minutes after I heard the last of them. When I climbed out, I sat for a minute listening and searching the night sky. I felt like a cigarette, but I decided against it. Sometimes a smoke can be deadly in more ways than one.

I was already thinking of climbing the ladder and getting out of the hole, when I noticed the oil drums I'd spotted when I was looking for a place to hide. Why oil drums here? There was a large tank next to the fort for refuelling the back-hoe. What was going on? I sniffed around and then it hit me. What the hell was I looking for all over the county? I was looking for toxic waste. And here was a cache of at least three barrels of it. Was I beginning to get somewhere, or was it only wishful thinking? I took up a shovel again and found the base of a fourth drum under the recently filled-in section. After a little more excavating of my own, I uncovered a fifth. I was beginning to get the idea. The tunnel was full of drums. Drums and more drums of toxic waste! Suddenly, I wanted to put my feet on the ladder and get out of there. I had spent my share of luck in that hole. The powers that be didn't owe Manny Cooperman's boy another minute. That was when the end of the shovel struck not a sixth metallic barrel but something else, something that took my mind off toxic waste, something that gave me a queer feeling under my belt. For a moment, I just stood there, not quite taking it in. Then I went back to digging. I kept at it, digging now with the shovel and now with my hands, until I could see what I had hit. I nearly brought up the undigested portion of my last meal.

I cleared the earth around what I'd found. It was a shoe, a brown Rockport, like the pair I had back at the apartment. Inside this shoe was a foot and it was cold.

Chapter Thirteen

I phoned Pete Staziak of the Niagara Regional Police from the pay-phone in the lobby of the Prince of Wales Hotel at the corner of King and Picton or King and Queen, depending on which street signs you read. I was feeling a little light-headed, like I'd just finished off a bottle of rye, which I hadn't. In fact, I've had the heel of a bottle in a cupboard for the last six months. Pete told me to have a drink and to stay away from the scene of the crime. As I came away from the lobby, the idea of a drink began to look good. What better way could I put in the time until Pete finished up at the fort. He said to stay put and that he'd want to talk to me. The Prince of Wales's bar was as comfortable a place as I knew in those parts.

When I caught my reflection in a mirror, I detoured to the men's room to repair my face and clothes. I was a mess, but it made me feel better. At least finding a body hadn't become routine. Sure, I became light-headed and even wanted a drink, but it took the sight of my face in the mirror to tell me that I hadn't become a total professional when it comes to dealing with death. I valued my amateur status. While the tap-water was running into the sink, I thought again of the cold foot in its Rockport shoe. Now I could remember the scramble up the ladder and back over the earthwork and down the bank to the rowboat. The tugging of muscles in my back told me about the difficult trip back to the silhouette of the movie-maker's gazebo outlined against the night sky. I'd been helped by the river in my outward journey; the way home was all against the current.

I got rid of some of the mud on my pants with a wet wad of paper towels. I discarded some Dame's Rocket that had attached itself to me with a length of bindweed. There wasn't a lot I could do for my clothes after I'd got rid of the mud. My shoes were as soaking after a first aid job as before. The lights in the bar are lower than in the John, so I put my comb away hoping that I would pass the dress code when I got upstairs again. I found a seat in a dark corner and persuaded the waiter to get me a sandwich as well as a rye and ginger ale.

As far as I knew, no prince of Wales ever slept in the Prince of Wales Hotel. In a brochure I'd seen that the Duke and Duchess of York had visited Niagara-on-the-Lake. A guidebook documented a visit by the Duke and Duchess of Cornwall. Both of these visits took place well before my time, in 1901. For some reason I found it very relaxing trying to imagine two ducal couples running around in Niagara trying not to run into one another.

The bar at the Prince of Wales was, of course, everything that a bar should be. There was dark wood; engraved, frosted glass; lots of brass and crystal as well as beer pumps of porcelain. I'd been there only a few times before this, and each time I regretted my usually temperate habits.

"Sorry to be so long," said the waiter as he set down knife, fork and spoon wrapped in a paper napkin. The waiter sorted out my order from the other two he was carrying. I found myself grinning at him, foolishly. This was so ordinary: sitting in a bar and eating, surrounded by lively, talking people who didn't have anything to do—as far as I knew—with the body back at Fort Mississauga. I was almost chuckling to myself as I cut into the chopped egg on home-made white bread with my knife and fork. In a place like this, I didn't think you lifted anything to the mouth with fingers, not even the pickles.

"Aren't you Sam Cooperman?" the waiter asked. In spite of the error, I jumped. Family is close enough.

"No. That's my brother. I'm Sam's younger brother, Benny." I almost withheld my name. No sense throwing security out the window.

"Well, you sure look like him. I seen you come in and I was sure it was him. I could of sworn it was him."

"Yeah, well, Sam's in Toronto. I'm still in Grantham. He's head of surgery at Toronto General."

"That a fact. I used to sell brushes with him one summer." I shot a glance towards the entrance, but the big figure coming into the room wasn't Pete Staziak. I had more than an hour to kill before I could reasonably expect to see him, but I hadn't taken the pledge to be reasonable, especially not after digging up a body. The big fellow joined a party of three ladies in hats in the centre of the room. I didn't think ladies wore hats this late in the day. But what do I know?

"He won awards selling brushes in the summer," I told the waiter when I remembered that he was still standing there. "What's your name?" I asked. "I'll tell Sam when I see him."

"Oh, ah, Des Dwyer."

"Des, can you tell me what's going on out at Fort Mississauga? They've got it fenced off and I see trucks coming and going."

"Ah!" Des said with a new light in his eyes, "They're putting in a lot of money there." He rubbed the point of his lapel with his thumb and forefinger and slipped me a wink.

"Sangallo's doing a major job on it. Going to make it into a show-place. Like the other fort." Des pretended not to see a customer waving from a table in the corner. "They're putting the earthworks in where they used to be according to some plan that was discovered somewhere. They're fixing up the old ammunition bays and rebuilding the sally-port, which was just about ready to cave in."

"What's a sally-port?"

"That's where they send the girls home when the colonel comes looking, I think. I dunno, really."

"How long has this been going on?" I asked.

"Soldiers have been wenching since Napoleon was a pup, Mr Cooperman."

"I meant the construction."

"Summer of last year as close as I can remember."

"That's a long time for putting in a few berms."

"Well, you know it's all being supervised by some professor from Toronto. They've already found bones and musket-balls and bits of broken dishes." I remembered the string grid I'd seen and the trench next to it. But this was archaeology on a small scale. Did Toronto know about the rest of it? Or was that all Sangallo?

There were now two customers trying to get Des's attention. I watched the skill he displayed in not catching their waving hands in either of his eyes. "How big an outfit is Sangallo?" I asked.

"Hell, they're about the biggest bunch in the restoration business around here. They'll sandblast your old brick house, or reglaze your windows with wobbly glass made the way they used to make it in the olden days. They can imitate old plaster fancy-work on ceilings, replace the missing spindles in your prize staircase and even make a four-car garage look like it was an old driving shed. Oh, you see that yellow sign of theirs all over town, especially in the old parts where the houses go back a few years.

At last Des responded to his customers' requests. He was greeted by them as a long-lost friend. I went back to my sandwich. Soon I could look down into my plate and say, "I've really accomplished something today." I tried to think of the fort, the excavation and the tunnelling under the earthworks, but it was no good. I sipped my drink and waited for Staziak.

The time went quicker than I would have guessed. A collection of familiar faces began to gather in the lobby. I could see them clearly from my seat in the bar. They stood quite close together for the convenience of five or six photographers who were busily snapping their pictures. One of their number, a red-whiskered man in a kilt, escaped into the bar briefly, then rejoined the ever enlarging crowd in front of the main desk. I began to recognize them as celebrities seen on television. There was a famous anchorman, a forthright interviewer, a tall bald-headed historian, towering over the others who stood as close to him as they could. I recognized a recent attorney general, a few newspaper columnists, a clutch of talk-show panellists and a few faces I might have recognized if I'd spent more time in front of the television set. My mother would have been able to name them all. I wondered what brought them to the Prince of Wales. Maybe it was the inauguration of a new fudge franchise on Queen Street. I grabbed Des the next time he passed my table and asked him.

"They're celebrating some book that's getting published," he said. "Don't they look like they're having a grand time?" I watched and couldn't help agreeing with the waiter.

It wasn't long after the lobby cleared that Pete Staziak paused at the entrance to the bar, spotted me and came over.

"Benny, you amaze me." He pulled out the chair opposite and sat down. When Des came over, he asked for coffee. He was still a working man. "Now, how the devil did you stumble across that? This better be good."

"I was just exploring the fort, Pete."

"Yeah, like I'm having a wonderful time in your company."

"I was just nosing around," I said, but Pete wasn't going to let me off with that. I decided not to try the shipwreck approach either. He glared at me and waited.

Pete and I went all the way back to grade nine together. I'd been in a play with his sister and we traded notes once or twice in five years. He'd been on the football team. I'd been about as athletic as Charles Atlas before he sent away for help. Since then, we had run into one another professionally from time to time. Pete was a good cop and I respected him, even though he was often more of a wall than a door in some of my investigations. I think that deep down he knew I wasn't out to steal hubcaps or the fillings out of his mother's teeth, but that didn't stop him being careful where I was concerned. I tried to return the glare he was giving me, but I never win contests like that. That's why I stay clear of people who show off with their bone-crushing handshakes.

"Okay, Benny, let's have it. Nice and simple."

"I'm working, Pete. I was following a truck into the fort, ran into the fence, so I went under it when it got dark."

"Uh-huh," he said. "You haven't confused me yet."

"I went down into the hole to see what was going on, how it could involve my friend in the truck."

"Who shall remain nameless?"

"At this stage, Pete, I'd just as soon." Pete neither nodded agreement or made any comment. He was reserving as many options as he could. I didn't blame him. In his place, I'd play tough too.

"Go on."

"I'd just dug a couple of those metal drums out of the dirt. He was behind the fifth one. That's all. I stopped digging when I saw the foot. That's when I called you. The only thing I know about him is that he isn't one of the garrison of the fort from back in 1837. Honest, Pete, I didn't touch anything and I don't know anything."

"What's your guy in the truck mixed up in?"

"Hauling toxic wastes. There, I've said it."

"Into that, eh? How far?"

"As deep as that hole, anyway, I guess."

"Benny, you wanna watch yourself. You could end up dead too, you know." Pete was looking at the drink I'd ordered over an hour ago. To me it looked old and warm, but I wasn't a couple of hours away from going off duty.

"Do you know who it was?" I asked.

"We've got a pretty good idea, but no positive ID yet." I nodded at that and then Pete nodded and we both sat and thought about naming the dead man. Once you name a dead man, there's no way to take it back. When you hear the bad news, you may not believe it, but the words have deadly magic in them and you already begin to see the world without the named person.

"Are you telling, or do I have to wait until I read about it in tomorrow's *Beacon*?"

"The body was wearing clothes that had this in the pockets." Pete took a plastic-wrapped wallet out of his coat pocket and put it in the middle of the table. Through the plastic, I could see worn leather, plastic credit-card holders and underneath a ring of keys.

"May I?" I asked looking at Pete, who inclined his head ever so slightly. I opened the plastic bag and took out the wallet. I didn't want to open it, but I had to know. Chances are that the dead man was someone I'd never met. Hell, I'd only been working the case for a few days. I hadn't even met the principals yet. The name in the wallet read *Alexander Pastor*. I'd had a conversation about that name with Alex Pásztory, the guy from . . .

Then it hit me, just the way I've just described. I said it over again to myself: The dead man is Alex Pásztory, the man from Environment Front. The second-last smoker in Grantham, the man who spotted Dr Carswell at the Turkey Roost, the man who interrupted himself after saying,

"I'm off to meet the AV," was dead. The second date on his tombstone was now available to the carver. I remembered the leather patches on his sleeves and the tobacco burns in his old sweater. I could suddenly see Pásztory's lopsided grin, like he was making some ironic comment on his own murder.

"You pretty sure it's Pásztory?" Pete dug into a pocket and handed me a photograph. It looked like a failed likeness of the man I'd talked to at the Turkey Roost, discarded by an apprentice sculptor in wax.

"It's a Polaroid I had taken. Is this the guy you know?"

"Wish I could say it wasn't. It's him, all right. How did he get it?"

"I'm no expert on that, and the lab hasn't even taken delivery of the remains yet, but, to me, it looked like he had taken a single shot in the pump. I'd say it was from close up too."

"Poor bugger! He was a nice fellow. You ever run across him?"

"Only in his letters to the editor. And those articles. He was always beating the drum, wasn't he?"

"Who's going to beat it now?"

"Aw, come on, Benny. You'll never survive in this racket if you're going to be a bleeding heart. You gotta see it as just another file, just another number."

"Yeah, I've seen the way they tie tags on the big toes of some of my best clients when they put them in a drawer at the morgue. Different numbers, different filing system."

"You mind if I sample this drink you're wasting?"

"Help yourself." Pete glanced around the room to see whether there were any spies from the NRP or any local peace officers in sight. The coast must have been clear, because he had the glass in his hand and returned to the table before I could take in the fact that he was breaking the rules. Of course, I only found the body. I didn't have to stand by while it was being dug out of the tunnel. I didn't have to scrub off Pásztory's face so that the mud and clay wouldn't get in the way of the Polaroid flash.

"Thanks," Pete said. "That picture won't be good enough to get a positive ID, but it will do until we can get to Environment Front's office in the morning." He was looking at my glass again, but keeping his hands clear. "Benny, if you were sniffing up the same tree as Pastor, I'd take a holiday. I'm not joking around. This was no case of manslaughter followed by a cover-up. This was murder in a neat, professional package." He underlined what he was saying by holding onto my eyes with his while he was talking. "Is there anything more I should know about this?"

"Look, Pete, I don't have anything but suspicions. By now, you're going to have the same suspicions. I've been working on this file since Tuesday. So far I've only been doing research. I haven't even met all the characters yet. I've been going sideways three steps and backwards two steps for every half-step I move forward. I haven't been able to get very close. The only thing I know is that there is a lot of money involved. Maybe finding Pásztory will blow the lid off. Maybe it will all have to come out into the open now."

"Yeah, maybe getting himself killed like this is going to accomplish more than all those pieces for the paper and those damned letters to the editor. Funny, eh?"

"Yeah, funny."

Pete and I talked for another ten minutes. I tried to quiz him about how Pásztory's death, and more particularly where it had taken place, was going to be received downtown. Pete pulled his big head closer to his collar and shook his head. "Nobody's going to thank me for tonight's work, Benny. It opens the lid on a can of dead bait and I can already smell it all over town."

"I thought you might say something like that. What are you going to do?"

"Hell, I'll just write it up and treat it like any other homicide. In cases like this, you have to go through the book without skipping. If I skip a line, they'll nail me and say it was all my fault. No, Benny, when I write this up, it's going to be a model in procedure."

We got up after I settled the check with Des. Staziak and I started for the door together, when Des called attention to a tangle of weeds adhering to Pete's left trouser leg, above his muddy boots.

"You got some weeds wrapped around your cuff, sir!" Pete looked down, holding his leg at an awkward angle to see it better. I saw that a scrap of bindweed was making itself at home on his pant leg. With it, an old friend, I helped Pete remove the bindweed and the familiar long pods of Dame's Rocket. It was a nice note on which to end the evening. I went home to bed.

Chapter Fourteen

The next morning, Friday, I had to get ready for a court appearance in Toronto. It had nothing to do with Kinross or Phidias and, as such, it was a welcome change for me. I enjoyed cleaning current work out of my briefcase and filling it with *Fermor vs Tutunjian*. The Queen Elizabeth Way was crowded, but traffic moved steadily until the beginning of the Gardiner Expressway, where cement baffles reduced the number of lanes temporarily. In going over the bumpy bridge across the Humber, I got a good look at the CN Tower. It set a challenging mark for developers to shoot at. The tower seemed to be saying, "I dare you!" to the powers within the Queen City. There was a new bridge over the railway lands at Spadina. From here I got a good view of the SkyDome, the fancy new stadium with its retractable roof. It spread an impressive curve over the vanished shunting yards that used to separate the waterfront from the rest of the city. The Dome, according to the papers, has displaced the centre of gravity in the city southward, making a serious traffic problem possible. For instance, I nearly had to mortgage my Olds to get a parking space within an easy hike of the Provincial Court Building across from Osgoode Hall. At least that historic site hadn't been turned into a parking lot. It still looked like the calmest place in town with its Greek columns and the expanse of lawn surrounded by a high ornamental iron fence. I caught a glimpse of the wide, ornate gates, which had been built to keep cattle from wandering into the precincts of the courthouse in the middle years of the last century. It was hard to imagine that as I looked for a way to cross Queen Street.

While I was waiting to do my bit in the case of *Fermor vs Tutunjian*, I put in a call to the Royal Archaeological Museum of Ontario and had a brief chat with the head of the North American section, a Dr Walter Graves. From him I learned that the man in charge of the Niagara-on-the-Lake dig was Dr John Roppa. From Roppa I heard that there hadn't been any archaeological work going on at the fort since a week after Labour Day. All of the digging, he told me, was confined to small sites near the wall of the fort proper and a narrow trench on the west side (which I had missed). When I asked him about the large-scale earth-moving equipment, he said that that had to do with Sangallo's restoration of the earthworks. "That's tourism," he said. "It's only of marginal interest to us in that Sangallo will be following plans that were discovered at Fort York in Toronto."

"Is that right?" I responded, hoping I was priming him for further disclosures.

"Perhaps you've heard of the Ridout Papers, Mr Cooperman? The plans were found among them, undisturbed for the past—"

"I'd like to hear about that sometime, Dr Roppa. I really would."

"Yes, well I was looking through my log-book only yesterday and found—"

"Dr Roppa do you keep a daily log on all your jobs?"

"Oh, yes. In fact the Ridout papers came to light when—"

"And that includes the dig at Fort Mississauga?"

"It's normal procedure. If we didn't we'd quickly lose track of where we were. You see—"

"Excuse me, Doctor, but I wonder if you could look something up for me. I'm looking for a break in the routine at the fort, an unusual event, a departure, something like that about fifteen months ago."

"I see," he said, drawing out the vowel as he thought. "That would have been fairly soon after we started. Hmmmm."

"Dr Roppa, I didn't mean you should look it up right now. I don't expect you have your logs sitting right in front of you. Even I'm not that organized. But, if you could give me a call—" Now it was his opportunity to interrupt me.

"Oh, Mr Cooperman, I'm a great believer in staying on top of things. You can't let things get out of hand, you know. Look what happened to Schliemann at Hissarlik!" I didn't catch his allusion, but I got the sense of it.

"Dr Roppa, I don't expect that you'll be able to—" Again he chopped me off with enthusiasm.

"I am looking at the logs of twenty-three years in the field, as I'm talking to you. A year and a quarter ago, let's see, a break in the daily routine. Let's see. . ." This was followed by a silence that was punctuated from time to time with remarks the doctor was addressing to his own thought processes and not to me. They were grunts that ran from deep in the base clef to squeals high in the treble upon discovering half-forgotten treasures. "I don't seem to be doing very well, Mr Cooperman. Nothing in the spring that was out of the normal routine. But, I'll keep trying."

"No need to take time, right now, Dr Roppa. I understand that you're a busy man and—"

"Who told you that, I wonder? Oh, just a minute! Here's something! But you wouldn't call that a break in the routine probably."

"What was it?"

"Here's a reference to a visit by the head man. Yes, I remember now, fine old gentleman it was."

"Could you be more specific?"

"We were visited by—where is it—ah! Murdo Forbes, who was the chairman of Phidias Manufacturing. I remember he came out to watch us one morning."

"So, Murdo Forbes, the Commander, came to see the dig?"

"Yes, as I said, a fine old gentleman. Actually, for an old-timer, he was there bright and early. He was trying to smooth over some damage his workmen had done to the parging on the fort. Let me see if I can find it. Yes, here it is:

> Work delay while giving a tour to Commander Murdo Forbes (RCN, Ret.) C of B Phidias Man'f'ing. Inspected slight damage caused by equipment. Parging damage slight, showing healthy red brick underneath. Whole site inspected. He knows a great deal about local history. Took me to local hotel for coffee and further talk about our findings. Bone fragments found yesterday definitely not human. Possibly canine . . .

"It goes on from there, Mr Cooperman, but I've gone past the break in our routine. We were able to accomplish very little that day until well into the morning. Is that the sort of thing you're looking for?"

"That's just what I wanted, Doctor. What was the date on that entry?"

"Ah, that's marked July 13, 1989. It's from Book One for this assignment, in case you need the text. I'll leave it to you to remember; my mind's rather too full of things like that. I suspect it's old age creeping up on me. What do you think?"

"Well, I'm sure—" I don't know what I was going to say. I was prepared to make it short, because my case was due to be called at any moment, when Dr Roppa interrupted me again. He had a call on the other line, a

policeman from Grantham, he said. I told him to give
Sergeant Staziak my regards and thanked Dr Roppa for his
help. I slipped his phone number into my wallet for future
reference and beat it back to the courtroom.

My client Mr Tutunjian was very happy with the result
of my performance on the witness stand. He was in a
mood to celebrate, but I got back to the highway as fast as I
could. I did stop off at Switzer's on Spadina for a corned
beef sandwich fix followed by a Vernor's ginger ale, stuff
you can't find in Grantham, but that's not important to the
story.

When I got back to town, I stopped at the first newspaper box I saw and picked up a copy of the *Beacon*. Opening
the first section over the steering wheel, I could see that
Pásztory's death was being given a prominent place, but
under his pen name, Pastor. LOCAL ENVIRONMENTALIST FOUND
SLAIN. I skimmed through the story quickly and was glad
to see that the police "went to the murder scene acting
upon information received." That was as close as it got to
me, and my breath came easier. Usually, I get a kick out of
getting my name in the paper, but this time I was glad to
hide behind Staziak's reticence. In the story, there were no
references to the drums of toxic waste found along with
Pásztory. The writer didn't guess at what was going on at
Fort Mississauga. No connections were made between the
rebuilding of the fort's earthworks and the disposal of a
large quantity of dangerous and unwanted chemical waste.

I parked the car in its usual spot behind my office and
went up the stairs carefully, because it was no secret that I
hadn't been going as placidly amid the noise and haste as I
could have. Nor had I collected as much peace as I might
have from an equal measure of silence. At least there was
no new warning shoved through my door when I unlocked it. I checked with the answering service and found
that Martha Tracy had called. I put the copy of today's
Beacon on my desk where I could see it and called her back.

That evening with the beer and pizza seemed like a month ago.

"Martha?"

"M'yeah. Cooperman? I've got that information you wanted."

"Great, Martha! That's wonderful!" I was trying to remember what it was I'd asked her to do.

"I pulled out the city's contract with Kinross, Benny."

"Great!"

"It ran to forty pages without the appendices."

"Martha, I can't wait to buy you lunch."

"Cooperman, you're a real womanizer, you know that?"

"Now, don't *you* start! Tell me about the contract."

"The main thing is that the city can't be held accountable for anything Kinross does. There are two clauses covering that. In one Kinross promises to assume the defence of and indemnify the city against all claims, and in the other it accepts all responsibility for its operations and employees. So, if Kinross gets caught with its hose in the Niagara River, the city can hold up its hands in shock at how it has been misled and abused."

"That's wonderful stuff, Martha!"

"M'yeah, I thought it was worth a phonecall. Now, don't you go thanking me again, Benny. You never could do 'sincere' if your life depended on it. We'll do lunch like you said and forget all about being sincere. Okay? Right now I've got to put my face on and go out. G'bye!"

"Goodbye, Martha, and thank you from the—" She cut me off with a click.

The *Beacon* on Saturday was usually a plump paper, except after Christmas, when it was as thin as boarding-house gruel. This Saturday the paper confirmed Pete Staziak's guess about how Pásztory had died: a single shot in the chest. It also explained that Alex Pastor was the pen name of Sandor or Alex Pásztory, but kept on calling the deceased "Pastor," which meant that I kept having to

translate that back to Pásztory, remembering what he'd
said about fine old Hunky names. There was not a word
about the scene of the crime apart from a reference to the
golf course. That was all. The fix was obviously in at a high
level. If Ross Forbes was behind this, he must be calling
home all the favours people in high places owed him. It
wouldn't take much journalistic digging to link Sangallo to
Phidias. Or to Tony Pritchett and the mob. Where are the
newspaper bloodhounds of yesteryear? One of them, it
suddenly occurred to me, was recovering from the shock
of a post-mortem examination.

Saturday night I took Anna out to the movies. While it
was more enjoyable than most of what happened to me
that week, my date added nothing new to the case.

Sunday? At least Sunday didn't add anything new to
the story since, as I've already mentioned, there is no
Sunday *Beacon*. The out-of-town papers were still letting
the story alone. There wasn't a mention in either the
Buffalo or the Toronto papers.

On Monday I got a call from the office of Jim Colling,
Teddie Forbes's lawyer. He told me that he'd just had a
favourable FAX message from Phidias about the proposal
he'd put to them.

"Whoopee!" I said. "When do I start?"

"As soon as their treasurer gets back from his vacation.
How does Thursday suit you?" I thanked Colling and,
while I was doing it, I was still wondering what he was
getting out of this. It was hard to get a lawyer to say hello
to you without him running up the meter. So why was Jim
Colling such a bundle of friendly helpfulness? If he was
sinking his personal hook into Phidias, I didn't want to be
the worm.

Chapter Fifteen

T he main office of Phidias Manufacturing was in the new complex that filled in almost all of the space between St Andrew and King east of Queen and west of James. They called it City Centre when it went up in the early 1980s. It had been intended to give the sluggish old centre of town a shot in the arm. After all the hoopla died down, it became just another office building with a walk-through mall full of stores selling things you could live without. But a few important companies were located here, as was our leading criminal lawyer, branches of two banks and the order office for a Toronto department store. I got off the elevator at the sixth floor and asked for the treasurer, who was expecting me. He came at me beaming from his corner office as soon as my name was taken in to him.

"Mr Cooperman? Good to see you. You didn't waste any time. Glad to see you're ready to get started. I have Mr Colling's letter, of course, and I even think we can find a corner for you to work in for just as long as you're going to be with us." Mr F.P. McAuliffe was a quick little man in brown, with wispy red hair around his ears and nowhere else except for wild eyebrows of the same colour. He looked tweedy, and from the signs of ash about him, he was a pipe-smoker.

He led me into his office and told me to make myself at home at what he called a parson's table. Not knowing very

much about parsons, I took him at his word and settled
my briefcase on a long table without much depth to it. It
wasn't literally in a corner, but it did occupy space along
the cold north wall. Over my head was a framed map of
Grantham during its heady days as a busy canal town.
There was an inset of the old courthouse at the bottom
right-hand corner. I tried to find the location of my office
on St Andrew Street. McAuliffe saw me distracted and
smiled with a set of discoloured teeth.

"That's the Brosius map of 1875. It's one of the first run,
not a reprint," he said. "I got it from my father and I
coveted it every day it hung in his office on Queen Street."
He came over to look too. For a minute, we both did that.
"Hasn't changed much, really," he said. "It's still an Indian
trail or two, only now they have a modern camber. The
original survey lines didn't make much of an impact in the
downtown part, did they?" I smiled. I couldn't tell where
the original survey lines were on the map, but I could tell
that he could. McAuliffe smelled of bay rum and tobacco,
a very comfortable smell. "My father was a collector of
these old maps, Mr Cooperman. Got interested while he
was building the present canal. He was one of the engineers working on it beginning in 1919, as soon as he got
out of the army." McAuliffe pulled a large black book from
a shelf and opened it near the end and pointed at a list of
those who had built the canal. There the McAuliffe name
appeared twice, once as a junior engineer and then as an
assistant engineer among scores of others.

"That was quite a piece of work," I said, embarrassed by
his concentration.

"Labourers, pipefitters, pitmen in those days were getting twenty cents an hour. Imagine what that canal would
cost today, eh?" I shook my head in tune with his. He
closed the book, giving me a glimpse of photographs of
the Welland Canal in different stages of construction as he
did so. He replaced the book and leaned back against my

parsons's table. He seemed lost in thought. Was he thinking of what the pyramids could be built for if you only
paid the slaves twenty cents an hour? I guess you don't
have to pay real slaves anything. He held on to his version
of the thought, shook himself like an old dog, and returned to his side of the room.

"Mr Cooperman, I have some of the minute books you
need right here on this shelf," he said indicating a wall of
books between two windows. "The rest are in the
boardroom, which doubles as our library." He sat down
behind his large, cluttered desk and looked back in my
direction. "If there's anything you want to know about
Phidias Manufacturing, please ask me," he said, selecting a
pipe from a rack of them next to his telephone. "I've been
with the firm for most of my sixty-four years. I remember
Miss Biddy Forbes's father. Not Miss Teddie's father—
although I knew him too; I mean Miss Biddy's father,
Sandy MacCallum. He was a friend of my father's in the
Royal Flying Corps, and he started all this when he got
home from the First War. He established an airline first,
but the only biplane he had crashed, so he went into
making safety bicycles. Now who would think that that
would lead up here to the sixth floor of the City Centre,
eh?" Once again I took the cue and gave him the required
response. From his manner I began to suspect that F.P.
McAuliffe was not the only chief financial officer of Phidias
Manufacturing. He was the financial end's equivalent of
chairman of the board. He held an impressive title, salary,
office and had very little to do except pass the time of day
with strays who got past the reefs of secretaries and
receptionists closer to the door. I couldn't connect him
with the death of Jack Dowden. Maybe he was part of the
scheme, but I doubted it. It was a long way from this room
in the offices of Phidias to the yard of its subsidiary,
Kinross. It was most likely that the death at Kinross
involved people working closer to Dowden and the

trucking end of things than the people, like McAuliffe, here at head office.

"Now," McAuliffe said, getting up again, "I suppose you want to see some books." He left his half-loaded pipe on his blotter next to a flat tin of tobacco, and went to the wall of books. His right hand went limply to his chin as he scanned the possibilities. "Now, where shall we start? Where shall we start?"

At this moment I heard a huge laugh come from elsewhere on the floor. It was too big to be contained by the flimsy space dividers and partitions of modern builders. The laugh was repeated and this time a woman's voice said something that sounded like a joking protest. All typing in the reception area stopped. I looked to Mr McAuliffe for guidance. "That would be the Commander," he said in a near whisper. "He's come back for the wedding on Saturday. They've been in Fort Lauderdale, him and Biddy."

I heard a door open and shut, a bigger-than-life roar and laugh, like Citizen Kane was walking down the corridors of Xanadu. "Where is that old rip?" a deep, radio announcer's voice shouted. "Where is that useless reprobate?" McAuliffe brightened.

"He's coming in here!"

"Fred? Where the hell are you?" The door opened and the Commander easily filled the doorway. He was about the size and shape of Orson Welles.

"Welcome home, Commander!" McAuliffe said, without actually pulling his forelock. The elder Mr Forbes kept shouting abuse while the two men approached one another and embraced in the middle of the room. McAuliffe almost disappeared in the arms of the bigger man. When they separated, the Commander held McAuliffe at arm's length, like a brown doll, and examined him carefully.

"You don't change, Fred. You never put on the years.

Hell, man, what's your secret?"

"Well, sir, I just try to stay busy."

"'Busy?' Hell, you never worked a day in your life. You can cut the crap when you're talkin' to me, Fred. You—" He had finally noticed that he wasn't alone in the room with McAuliffe. "Who in God's name is that, Fred? Don't tell me you have an assistant! I'll put an end to that fast enough, you old scallywag!"

"Oh, Commander Forbes, this is Mr Cooperman who's doing some work for Miss Teddie."

"How do you do, Mr Forbes?" I said.

"What's Teddie need with anything here?" he asked. The question was addressed to McAuliffe. He had ignored my greeting. Maybe it was the *Mister*. I should have brought him aboard with a toot from my handy boatswain's whistle. Meanwhile, he had fixed McAuliffe with a bulging eye so that the little man's eyebrows moved up and down in confusion. "What are you up to, Fred? What's going on here?"

A slim woman wearing a silver grey suit that matched her hair came into the room quietly and stood by the door. McAuliffe couldn't see her on the far side of Forbes's broad back. She nodded her head slowly in my direction, acknowledging my existence and then called:

"Murdo, they can hear you all the way to City Hall." The Commander turned and stared at her. She gave McAuliffe a warm smile when Fred moved to get a clear view. "Hello, Fred," she said.

"Miss Biddy. Well, I declare! You don't both of you come to the office often enough. How was Florida, Miss Biddy?"

"Everybody's getting older, Fred. I wouldn't be surprised to read that the whole population perished on a single night at the average age of eighty-four. They could just 'cease upon the midnight with no pain' and there'd be nobody left to notice."

"Oh dear!" McAuliffe said in mock surprise. "I don't think Keats was contemplating such large numbers."

"What the hell's going on with you two?" The Commander looked from one to the other and then to me to see if I knew what they were talking about. I shrugged complete ignorance and that settled him for the moment. He took a breath to show that he had decided to skip along to something important, but came around between his wife and McAuliffe, facing me. I felt the parson's table cornering me from behind.

"Fred, you still haven't told me what Teddie's doing with a man working in this office!" Again he fixed me with his eye. I felt like a notice pinned to a bulletin board. McAuliffe moved back behind his desk, sorting through a pile of papers under his pipe and tobacco tin.

"I'll show you the letter, Commander. I think you'll find that everything's in order."

"There hasn't been anything like order around here, Fred, since I took my paws off the wheel. That's a fact. You know it and I know it." He looked at Biddy as he said this, seeing how the colour came to her cheeks and hoping that with McAuliffe in the room as well as a stranger she wouldn't pick this moment to argue the point. Biddy held her tongue. The Commander took courage and went on. "Since the boy took charge, Fred, we've all been headed downhill on a runaway toboggan."

"Murdo, the *boy* is about to give his daughter away in marriage!"

"I never said he couldn't breed, Biddy! He couldn't get me grandsons, though. Sherry's a fine girl. I never said a word against her. And she's marrying a fine man. Damn it, I don't care what you say: Norman Caine will put new life into this business. You know as well as I do, both of you, Ross has never taken hold here, damn it!"

"Murdo! You're talking about your own son!"

"Mother, don't pretend you haven't heard that line before. Hello, Fred. Good-afternoon, Dad."

"Ross!" Ross Forbes was suddenly standing there and none of us had seen him come in. The Commander made a sort of bark at the back of his throat. Ross and his mother exchanged smiles. The old man looked his son up and down without, apparently, finding anything to write home about. Ross hadn't changed much. There was still the look of a spoiled child and the private school in every line of his face. He had that unbarbered look of an aristocrat.

"Wonderful to see you, darling!" Biddy Forbes presented a well-powdered cheek to be kissed. Ross pecked her there and held her around the waist, still keeping a wary eye on his father. When he straightened up, he maintained his hold on his mother and Biddy locked her fingers around his.

"I thought we'd declared a truce until after the wedding, Dad? Have I missed a round of negotiations?"

"Would you like to sit down, Miss Biddy?" Fred said trying to remember to be polite. She shook her head and stood near Ross with her hand in his.

"Place is going to hell, I said, and I'll say it to your face, Ross. It needs managing not coddling. We knew the difference in my day."

"We're not going to settle longstanding differences in the middle of Fred's office, are we?" He smiled and took a step in his father's direction with his hand stretched out. The Commander deliberately put his right hand in his jacket pocket, where it made him look both fey and petulant. Biddy's head tilted and she regarded her son with moist eyes.

"I think I'm going back to the club, Ross," she said. "There is still so much to do before the wedding." She looked around the room, gave Fred a warm apologetic smile and went out into the reception area, where I could

hear her talking to one of the secretaries as though nothing
had happened in Fred McAuliffe's office that was unfit for
the ears of everyone on the payroll or for scores who had
never heard of Phidias Manufacturing.

"Well, Dad," Ross said at length. "Here we go again. I
hope we can agree not to get into another row with Mother
around. It can't be good for her heart."

"I wasn't saying anything behind your back I wouldn't
say—indeed, haven't said—to your face."

"We agree on that much at least." It was as though the
room had suddenly released a breath it had been holding
for the last forty to fifty seconds. "When did you get back?
I haven't seen a light at the house."

"Nearly a week now. We've been keeping to ourselves.
Hiding out at the club. Once the family knows we're back,
and with this wedding thing, well, there'll be no peace for
either of us. I hope there are no changes in the plans you
wired your mother?"

"Nothing important. Sherry still wants to go through
with it. I've given up trying to get her to see reason."

"You mean to see things your way! Well, Ross, the girl's
a match for you, eh? The women in this family always did
have the balls. Take your mother. Bloody stoic. Bloody
Spartan, if it comes to that. Your mother could lead a
charge down St Andrew Street."

Ross looked about to go, not to retreat, but simply to
leave the field on equal terms with the enemy, when he
spotted me. "I remember you," he said. "You're Sugarman
or Goodman or something."

"Cooperman, Mr Forbes."

"Well, what the hell are you—? Wait a minute. That
letter from Colling. I remember it now."

"I have the letter right here, sir," said McAuliffe, putting
on his manners for the CEO. Was he the AV as well? I'd
have to find out. McAuliffe passed the two-page docu-

ment to Ross. It was intercepted without comment by the
Commander who quickly glanced down each of the pages
before handing them on to his son. He let loose something
like a stifled growl in the back of his throat. Ross studied
the letter too and seemed to find something amusing in the
contents, so that, when he looked up at me, he was almost
smiling.

"I know what it's like to have the tax people on my
back. If it wasn't my former wife, I'd be full of sympathy.
You may tell her I said that."

"Messenger boy," said the Commander, fixing me with
a cold eye. "Is that what he is? Come to spoil things for
Teddie at a time like this?" I could tell he wanted me to
wither up and blow away. Instead, I thought it was time to
strut some of the things I'd learned from Jim Colling.

"Mrs Forbes's tax status is in dispute, Commander
Forbes. We are just trying to clear it up as simply as
possible."

"What Mr Cooperman is too polite to say, Father, is that
Teddie has clout enough to demand a full-scale audit if we
don't cooperate."

"And you cave in at the first blast of a gale? Ha!" The
Commander made another of those croaking noises in the
back of his throat and wandered out of the room shaking
his head as though he had just come into the office and
found it empty.

After a moment, Ross pulled his attention back to me
and McAuliffe. It was plain that he had trouble sharing the
floor with the old man. "Fred, you keep an eye on Mr
Cooperman here, will you?"

"I'll be sure to do that, Mr Forbes."

"Try to remember that we're doing Teddie a favour, Mr
Cooperman. If you have any problems that Fred here can't
help you with, which I find hard to imagine, since he's
been here longer than anybody except Father, you bring it

to me. Is that understood?" I nodded but refused to pull my forelock. I was still trying to be my own man. "See you at the wedding, Fred."

"Oh, we wouldn't miss Miss Sherry's wedding, Mr Forbes," said McAuliffe. "Oh, no. We were at all the family weddings, you remember. Oh, May and I'll be there with bells on—wedding bells!" Forbes smiled at the older man's little joke and sucked in his largish belly so that it vanished under the shelter of his barrel chest, giving the illusion of fitness and health. Of the whole Forbes clan and throwing in McAuliffe and me for nothing, the Commander looked about as trim and healthy as the rest of us put together. For a man on the brink of eighty, he was putting us all to shame in the health department. I still wasn't ready to live under his whimsical, iron tyranny. There might be some hope for the son, but I doubted it. With the slightest of glances in my direction, Ross Forbes left me in McAuliffe's custody.

Chapter Sixteen

The first piece of interesting information I learned in the head office of Phidias wasn't about Kinross Disposals at all. It was about Sangallo Restorations. Recent events had partially obscured my primary mission to the extent that, when I found a description of Sangallo, I ate it up greedily. As I expected, it was a small firm with an office and small yard on the outskirts of Niagara-on-the-Lake. It had been a subsidiary of Phidias Manufacturing since 1988 and, like Kinross, appeared to operate with a measure of autonomy from the mother house. What raised my eyelids to fully open was the discovery that the chief executive officer was Harold Grier. Grier was a family name I'd run into before in this investigation. With a little discreet questioning of Fred McAuliffe, I learned that Harold was the brother-in-law of both Ross Forbes and Paul Renner of the city's sanitation department. Harold was the brother of the women they married. I tried not to show my delight at this piece of news. But I could almost hear myself whispering under my breath, "Rub-a-dub dub / Three men in a tub / The butcher, the baker, the candlestick-maker". And I was forgetting that Grier must be the front man for Tony Pritchett and his boys. The tub was more crowded than I thought.

From his desk across the room from me, McAuliffe sat surrounded in a cloud of his own pipesmoke. He had had a blower unit installed above his head, something he called his "ceiling-hung blower unit," which had no doubt been put in to obey the smoking by-laws, but from what I could see, McAuliffe rarely bothered to turn the thing on. Wherever I went with him in the office, on any of the floors and once down into the basement to the dead-files room, Fred ignored all NO SMOKING signs posted by the elevators and stairs. He was too old to change his spots, he told me. He spent a good part of his day scraping, cleaning, reaming, filling and, on occasion, smoking one of his fifty briars. They were all a big part of him. Like the burned holes in his desk blotter and the ashes—I've seen them even in his eyebrows—everywhere, McAuliffe was a leftover from an earlier day. I hadn't come into the office with any high regard for Phidias or any of its tentacles, but the fact that it gave office space to this tweedy, Dickensian character, who always had time to digress and give me the history or background on any matter that came up, made me respect it and give it the benefit of the doubt.

I had never been a whiz with figures, but Fred McAuliffe could breathe life into a ledger. He seemed to remember every entry. Sometimes he would explain the reason for a group of figures as though he were lecturing to a large class of students; another time he would close the door and whisper reasons to me that I was too thick to follow. I got the general idea that Phidias had an insatiable appetite for small companies that had expanded as far as they could on the available capital. When it came to blocks of shares and values before and after splits, I was over my head, and only McAuliffe's gentle patience helped me keep one toe on the bottom and my nose clearing the waves.

What made working this close to Fred agreeable was that he enjoyed distraction from work as much as I did. I learned more about all four of the Welland Canals than has ever been printed in books. He was a walking encyclopedia. For instance, he told me his name, McAuliffe, came from the same word as Hamlet and that they both were fancy forms of Olaf.

I asked Fred if he knew anything about the excavations at Fort Mississauga in Niagara-on-the-Lake. He didn't suddenly change. In fact, he smiled.

"Ah, yes!" he said. "That's one of the Sangallo jobs. Yes, I'm glad to be associated with that. You know the supervisor is Dr John Roppa of the RAM in Toronto, same fellow who discovered the remains of those American soldiers from the War of 1812 at Queenston three years ago."

"What's he finding at the fort?"

"Well, he's keeping it very hush-hush at this stage. But I know this much: they are putting the earthworks back where they were originally, as well as making general repairs and restorations to the main structure."

"The last time I saw it, it looked like it had a skin disease."

"Ha! That's pargeting," said Mr McAuliffe.

"I beg your pardon?"

"Parging, pargeting, covering the brick with plaster to keep the weather out. What the English call roughcast. The golf club's lease on the property ends in 1991. After that, it will probably go to the Parks Board, like Fort George. The golf club's moved a couple of tees and the old green beside the tower so that the historic landmarks people didn't stage a protest. There've been more letters about that damned fort in the paper than there have been about the local water supply, which, to hear them, comes directly from the Love Canal over the river."

From the records I was looking at, it appeared that the Commander had retained active control of Phidias until recently. It was only when advanced age and crotchetiness had got the better of him that he had reluctantly stepped aside in favour of his son. But Murdo Forbes was still an important shareholder. Without owning an overall majority, he could at least match with his own shares anything that Ross could put up. Teddie's interest in the firm amounted to a tidy ten percent. I couldn't see why she had hung on to her shares since the divorce, but Fred explained that she would need the consent of the other board members to sell, and that permission had not been expressed in the minutes.

"Oh, I've seen it more than once," Fred said, "where an unwilling shareholder is kept involuntarily. It keeps the board from having to buy her out and it keeps newcomers away. On Mr Forbes's side, too, I think there may be something personal."

"Like spite?"

"That's your word for it, Mr Cooperman, not mine. Teddie's family is an old one in this town, you know, and Teddie herself has been a credit to her name."

From Fred I learned that Ross had never really taken charge at Phidias, not in the way the old man had. "The boy doesn't have the grit of the Commander. He's never had to worry about where his next meal was coming from, eh?" he said with a grin, while sending a shower of sparks up towards the ceiling-hung blower unit. "The Commander wasn't born to a bed of roses. He made his own way, same as I did."

"Did Ross Forbes ever have a chance around here?"

"Chance? Why, what are you talking about? There's an opportunity born every day. And most days Mr Ross comes in at ten in the morning. The Commander was always deep at work when I came in at seven in the old days. Seven, eh! And he'd be still hard at it when I went home for my supper at seven at night. Oh, the Commander loved making this place tick. And he kept all the subsidiaries ticking too. Why, I remember once he bought a failing dairy. He did everything but milk the cows until it turned a profit a year and a half later. Mr Ross isn't a detail man like his father. He goes for flow charts and graphs and printouts I can hardly read. The Commander can call any worker by his first name and tell you his wife's name too and how many youngsters they have. Oh, the Commander's a remarkable man."

"It's a remarkable family," I agreed. "And I guess they will all be on their best behaviour for the wedding?"

"That's where class shows, Mr Cooperman. There may be problems. I'm not saying there aren't. But in public it will be smooth as silk. Oh, the Forbeses are the salt of the earth."

"I'm sure you're right," I lied. I was trying to cut down on sodium like the Forbeses. They were bad for my diet.

"The interesting thing, Mr Cooperman, is that this wedding is a case of history repeating itself."

I thought I'd heard the story before, but I thought I might learn something new. "How's that?" I asked.

"Sandy MacCallum didn't have a son to carry on his business, so he married his daughter to a capable young lad with lots of get-up-and-go. He could see that the Commander, even in those days, had as much stick-to-it-iveness as he had himself. That's why he became more of a son than a son-in-law. Now the Commander is looking at Mr Ross's girl, Sherry, as a second Miss Biddy. You see? He thinks the world of Miss Sherry's young man, Mr Caine. Mr Caine will be grand for the business, Mr Cooperman. I think he's the Commander all over again."

"I hope you're right." Fred had repeated the story as I'd first heard it; so it must be common knowledge. In my business a little confirmation is a big help in taking the next step.

"Oh, I am," Fred was saying. "I know I am. You see, it's not just breeding, it's the military training. Mr Caine was in Central America with the Americans for a year as a volunteer. Before that, he was in the Canadian Forces. You can't beat military training, Mr Cooperman. It cuts out fuzzy thinking. They all had it, you know: the Commander, of course; Miss Biddy in the Canadian Women's

Army Corps; even Mr Ross held a commission at one time and he had all those military academies one after the other."

"They sound like dangerous people to know." I said it as a joke, but Fred pondered it seriously. There was no trace of a smile on his face when he answered.

"I wouldn't want to cross them. I'll say that. But they all work like Trojans. They expect as much from the people around them. Still, I see what you mean. Medes and Persians, eh?"

"Pardon?"

"'According to the law of the Medes and Persians, which altereth not.' They, as a family, are rather rigid once they've settled on a question."

"Inflexible?" I asked.

"Well," he hedged, "a close cousin, I'd say. You know I've been with them for many years. I don't want to bore you on that score, but I know that there will be a pension for me when it's time for me to go. There's nothing written down, mind. But, I know. It's their way of doing business. You can't find many examples of that these days, Mr Cooperman. There was a time . . ." Here he headed off into one of his sketches of contemporary practices that made business seem knowable even for people like me. I felt like I could pick up the *Report on Business* in the *Globe and Mail* and understand every word. Of course he'd missed things like organized labour and other non-paternal things that had been going on during the last twenty years, but it wasn't my job to put him straight.

"Here's something I think might interest you, Mr Cooperman." He handed me a framed photograph showing a very young Murdo Forbes standing beside a middle-aged, lean man with one lens of his glasses frosted over. Sandy MacCallum, even in a black-and-white picture, looked like a man in a brown suit. I could see him getting along with the man at my elbow. The Commander, seen some years before he had earned that rank, looked like a man on the make. He still had hungry lines on his face, which had not widened to the familiar patrician face of the present. His features were as good as a look into his antecedents. You could see from his eyes how much the moment recorded in the photograph meant to him. For MacCallum it was just another photograph. I handed the picture back to Fred. "Nice," I said, "nice." After McAuliffe handed me a picture showing the Grantham Hunt, all mounted up wearing hunting pink jackets and drinking stirrup cups in the front yard of the MacCallum house on Church Street, even I thought that it was time to get back to work on the company books.

On the front door of the Phidias office, a marvel in glass and boards stripped from the last of our old barns, I noticed the little decal that told me that security at Phidias was being handled by my rival in the private investigations business in town, Howard Dover. When I got a chance to call Howard, I did. Since Howard knew that I wasn't interested in the rent-a-cop business, we got along reasonably well. By the end of our conversation he'd told me several interesting things:

"Working for Phidias, Benny, is like working for Jack Benny. They're so cheap they'll skin a mouse to sell its pelt; they'll have the hide off a cockroach, I'm tellin' you." In addition to this, I learned that the man on duty downstairs that night was named Boris Jurik and that he was reasonably dim in spite of having been on the job for a year and a half.

Later in the day, on my way back from the bathroom, a sudden voice behind me made me check to see if I'd forgotten to zip up. "Hey! Cooperman!" It was Ross Forbes. I stopped and turned around as he caught up to me. I got the feeling that this might be the end of my intimate association with Phidias Manufacturing. And just when I was getting used to Fred's informal course on local history.

"Will you come back with me to my office, please?" He didn't say it like it was really a question. I wondered if I'd ever willingly accepted that tone of voice. I doubted it.

"Sure," I said. "What's up?" There was no answer, so I kept a half a step behind Forbes and followed him into one of the big corner offices. Its carpet was deeper, its furniture newer and with a designer's imprint on the glass and blond wood. There was also a better view over the city from here. How had he arranged that?

Standing in the deep plush in the middle of the room were the shoes of Norman Caine. The face a little over five feet above them was not smiling, but I recognized it from I'm still not sure where.

"Is this Mr Cooperman?" He looked at Forbes for his answer. Maybe my word wasn't good enough. Forbes nodded.

"Mr Cooperman, Mr Norman Caine," he said. "Mr Caine is in charge of Kinross Disposals, a subsidiary of this company. He wants a word with you." From the way Caine was looking through me, I was wondering whether I had disappeared without knowing it. His failure to make contact reminded me of somebody. Of course, it was the Commander.

Apart from his slight stature, Norman Caine looked like he could be a formidable antagonist. But he had to work hard to make his cherubic face frown. There was a fuzzy, boyish quality about him that his tweedy jacket accentuated. His hands were joined by a length of yellow pencil. "Mr Cooperman," he began, "is it true that you are looking up material for Teddie Forbes?" I fielded that question fairly well, I thought. Forbes bobbed his head as I explained. I think I did a better job on Caine than I had done to date. I had mastered the phrases that Jim Colling had given me and to them had added fresh lines of patter from Fred McAuliffe. Caine didn't look convinced for a minute. I came to the end of the speech:

"Anything wrong with that?" Caine levelled his pencil at me.

"What do you know about a man named Alex Pásztory?" Ah-ha, this was no casual encounter.

"Well, I used to read his stuff in the *Beacon*. But I have a low tolerance for stuff about pollution, so I make a poor advocate for a pure environment. I'm for it, you understand, but I'm no fanatic. I may get to the barricades, but I won't be among the first, if you know what I mean."

"Have you ever talked to him, face to face?"

"Sure. Pásztory's an old drinking friend of mine. I've known him for years. I don't lumber him with my transom gazing and he keeps his acid rain to himself. What's wrong? Is it wrong to know Alex all of a sudden?" I don't usually think fast on my feet, but from my memory of the figure sitting opposite me at the Turkey Roost, I thought that I was making a reasonable invention. I was sure that he knew that I had seen him at the restaurant.

"Did you know he was found dead at Fort Mississauga on Thursday night?"

"Sure. I read it in the weekend papers. I'm sorry he's dead. He was a funny guy. My big brother used to date his sister. So what? Is it a crime to have known him?" I'd thought of showing shock at the news of his death, but decided that I couldn't play it in the round. As it was, I'm not sure either Caine or Forbes was buying my act.

"He was found murdered, Cooperman," Caine said. "And I think you know more about it than you're saying."

"Great! You think I killed him? I didn't even know he was found at Fort Mississauga until you said so. That wasn't in the paper. So right now I'd say you know more about this than I do." That was a bad move; I'd put Caine on the defensive. I tried to think what I could do about it. "Alex always said it would be our smoking that got us in the end. He said we were the last of a happy breed of men." What I'd added was irrelevant, but it seemed to oil

the troubled waters. For half a second mortality was
contemplated in the blond office, then Caine was right
back in there reaching for my jugular vein.

"I think you know a lot more about Pastor and the
things he was playing around with than you're letting on.
I say you're lying."

"Look, I told you, I know—knew—him casually. Since
when is that a crime in a town this size? I had coffee the
other day with a zoologist. What does that make me? A
petunia?"

Caine took his eyes off me and glanced over at Forbes.
"I don't like this, Ross. I say get him out of here."

"But he's only—"

"Yeah, that's what he says. But I say unload him now
and forget all about what he's doing here. Teddie's not
your business any more. I say he's an inconvenience at
best, at worst he could be trouble." Ross looked at both of
us and then at a glass polar bear, which was the only
decoration on a bare bookshelf. He did a thing with his
lower lip and moved his jaw from side to side, as though
thinking didn't come easy.

"Cooperman is here for a good reason, Norm. Teddie's
ten percent gives her a lot of clout. She could demand an
audit and that could run into big numbers. I don't want to
run afoul of the Business Corporations Act if I can help it.
Mr Cooperman here is a very convenient solution." It was
smoother than I'd heard him talk before, reasoned for a
change and calm, which put the wind up Caine who was
facing him.

"I still say he's a pest. Get rid of him! I don't like his
timing."

"Cooperman's not going anywhere close to Kinross
affairs, Norm. McAuliffe's got his eye on him. I suggest
you leave this to me."

"McAuliffe? Get serious, Ross." Caine threw a scornful
glance at Forbes and even included me in it. It was nice to

be part of the party again after being the thing they were arguing about. "Now, Ross, I've talked this over with the Commander and—"

"I don't care whether you've had direct communication from God Almighty! Phidias is my affair. So is Teddie. I think you should spend more time down at the yard and less up here looking over my shoulder!"

"The Commander isn't going to like this! He *is* Chairman of the Board, you know."

"Norm, my father can't order a box of paperclips in this office without my okaying it. I'm in charge here and the sooner you remember that the better!"

"Look," I put in, just to show I wasn't a lifelike replica of Benny Cooperman but the man himself, "if I'm in the way . . ."

"Cooperman, keep out of this!" Ross said and I did that, while the two continued to wrangle. I hoped that some crucial information might fall my way, but they were both too clever for that. The altercation ended with Caine storming out of the room, red in the face and with white knuckles.

"You've made a bad enemy, Mr Forbes," I said at length.

"Caine? Oh, we've been at each other's throats since he arrived. This is nothing new."

"He could be right, you know."

"If I unload you, Cooperman, Teddie will have everybody in town talking. I know what I'm doing. It's business as usual at Phidias Manufacturing."

"Well, thanks, anyway," I said.

"Look, my friend, don't imagine for a moment that you played any part in what just occurred. Caine and I have been jousting like this for the past three years. If he'd suggested that I keep you here, you'd be on your way out of here this minute."

"He seems to think the Commander—"

"For Christ's sake, Cooperman, get out of here before I change my mind!"

I turned and tried to walk calmly through the open door and down the corridor. I got back to the office just as McAuliffe was putting on his coat. It was about five after five.

"Well, good-night there, Mr Cooperman," he said.

"I suppose you heard most of that?" I asked. He would have had to be stone deaf not to have caught at least part of what went on.

"I think you're a lucky man, Mr Cooperman. You have been given a very rare privilege to come and go here. I hope you appreciate that?"

"Oh, I do, Mr McAuliffe, but I didn't want to become a cause of dissension." His fingers stopped buttoning.

"I'm sure it was a considered decision, Mr Cooperman. You know Grantham is in many ways still a village. People from Toronto don't always remember that. Well, at least for the moment anyway, it seems our acquaintance is not going to be cut short." McAuliffe looked a little shaken by what he had heard, and I remembered Caine's sneer at the mention of Fred's name. I tried to think of something to get him over this rough patch.

"Mr McAuliffe," I asked, remembering what Pásztory had said just before we went to look at the parts of an enormous clock behind a shed in the Kinross yard, "have you ever run into the term 'AV' in your work? It's probably a common shortening, but I've never heard of it." The fingers remained motionless on the coat buttons. Fred reflected.

"A business term, you say?"

"I think so. Something like CEO, I think." McAuliffe let his lower lip droop rather dramatically, but in the end he shook his head.

"It's not a term I'm familiar with, Mr Cooperman. Perhaps it's computer jargon. You might ask one of the younger people tomorrow." His fingers began to move again. They continued down the front of his coat and then reached for the green Irish tweed cap. "Well," he said, half-turned towards the half-closed door, "well, well, well, well." And he was gone.

Chapter Seventeen

I n the lobby of the City Centre, behind a desk and in uniform sat a security guard making an attempt to look like he was keeping track of comings and goings after the day people had signed out. I picked up the pad from his desk and put my name down and added the time. It was just ten after five. As I did this, I noticed that both Forbes and Caine were still on the premises.

"You're Boris Jurik, aren't you?" I asked the guard. He blinked back to being semi-alert.

"Yeah, that's right." He checked the book to see who was asking.

"My name's Cooperman. I'm in the way of being in the same line of work myself. Howard Dover, your boss, and I go back a long way together. He's been talking to me about you."

"No kidding?" I got a peek at some complicated dental work under his sparse moustache. "Are you into corporate security?" he asked. I smiled at the term.

"No, I do private investigations. Undercover, surveillance, that sort of thing."

"Are you looking for a man?" So much for employee loyalty.

"Always on the lookout for the *right* man," I said. I shot him a confidential glance and added: "Somebody who knows his way around." Boris hitched his belt a little higher on his hips. "Things seem pretty secure around here," I said. "Any problems?"

"This job? Naw. Nothin' to it."

"I'm a little concerned about the storage room downstairs. How secure are you down there?" Boris's face emptied. I had obviously hit upon someplace he hadn't even been told to worry about.

"We've had no trouble down there," he said evasively. I smiled at his answer and let it sink in.

"That's just the problem, isn't it? Your average security man wouldn't even check down there. But I'm sure that a guard of your calibre, who's been with Dover for the last year and a half—"

"Almost coming up to a year and three quarters."

"There you are! Practically two years!"

"Is there something not right down there, security-wise, Mr Cooperman? I want to get on top of it if there's a loophole somewhere."

"Well, as a favour to you, I'll duke down there and have a fast look and let you know. Might be just a little thing. I'll let you pass the word on to Phidias yourself, so they'll know you're on your toes."

"Gee, that's great!"

"Oh, I'm going to need your keys," I said as an afterthought. He handed them over like they were cut glass. "Have 'em back to you in a few minutes."

"Take your time. And thanks for doing this, like they say on TV."

I took the elevator down to the place marked "B" on the floor selector. Part of the area was given over to underground parking. The rest was deeply involved with storage. I opened the door marked "Phidias" with one of the keys on the ring, and stepped inside. It was a long narrow room with green metal shelf units up and down the middle of the space and along each wall. At first my heart sank. I'd never get through to the things I needed. But right from the first cardboard box I looked at, my heart grew a bit lighter. Each box was clearly labelled as to date and company of origin. First of all I checked the Kinross section. There were columns of boxes which I quickly dug into. I was looking for paper having to do with the date of the accident and immediately afterwards. It took longer than I thought to find anything. Why is it that I grow thumbs on all my fingers when I need the skill of a brain surgeon?

Then I had something. It was the dispatcher's list of business in and out of the Kinross yard on the day Jack Dowden died. I pulled it from the rest of the pack of similar reports and put it in my pocket. Then I found the personnel records for the same time period. Whoever kept these records kept them very well. I followed down the list of names looking for the familiar ones. There was Jack Dowden's name leaping off the page. There were the amounts paid to his widow that she'd told me about. Further down the page I saw that O'Mara, Tadeuss Puisans and Luigi Pegoraro were given bonuses. Their hourly rate was increased until, in Puisans's and Pegoraro's cases, they left the firm, both with parting bonuses as well as a handshake. I thought I was all finished, when I saw an extra bonus, this time to Rory O'Mara for hockey camp. So that's what he practised. I'd been wondering about the black-clad lout in O'Mara's living-room.

I helped myself to the pages concerned and stuffed them with my other papers into the files in my briefcase. After closing the boxes, I hefted them back to the shelves upon which they were allocated to spend eternity and dusted myself off. Back upstairs, I told Boris that he should suggest a steel door be added to the arrangements in the basement. "It's too easy to get in there from the parking garage." He nodded vigorously, having had the same notion himself, I'm sure on many occasions. "I could put this in my report," I said, "but it would look even better coming from you, Boris." Boris showed me his metallic smile again. "I'll leave our little conversation out of my report completely, so the whole idea will come from you. You'll get credit for the whole deal."

"Gosh, Mr Cooperman, I don't know how to thank you." I flipped him back his keys, which he caught over his right shoulder.

Chapter Eighteen

The sun was going down over the city. In fact, except where you got an east-west street running straight to the horizon, which wasn't often in downtown Grantham, it had gone down already. I found the car, dusty from blowing leaves and neglect, behind my office. As I opened the door and sat down behind the wheel, I remembered the warning contained in my personal copy of the *Desiderata*. Had anybody ever been blown up in his car in this town? I tried to remember. I wasn't sure what to expect as a follow-up, when it became plain that I didn't know how to mind my own business. I thought of Alex Pásztory and turned the key in the ignition. The motor caught, and for a minute drowned out the racket of the textile mill on the edge of the canal below me. I turned the car in the limited space, then climbed up the narrow alley to join the one-way traffic of St Andrew Street.

It was still light enough so that I didn't have to turn my headlights on as I headed towards Junkin Street for a return visit. Kids were playing in a great heap of leaves at the corner of Geneva when I began looking for a parking place. I left the car on Geneva nearer St Patrick than Junkin and walked back the block to the O'Mara house. I couldn't see anyone behind me, but what did I know? If I was following me, I'd keep out of sight too. Except for the school kids jumping in the leaves below the black trunks of the old maples, the neighbourhood was quiet as I walked up the steps and knocked on the door.

"He ain't here!" Mrs O'Mara was again playing protective games. I pointed out the car in the driveway and her defence broke down. I was glad her boy Rory was out peddling dope to school kids or whatever he did to amuse himself between meals. Against very little opposition, I pushed the door open the rest of the way and she retreated ahead of me. A flushing sound from the back of the house told me that there were at least three of us present. In a moment, O'Mara arrived upon the scene with a blue towel in his hands.

"You again!" he said, throwing me a look that tried to make me feel guilty of breaking our bargain. "I told you, Mr Cooperman, that I can't go around blabbing all day just because Irma Dowden wants to waste her insurance money on a rent-a-cop! I want nothin' to do with you. You already got me more heat than I want."

"There's going to be more heat from now on, Mr O'Mara, not less. And it won't be coming from me. I saw what you've been hauling from the City Yard to the fort. All of that's going to come out before long. Now we both know what was in those oil drums." O'Mara's expression changed. He sent his wife out to get some beer from the kitchen.

"Shit, Cooperman, I don't want Dora knowing about this. Where'd you leave your tact and good manners, eh?"

"I can listen anywhere you say, Brian. It's your call."

He thought about that. He was just about to speak when Dora arrived back with two unopened bottles, no glasses and a rusty opener. I think she was beginning to like me. "What about the Men's Beverage Room at the Harding House on James at King, say, seven-thirty?"

"How do I know you'll be there?" I asked, getting a lot of foam in my mouth from the warm beer.

"I'll meet you. I'm tellin' you I'll be there, okay?"

"If you let me down, I'll come looking for you up the hill, Brian."

"Yeah, I figured you might. I'll be there like I said. After supper. Seven-thirty."

I took a polite deep swig of the beer in my hand, smiled at Dora and bowed out of the house. I wasn't used to threatening people. I never thought I'd be any good at it. In this case, I was pretty sure that he would show up, unless Dora tied him to the television set and had Rory lock the door.

Nobody had thought to slash my tires. The car started, and I treated myself to a good meal at the Diana Sweets. They had vegetable soup and a sandwich on special, with coffee thrown in. I tried to kill the hour or so I had in hand with a bum-flattened copy of the *Beacon* I'd found in my booth. I worked my way through it from the front page to the obituaries. It is always a lift to read the obits and discover that I'm still numbered among the living. After I got my change from the cashier, I wandered up St Andrew, bought a fresh pack of cigarettes before I discovered that I had most of the present package unsmoked in my pocket. I selected a cigarette, like they say in books, and rounded the corner of James Street.

The Men's Beverage Room at the Harding House was a throwback to less enlightened days when the sexes were separated for the purpose of drinking. The room next door was set aside for "Ladies and Escorts." It was a fancier room, its walls were decorated and its floor got swept more regularly than in the Men's. I was sitting at a round table for two with my back to the service bar at about twenty-five after seven. I was so sure O'Mara would show, I'd ordered the waiter to cover the table with draft beer so that now it looked like the other tables in the dim, smoky room. The beer was cold and I sipped one while watching the waiter move in and around the tables, dropping glasses, removing empties and giving change. He looked like a ballet dancer with an apron full of silver instead of a tutu.

I'd been there long enough to start worrying what I'd do with all this draft beer in case O'Mara didn't show up. Pubs don't stock the equivalent of doggy bags for customers who order more than they can swallow. This problem was developing nicely when O'Mara pulled out the chair opposite me and sat down. He was wearing a quilted hunting jacket over a plaid shirt. The cap he was wearing had been made for a sportscar driver, but it was a close enough equivalent of the traditional working-class cloth cap to pass if you didn't look too closely. It's funny about clothes and class. I'll have to think about that some time.

"You didn't think I was coming, I'll bet," he said, lifting the nearest beer to his mouth.

"I wasn't making bets either way. I just know we've still got lots to talk about. For instance, if you have the bad luck to get hit by a big truck, you get your pelvis crushed, not your chest. You don't get your spine damaged where Jack's was. So that means the story of Jack being on his feet when the truck hit him is made of rhubarb, Brian." O'Mara was studying my face, looking for what was going on inside, I guess. He put his first empty glass down hard on the red Formica top of the table. "Another thing, Brian: if a Freightliner nudged me with all of its weight, I'd end up pinned against the wall I was standing against. I wouldn't slide under the truck. Not unless the truck was in gear and there was somebody behind the wheel to put it in reverse."

"You're crazy if you think that!"

"Yeah, then I'm crazy then. And you and the other witnesses weren't paid off to dummy up and say what they were told to say at the inquest. Maybe Rory paid his own way to hockey camp. What do you take me for, Brian? Some kind of idiot who can't count his feet? O'Mara, if you can't tell talk from bullshit, stay away from me. And when they find you in a ditch along Old Number Eight because you knew too much, I'll laugh my head off." I pretended that I was getting up. We both thought about Pásztory without saying his name out loud.

"Sit down, Mr Cooperman," he said. "I didn't know you were into this this deep. I gotta be careful, you understand?"

"Nobody ever rubbed out anybody who shared a secret with enough other people, Brian. Right now, you're hot. With Pásztory out of the way and what he'd been digging up about Jack Dowden's death probably in their hands, you're on deck, kid. Don't neglect your life insurance."

"Okay, I'll level with you. Is that what you want?"

"It's your only hope." O'Mara nodded sadly. He could see I had a point. "To begin with," I asked, trying not to waste the opportunity, "what did you really see up there?"

"Nothin'. We didn't see nothin' movin'. He didn't scream. Jack was under the cab of the tractor. You could see he was done for. We pulled him out and Puisans ran to get the doctor."

"Carswell."

"Yeah, he'd been waiting to have breakfast with Mr Caine, but Caine didn't show up."

"When did he come on the scene?"

"Caine? Oh, he didn't get there until around ten-thirty, which was late for him. By then the ambulance had gone and the cops were all over the yard like a tent, takin' pictures and measuring stuff."

"Who put you up to the testimony you gave?"

"Webster. He was in charge of the yard, chief dispatcher. He checked everything in and out from the office at the front of the yard."

"Keep going."

"He ran the place, made up our cards. What more is there to say?"

"Find it."

"He said it would be best if we got our stories straight. He said anybody could see it was an accident, so where's the harm in saying so."

"So, you were just doing your duty?"

"Come off it, Cooperman! I'm tellin' you what I'm tellin' you."

"You're just beginning. Keep going; it gets easier."

"Webster was the guy we had to deal with, so what were we goin' to tell him? Webster was callin' the shots. We just said what he told us to say."

"So he knows where all the bodies are buried, eh?"

"*Knew*, Cooperman, *knew*. Webster ain't with us any more. He got the Big C and he died just after the Civic Holiday in August. So, go ask him some questions."

O'Mara emptied another glass of beer and started on a third. I'd got to within a swallow of the end of my first. For me, that wasn't bad. The cold of the coming winter crept along my bones as I picked up the second draft. Maybe I was coming down with something.

"So, although you admit to no inside knowledge about it, you're saying that the Kinross brass might have had a good reason for arranging an accident for Jack Dowden."

"You said that, not me!"

"Would you swear that there's nothing to what I've said?"

"Well, you know, anything's possible."

"That's right. Unfortunately, it isn't proof of anything. Now tell me about the fort."

"You were in my mirror all the way from the City yard. I could have blown the whistle on you."

"But you didn't. That's why I didn't come **blundering** in the front door right after you." O'Mara nodded. He'd been thinking about that. He finished another glass, still looking as uncomfortable as when he had sat down. He was sitting like his back hurt and it was driving him crazy.

"What kind of garbage are you getting from the city and why are you burying it there?"

There, I'd said it. I'd asked the big question. All O'Mara had to do was hit me on the nose or answer. He compromised by wetting his lips with his grey tongue. He had another half-draft and put the glass down again. Soon he was moving the glass around his end of the table, breaking up the wet rings of condensation and spilled beer. At last he lifted his eyes and looked me in the eye.

"The city has these cross-walk lights," he said. "The boxes that control the lights are full of PCBs. When they wear out or get broken, they have to go somewhere. There are other things too, other toxic garbage. The city gets us to dump it like we get rid of a lot of other stuff."

"But that other stuff doesn't all get buried in the new earthworks of Fort Mississauga."

"Right. We dump a lot of the liquid—the metallic stuff—into the lake from there. It's the perfect spot and nobody even guesses we have a pipe going into the lake. And that close to the river, if they spotted our stuff, they'd think it came from up the river someplace."

"So the fort's the main dumping spot?"

"Yeah, but we also store stuff there. Stuff that's too hot to keep in the yard. We sometimes rig a pig there if we're selling fuel oil over the river."

"Pig? What are you talking about?"

"It's an inflatable plastic bag, about the size of a swimming-pool liner. You fill it up with toxic garbage after sticking it into an empty tank of a big tanker, then you fill up the rest with regular bunker C, stove oil, domestic fuel oil or diesel fuel oil. It doesn't matter, as long as you've got a buyer on the other side. You know the scam from the papers last spring. They nearly put us out of business. We had to keep our noses clean for a while because they tightened up the border inspection on the few points they didn't close down."

"So this pig would get your PCBs through customs?"

"Yeah. Once on the other side, we would break the pig with steel rods and let the two substances mix."

"It would have served you right if the damned stuff exploded!"

"Hey, Cooperman, I was just following orders. Besides, PCBs are very stable and don't combine with anything at low temperatures. Like, they're inert."

"Gee, I wonder what all the fuss is about! Have you ever heard of dioxin? Did Jack Dowden ever mention TCDD? There's a whole alphabet soup of garbage you've been chauffeuring around the countryside! Didn't it ever bother you? Damn it, O'Mara, your grandchildren could be born with their belly-buttons where their chins should be. You should read up on this stuff you're messing in."

"Kinross has always treated me right, Cooperman. I'll say that for them."

"Well, you can't make a separate peace with them. We're all drinking out of the same trough. Same trough Webster was drinking from. I'll bet Kinross sent a big wreath to the funeral. They'll do as much for you." I let him think about that for a moment, while I went back over the list of questions I had stored in my head. When I found a new line of inquiry, I interrupted his drinking again. "The fort's only been available for a year and a few months. What did you do before that?"

"There was the old Hydro fill near Niagara Falls. That landfill is full of stuff. There's another twenty or thirty drums under the ornamental floral clock on the Niagara Parkway. The place is dotted with dumping sites. You want me to draw you a map?"

"Why are the hands of the clock in the Kinross yard?"

"A truck from Sangallo left it there. Sangallo has been keeping the damn thing going for the tourists to see."

"I get it. You even have to set out the plants and water them."

"That's Sangallo. We don't want strangers digging under the petunias, if you know what I mean." We were steadily progressing through the beer on the table. He was doing better than I was, and I was reaping the rewards.

"Tell me about Sangallo," I asked, picking up my third glass. "I know the head man's Harold Grier."

"Yeah, Grier is the front man all right, but there's somebody else."

"Like who?"

"I don't know, but I get the feeling—it's just a feeling—that Grier's fronting for—maybe it's the mob, I don't know. What I'm saying is that Grier may sign the cheques, but I think there's somebody standing behind his chair."

"You mean like Phidias is behind Kinross?"

"Naw, that's all in the open. This is more secret like."

"So you mean that this other element is working at the fort too?"

"I thought you were listening. Sangallo is the whole show in Niagara-on-the-Lake. We just drive and deliver."

"I thought Sangallo did historical restorations."

"Yeah, like an iceberg floats on the top of the water without blue ice underneath going down maybe a couple of hundred feet." O'Mara wiped his mouth on the cuff of his right sleeve and, at the same time, shifted his haunches. "I've got to get rid of some of this beer," he said getting up. "You want chips when I come back, Mr Cooperman?" His chair squawked against the tile floor and I watched him weave his way through the clutter of tables to the john at the far end of the room.

He was still holding things back, O'Mara, but he had moved his lines of defendable territory from our earlier talk. If he would help, maybe the Jack Dowden case could be reopened. If he wouldn't come forward himself to be a witness, at least he might be able to point me in the right direction so I could find some proof myself.

The balance of beer on the red-topped Formica was now tipped in favour of the empty glasses. The waiter danced over, removed the empties and without asking replaced them with amber reinforcements. I put a few bills in the waiter's hand and he dipped into his apron for some change. When I gave him a tip, it was pocketed silently.

O'Mara was taking his time in the men's room. I'd noticed other renters of the Harding House beer going to and coming from the toilet, some of them ignoring the suggestion of the management that clothing should be adjusted before leaving the room with all the porcelain fixtures. At last, I got up and walked between the tables myself. I was developing a need of my own, but it was less than serious. Mainly, I was beginning to worry about my friend O'Mara.

He wasn't in the john. He wasn't standing at either of the urinals, and the only occupied cubicle produced a stranger after I'd waited two minutes. O'Mara was gone.

Chapter Nineteen

There were only two things that could have happened. Either he had got tired of our conversation and gone through the back door to return home to Junkin Street, or he had been taken out of the Harding House by people who didn't like him talking to me. I looked around the floor of the toilet without finding anything that suggested one theory over the other. I followed his probable route out of the john and into the small parking lot. Not even the alley cats were moving. I caught just a cold whiff of the usual night smells of Grantham: papermills and beer from the exhausted air of the pub. I went back to my table and sat for ten minutes in case he sent a message. I was worried for O'Mara, but not nervous for myself. I didn't think the heavies from Kinross, or wherever they came from, would start anything in the crowded beverage room. I might have been right, because the only company I had was my own.

In the end I abandoned the last of the glasses of draft beer on the table and left the pub through the front door, the one that faced the old courthouse. It had recently been turned into a maze of boutiques. I honestly didn't know what to do. A phonecall to the O'Mara house in a few minutes would tell me if Brian had got tired and wandered home. It would also tell me if he was still out and unaccounted for. I didn't relish being the messenger with the news that he might not be getting home for some time. I didn't want to face Dora and tell her her instincts about keeping quiet were well founded.

I was saved from further speculation of this kind by, first, a vague feeling that suddenly O'Mara wasn't the only person I should be feeling sorry for, and second, pressure in the small of my back that only in the movies turns out to be the stem of a pipe.

"Keep walking," ordered a voice behind me. At the same moment my arms were grabbed tightly. My arms were held tightly and close to my body so I couldn't turn around. I tried, but was tugged back so that I was facing the street. The former courthouse saw what was going on but did nothing, having lost the power to preserve the peace when it was transformed into all those boutiques and shoppes. Of course James Street was deserted.

There were two of them. The one on my right arm was taller than the other, judging from the height of his grip on my arm. He was holding the gun, or pipe, or corner of a box of chocolates in his left hand. I wondered whether I had the courage to call out. I tried, but nothing happened. If I made a sound, it was swallowed up by the din from the Harding House. The emptiness of the street, an emptiness I haven't seen this side of midnight since I first started staying up late, daunted me, froze my vocal cords. Whatever was pressed into my back, I knew it could go off, leaving the field of private investigations in Grantham open to my chief rival. Right now, Howard Dover could have all my clients. I'd throw in Irma Dowden for nothing.

I don't know why I was thinking like this, none of it had much to do with getting me moved quickly around the corner and into King Street, where a dark green Toyota was idling at the curb. Here the noise from the Harding House was more mocking than ever. The back door was ajar. The man on my left arm opened the convenient right-hand, rear door of the car and shoved me inside. The man with the gun slid in after me, while the first guy got in on

the far side. By now I had seen their faces. They were new
to me. I didn't like that. Hired heavies from out of town.

"I hope you know that I'm being followed," I said, ad
libbing my part as I went along. "I'm going to be missed
faster than you figured." The driver pulled away from the
curb and joined the sparse one-way traffic moving towards Ontario Street. That was the only response to what
I'd said. On each side of me, my two captors looked
straight ahead and said nothing. "Well, I hope you know
what you're doing. There are people who will come looking for me." I got no rise out of either of them. The driver
turned right at Ontario, signalling the turn like a good
citizen.

The hood on my right was the taller of the two, as I'd
suspected. He was just over six feet, with no neck, and
shoulders that could have earned him a football scholar-
ship almost anywhere. His bland face, showing smallish
eyes and an unbroken nose, was impassive. The man on
the other side was smaller, narrower, with dark eyes deep-
set on either side of a thin hooked nose. He was losing his
hair early. What remained was spread to disguise the fact.
Of the driver, all I saw was a big head and neck that didn't
get smaller as it disappeared into his blue bomber jacket.

"Listen you guys," I went on, talking to the streetlights
passing us hypnotically as the car continued up Ontario,
"you are forgetting that I was expecting your little visit.
I've left a letter behind. Your boss isn't going to thank you
for this. Not if he finds his face all over the front page of
the *Beacon* tomorrow. Another thing . . ."

"Shut up and enjoy the scenery," the driver said, speaking to the rear-view mirror, which was turned so that I
couldn't see his face. "We won't be long now." We were
crossing the dip in Ontario Street where the road crossed
the grave of one of the old canals. I didn't usually think of
it that way. Must have been the company. There was a
good-looking farmhouse on the left, I could just glimpse

its lights through a small stand of trees, a survivor, the last of dozens of farmhouses that used to run all the way to the lake.

The car continued to the end of Ontario, turned left over the two bridges that beckoned the way to Port Richmond, once the Port Said of Lake Ontario, now a summertime marina and tourist haven. At this time of year it was quiet and self-contained. There were a few good fish restaurants that remained open through the winter. There were a few pubs that were lively enough to raise the ghosts of all the departed sailors who used to frequent them back in the last century. I could glimpse the lights as we curved around the inner harbour, until all light was cut off as we passed under the shadow of an old rubber factory. I watched those dismal windows slip past us. Beyond, I could again make out the lights of the street that faced the outer harbour. Facing this row of busy hotels, pubs and restaurants was the harbour, itself a bright circus of dancing lights in the summer, but now dark and deserted. I'd feared we might be headed here.

The man with the thick neck pulled off the road and parked the car facing the water. The nearest light from that direction came from across the water.

"Get out!" the driver said. "We've arrived." The door to my right had been opened and the big fellow now stood leaning into the car. Finally, I could see that what he was holding in his hand was not a pipe. At least I didn't have to guess about that any more. Narrow-nose gave me a push, so I moved out. At the same time, the driver got out and walked around to the trunk of the car. He unlocked and lifted the lid. I wondered if they wanted me to get inside. It wouldn't have been the first time I've seen the world from the inside of a car trunk. Then I saw that the trunk already had a passenger. It was Brian O'Mara. He was wearing a bruise on his forehead that he hadn't got from the beer at the Harding House. He looked out of that

dark hole next to the spare tire, first at me and then at the
other three faces watching him shift to his knees and
clamber out onto the pavement. His eyes were half-closed.
Nobody lent a helping hand. Is it a kindness to help the
condemned up the gallows steps? I could read panic in
O'Mara's eyes as he got his footing.

"Okay, you two," the driver said. "We're going for a
boatride." I felt a familiar hand on my arm pulling me in
the direction of the dark marina. A car's headlights passed
over the faces of the hoods I could see. "Get a move on.
Our friend doesn't want to wait around all night." At the
same moment, O'Mara was yanked into movement by the
heavy with the skinny nose. I tried to see what there was
out in the harbour that might still have life aboard this late
in the season. I couldn't detect a thing. I should stick to
tracing oil-company receipts.

"Benny! What are you doing here?" It was a voice from
behind us. A woman's nasal accusation. "We weren't
expecting to see you too." We all turned around to see the
newcomer. It was Edna Stillman. Edna Stillman? What
was a friend of my parents doing here, running into our
abduction? It was like seeing an animated Disney character walk into the middle of *Casablanca* or the *Maltese Falcon*.
A step behind Edna stood Edna's husband, Hy Stillman,
who was just locking the car door. Now I remembered the
headlights of a minute ago. They'd just parked beside us.

"Benny!" Hy chimed in, "I didn't think we were going
to see you too!" I wished they would underplay the stuff
about this being a chance meeting. I'd already begun
planning a strategy involving the Stillmans. I could say
that I was followed everywhere by Hy and Edna Stillman,
who ran *Lambkins*, a children's clothing store and baby
outfitter on St Andrew Street. It was the perfect cover for
surveillance work. Hy was still talking:

"Manny said it would just be the four of us." It wasn't
going to do me any good now to smile as though the plot

I'd been talking about in the car was beginning to unfold on time.

"They're late," I said evenly. I think that's how it came out. "Evenly" was my intention, anyway. At that moment a black 1980 Caddie parked beside us and my mother and father got out.

"Here they are!" said Edna with her usual oboe-like intonation. "We're not going to split hairs about being late." She went on to greet my mother and father. Pa gave Edna a kiss and Hy did as much for my mother, who hadn't taken her eyes off me and the rogues gallery I was standing with since she'd come out of the car.

"Benny, is everything all right?

"Hy and I were early for a change," Edna finished up what she had started to say. "Are your friends coming into the restaurant too?" she asked, giving the three hoods and O'Mara a bright smile. O'Mara pulled away from the guy holding him.

"I'm coming," he shouted. The driver and the thin-nosed hood stood back so that there never could be a question of their having stood in his way.

"Is Anna with you, Benny?" Ma asked, still looking the hoods up and down. "Your friends don't look like they enjoy seafood," she added in a lower voice. My father slammed the door on his side of the Cadillac and came up behind Ma. We exchanged nods as he gave the group standing by the open trunk of the car a careful scrutiny. The big guy, who now showed no sign of his gun, smiled back at him awkwardly.

"Anna's gone to Boston on a research project," I lied. I hoped that the hoods would know as much about research trips at this time of year as my mother did. "She'll be away until the end of the month," I added, in case my lie needed buttressing.

"What have you got, a case of bootleg beer in the trunk?" my father asked. "You look like a bunch of rubes with a bottle in the trunk." The hoods, and even O'Mara, moved away from the rear of the car to show that the trunk contained no illegal extras. "The way you were standing there, it made me want to get in line!" There were some poor attempts at grins, nothing to win any prizes.

"Benny," Ma said taking my arm, "when are you going to bring Anna over to the house? Your father and I would like to meet her. You keep her such a big secret, I'm beginning to think maybe you're not getting on so well. Is that it?"

"She has other friends besides me, Ma. We only go to the movies once in a while."

"But, I can tell she likes you. Just from the way you talk. But it's just as well you don't bring her over just yet. The slip-covers are still not ready. When they're done, she can come over and bring that father of hers too. I'll charm both of them with my chicken soup."

"Campbell's Chicken Broth?"

"Benny! That's *my* secret! Have a little respect for your Aged P!"

Hy Stillman came over and put an arm on my shoulder: "Benny, the reservation's just for the four of us, but I think it can't be too busy on a Thursday night. What do you think?"

"I think my friends have another date," I said, looking at the stout-necked driver. He blinked and glanced at his two buddies.

"Thanks a lot, but we gotta be gettin' back to town," he said. The other two grabbed O'Mara under the arms as though they were just having a little fun. In a second they would have had him stuffed back into the car. The back seat was an improvement on the trunk, but I felt obliged to protest.

"Just a minute!" I said. "I don't think Brian wants to go home yet. I'm sure the restaurant can find another extra chair." Brian peeled the hands that were clutching him off his arms and propelled himself past the hood and away from the car.

"You're pushing it, Mr Cooperman," said the driver slowly.

"It was fun running into you fellows. Sorry that our plans changed so quickly. That's life, isn't it?"

"We'll run into you again sometime," the driver said, going to his side of the car. Meanwhile, O'Mara had crossed over to the side of the good guys and was looking back at his erstwhile abductors.

"We'll see you again," said another of the hoods as he opened the car door.

"Maybe it won't be for some time," I added hopefully.

"Don't count on it," he said as he slammed the door shut behind him.

"Nice running into you boys," Edna said as the remaining hood stirred himself.

"Yeah, nice," he said, brushing back his scanty hair with the palm of his hand. He shut the lid of the trunk and climbed into the back seat.

At the same time, the car's motor jumped to life and a lot of unnecessary exhaust was piped in our direction. The car reversed, backed out and gunned its motor as it left the street to O'Mara, the Stillmans and the Coopermans.

"Those fellows look like they just walked out of television," my mother said. I nodded agreement. "There's still something not very kosher about this."

"What do you mean, Ma?"

"Since when have you become such a fan of seafood?" she said.

"I'll tell you all about it in the restaurant." We walked across the street and into the dining-room with its fishnets on the ceiling and a bar made from a cut-away lifeboat. O'Mara was still looking stunned, but Edna was talking a blue streak at him. I thought that with a little nourishment, he might come around.

Chapter Twenty

"He was a decent old skin," Frank Bushmill said as we sat in a booth at the Di on St Andrew Street. "He was the only man in town who could talk intelligently about rhetoric. And he knew books. I got my Swift from Martin." Martin Lyster had picked Friday the thirteenth to die in his room at the Grantham General. When I went to see him a few days earlier, he was still hoping to make it down to Florida to watch the Blue Jays in spring training. Frank and I were toasting his memory in Diana Sweets's coffee.

"He sure knew a lot about books."

"Sold me my copy of Flannery O'Connor."

"Yeah, he knew all that Irish stuff."

"American. O'Connor was American."

"Well, he was always talking about James Joyce and Yeats and all that gang."

"He should have died hereafter."

"You can say that again."

Frank and I drank up our coffee and I followed him out into the sunlight. I took a good look first to see if any green Toyotas were lurking at the curb. The sidewalks were clear of hoods as well as shoppers. Maybe it was too early for either group. I was going to miss Martin. He was always talking over my head, like Frank, but it made me feel good, like there was a real world out there far away from Grantham, where people didn't get bundled into cars against their will, where books mattered and where all questions weren't submitted to the test of "the bottom line." As a matter of fact, I don't think I ever heard either Martin or Frank use the phrase. I respected them for that.

Frank was trying to organize a wake for Martin. I agreed to go as long as it didn't collide with Anna's plans for my time during the next few days. Sherry Forbes's wedding rehearsal was the main obstacle that night. In fact, I was rather curious to see all the Forbes clan acting on their best behaviour in public. The promise of a good dinner at the Grantham Club was an extra dollop of jam. The following day, Saturday, the wedding itself was scheduled to take place. I had to be there as well. Frank said that he would try to work around these events and let me know the time and place. Together we climbed the twenty-eight steps to our offices, he to his patients with their corns and bunions and me to my notes on Kinross, Phidias and now Sangallo Restorations. I played about with this for a few minutes, then remembered that there was another office where I was expected. I didn't want McAuliffe's opinion of me to sink to the level of his regard for Ross Forbes as a manager:

> A dillar, a dollar,
> A ten o'clock scholar,
> What makes you come so soon?
> You used to come at ten o'clock,
> But now you come at noon.

It was close to ten when I arrived at the sixth-floor head office of Phidias Manufacturing. I don't know whether I beat Forbes in or not. By the time I was sitting at my parson's table, I'd passed several busy-looking people. I spotted a Harlequin romance behind one copy of the *Report on Business* section of the *Globe and Mail*. McAuliffe's greeting to me was warm but from a distance. I was sure that should he have asked me to show him, I would have been able to make a good case for Teddie's arguments with American Internal Revenue, which I could now document from sources at Phidias. When the phone rang, as usual, I made no effort to answer it, although an extension was within my reach. Fred picked it up quickly, almost as though it might snap at him. I guess it often had, judging from Murdo Forbes's boardroom manners.

"It's for you," McAuliffe said, almost as surprised as I was. "It's Mr Ross," he added with his hand over the receiver.

"Yes?" I said, as McAuliffe hung up softly.

"Cooperman, it's Ross Forbes here." I nodded idiotically and waited. "You and I have a score to settle from a long time ago. I've been thinking of it all night and it still bothers me."

"Why not have a word with your analyst about it?"

"Now, don't get on the defensive. As far as I'm concerned the past is over and done with. But that's because Teddie stays seventeen hundred kilometres away from here and I value each of them. Her coming back for the wedding has upset me. Everything about this damned wedding upsets me. But that's neither here nor there. You and I have to talk, Cooperman. What are you doing for lunch?"

"First you hit me in the nose and now you're buying lunch! I assume you're buying?"

"And I won't repeat my bad manners again, I assure you."

"What time do you want me to meet you?"

"I'm going to be tied up in a meeting until noon. Can you make it, say, twelve-thirty at the Golf Club?"

"Will they let me in? I'm not a card-carrying member."

"I'll fix it. You won't have any trouble." It sounded like a promise, so I believed him.

When I had hung up the phone, McAuliffe kept his face

in a series of printouts for a few minutes. The office seemed quieter than usual. I felt I had to break the ice. "He wants to take me to lunch," I said.

Fred McAuliffe looked across the room at me. "It's getting hard for Mr Ross to find people to lunch with him." He shook his head while dusting off the printouts which had collected a fine spray of ash from the pipe he was cleaning. "It's not just his drinking—there are plenty of drinkers over at the club, though most of them are a lot older than Mr Ross—it's the fact that he has been involved in the unsavoury stories about the marketing of contaminated fuel last May. People want to distance themselves from him in public."

"Was he head of Kinross in May?"

"Oh, no, he was in charge here. Mr Caine was in charge at Kinross."

"Then why is Mr Ross getting all the social heat? Shouldn't some of it rub off on Norm Caine?" McAuliffe opened his mouth to answer, but stopped himself. He caught his breath and tried it another way.

"You make a good point, Mr Cooperman. He should have let Mr Caine answer the questions. I told him that. I'm not telling you anything I didn't tell Mr Ross to his face. Phidias was not involved at all, until Mr Ross tried to get the story hushed up."

"But that story was too big for anybody to hush it up. It was a big international exposé. Nobody could have kept a lid on it."

"Yes, well . . ." McAuliffe got his pipe started, holding a box of wooden matches over the bowl and drawing down deeply. "Let's just say it's more complicated than that." I felt that I was on the verge of learning something important and I hoped it wasn't showing in my face.

"I don't want you to betray a confidence, Mr McAuliffe," I said hoping he would spill his guts to me then and there.

"I'll only say this," he said. "The stories in the paper didn't get it right where Mr Ross was concerned. Not a bit, they didn't. I wish more people knew the truth. Maybe some day they will. But right now, it's not my secret to break, though it festers inside me, I'll tell you."

I could see that that was the end of the conversation, so I went back to the papers on my desk before he did. Maybe it gave me a moral advantage, like not taking the last olive or not being the last person to leave a party. Fred returned to his seat as well, but, looking up, I could see he wasn't comfortable. I knew it wasn't the old chair with the green almost worn off the backrest. After a few uneasy minutes, he left the room for a short time and returned with one of the minute books from the boardroom. From his desk he took a ledger key and removed the heavy binder. At this point he glanced up at me, but saw that I was deeply involved with work of my own. Actually, I could get a good picture of what was going on on his side of the room from the reflection in the glass of the picture of the Commander and his father-in-law, Sandy MacCallum. He took pages out of the ledger and put them in his desk drawer. Minute books are serious documents, records of what the board of directors does while in office. They aren't to be added to or altered at will. How unlike Fred McAuliffe to remove pages; how like him to do it where he could be seen. What was the old man up to?

At exactly 12:05, Fred hung up his grey cardigan on a wooden hanger, put his jacket back on and removed his Irish cap from its peg in the old-fashioned hat-rack. He gave me one of his friendly twinkles as he passed my table and he was gone. I waited four minutes before discovering that he'd locked his desk. I didn't have the time or the tools to make a tidy entry, so I settled for a trip to the boardroom to see which was the missing book. It was easy to spot: 1985 was gone. There was a space between 1984 and 1986 the size of the ledger in Fred's drawer. Nineteen eight-five was long before Jack Dowden's death. It predated the digging at Fort Mississauga as well. It was food for speculation if not for thought. I deserted the high-backed chairs placed around the boardroom table. I could feel the eyes of all the board members on my back as I grabbed my coat and caught the next "down" elevator.

On the way to collect my car, I tried to place Fred's loyalties. He was surely in the Commander's camp. His age and manner would have him there rather than standing under the Ross Forbes standard. Ross was too sloppy for Fred, who was more the Commander's man. I couldn't imagine McAuliffe quite as antediluvian as Murdo Forbes, however. Fred was essentially a gentle man, whereas the Commander was probably still complaining about the fifty-hour-week, unions, social security, unemployment insurance, maybe even the vote. The more I thought of it, the more I could see that the Commander wasn't as out of touch with his age as I thought at first. A lot of this kind of thinking was very popular. I could almost hear him saying that it's time to cut our losses on the railways, time to deregulate, time to end farm-price subsidies. For an old robber baron who had cut his teeth before the Second World War, he was sounding a very contemporary note. Paternalism has it all over creeping socialism. Had the Commander got over the shock of discovering that the working man, whose friend he was, had been replaced by organized labour?

The car cut left down the hill near the old firehall, following the twisting road down to the bridge over the Old Canal. On the other side, the road twisted back up to the original level again. The Golf Club occupied prime real estate right in the middle of town. There are many odd things about Grantham, but none odder than this. Any map of the area confirms the truth, however. The Eleven Mile Creek curved sharply where it joined the Old Canal. On the outside of the curve, the old business section

followed ancient Indian trails, creating a maze of familiar
blocks and corners. Across the canal, on the inside of the
curve and reached by only a few bridges, the fairways of
the Golf Club separated the old town from its newer
suburbs.

From the street the club didn't arrest your attention. The
church next door did that. The club consisted of a random
assembly of hangars and sheds adapted to leisure pur-
suits. A bit of ivy ran up one stucco wall and landscaping
had improved matters, but it never could be said, for all
the terraces looking out over the tennis courts and greens,
that the Grantham Golf Club was an architectural prize.
From the outside it was almost an eyesore, but it was the
interior that mattered. Here you could find a shed to house
and repair hundreds of golf carts, a curling rink with a
heated gallery for onlookers and a card room for Manny
Cooperman to spend his time in. There was a huge pool
that could be opened up to the warm summer weather for
three months of the year. A large restaurant served de-
pendable if not inspired food, or so Frank Bushmill used to
tell me. I always thought the food there must be the best in
town since it was so hard to get a table when you wanted
one.

I found a spot reserved for guest-parking and walked
around to the deserted terrace in front of the restaurant. A
few hardy souls were playing golf. I could see the bright
colours of their jackets far away over the rolling landscape.
The parking lot reserved for members made a challenging
contrast to the guest lot with my beat-up Olds in it. Here I
saw three Rolls-Royces, an antique Bentley and a
Thunderbird of an early year. I didn't bother to count the
Corvettes and Triumphs. I was surprised to see a full lot
this early on a Friday. But what do I know about such
things? I suppose the restaurant was booked for every day
of the year. The door to the patio was closed; I had to walk
around through another door and enter the dining-room

in the approved autumn manner. I could see no sign of Ross Forbes.

A few heads turned when I entered. I asked a waiter if there was a table with Ross Forbes's name on it. I followed him to a place near a window and accepted the two menus he handed me. Naturally, he'd get a view. I was discovering that the club made me nervous.

I was looking at a rosy-faced bald-headed man with a white moustache as he dug into a portion of clubhouse curry. I was trying to discover why I was so sure it was curry when I could neither smell nor taste it. I'd decided that I had an irrational side after all, when Ross Forbes cleared his throat beside me. "Hello, Cooperman!" he said heartily. "Are you doing sums in your head or coming down with a migraine?"

"Oh! Hello! I didn't see you come in. I was woolgathering. I do a lot of it these days." I didn't know whether to get up or not. I made a gesture and left it at that. He seated himself opposite me and deployed his napkin against future problems on his lap. Mine was still nestled in a wine glass. I didn't want to copy Forbes in all things, so I left it there.

Forbes was well above medium height, in fact he was taller than he looked. His great barrel chest and round shoulders took inches off his apparent height. His wavy dark hair was going grey at the temples, giving a touched-up-by-professionals look to it. His brow was wide, but not high, and separated from the rest of his face by a nearly continuous dark line of eyebrow. The rounded end of his nose was echoed in the heavy chin. Add to that rather petulant brown eyes and a lower lip that returned to a pouting expression when his features were not animated with talk. He had a way of talking which seemed to add quotation marks around certain phrases in order to lift them to something more memorable than chat. His smile showed even teeth. I hadn't seen him smile before.

"Well, now, Cooperman, I hope that we can both agree that the past is dead and buried?"

"I'm on your side there," I said. "No sense keeping a feud alive."

"Exactly! So, the less said about our scuffle downtown, the better."

"It was outside your office at Kinross Disposals. But, sure, no hard feelings. I was just doing my job; you were just repelling trespassers."

"Glad you see it in that light." He let his eyes drop to the menu that lay across his plate, and curled his lower lip in thought. "The curry looks good," he said at length. The thought of strange pieces of meat in a pale greeny yellow sauce did nothing for my appetite. I scanned the menu looking for a friend. Where were the chopped-egg sandwiches hiding? My eyes went down one column and up the next. I couldn't understand what half of the words meant. I wondered whether on a menu in France they might not think it's chic to use English. I finally settled on the soup and pasta of the day and hoped for the best.

"Would you like some wine with that, sir?" the waiter asked, once he had written what he thought of me on his order pad.

"Not for me, thanks."

"Mr Forbes?"

"Bring a bottle of Perrier, Joe."

"Right away, Mr Forbes."

Once the pale green bottle came and I found myself sipping what tasted like seltzer; it seemed that Forbes was going to get down to the reason for inviting me to lunch. Some people can put business off until coffee, others bring it up casually over the last part of the main course, but Ross Forbes was a man for the direct approach. Before I had even dipped into the basket of warmed Parker House rolls, he was at me.

"May I ask why you continue doing business for my ex-wife here in Grantham, Mr Cooperman?" He held his glass as though he had had lots of practice holding glasses. I had been surprised about the mineral water. In fact I had been ready to trade him Scotch for Scotch well into the evening if I had to. But Perrier was a new direction.

"Let's agree not to talk about Mrs Forbes, okay? Either you're going to say something you'll regret or I will. Either way it will spoil the lunch. I'm surprised you aren't wining and dining out-of-town company for the wedding, Mr Forbes. Tomorrow's the big day, isn't it?"

"People are still arriving. I'll stay clear until this evening. There's a rehearsal."

I nodded, keeping quiet about the fact that I would be there. I could see him trying to think of a new way to ask the question that was bugging him.

"Do you do a lot of income tax work, Cooperman?"

"When I can get it. It makes a change from waiting around for people to check out of the Black Duck Motel. Nowadays a lot of the work is going through credit-card receipts, telephone bills, that kind of thing. It's not like in the movies."

"I suppose not. I used to have a first edition of *The Big Sleep*," he said. I wondered what he was thinking about when he talked like this. "Bought it from that book dealer, Martin Lyster, who you can never get hold of when you want him. Do you know him? A most lubricious fellow."

"As a matter of fact, I heard he died this morning. It was not unexpected."

"Well, sorry. Hope he wasn't a particular friend of yours?"

"I don't collect books, but I knew him slightly." Forbes was handling the Perrier water pretty well. After the stories of his drinking (mostly retailed by Teddie), I was wondering what sort of new leaf he was showing off here.

The waiter cleared away the soup cups. Mine had tasted of green cheese. I guess there are places where soup is made with green cheese. Now I know where to find it. "Is book collecting what you want to talk about, Mr Forbes? It's not something I know a lot about. And I guess it hasn't much to do with why you're buying me lunch."

"How long will you be in McAuliffe's office?"

"Couple of days more. I shouldn't think I'll still be there by this time next week. Today's a short day and then we are into the weekend . . ."

"Will you be free by, say, next Wednesday?"

"I might be. Why?"

"I might have a job for you."

"Me? Why me? I thought Howard Dover worked for you? Don't tell me you hit him in the nose too?"

"I won't say I've liked you much, Cooperman, but I know to my cost that you give value for money. Dover's busy doing security for Phidias. What I want has nothing to do with the office." This was going a little too fast for me. One minute I'm on the outside trying to find a peephole to the inside, then I'm shown the red carpet to the inner sanctum itself. I didn't know whether to burst out laughing or to cry.

"What kind of job do you want me to do, Mr Forbes?"

The curry and pasta arrived. Forbes was quick to dig into his, after complaining to the waiter that he did not want his salad served on the same plate. The dish was removed and returned a minute later without the offending salad, which arrived seconds later on a side dish. "There are parts of this town where they still bring you coffee with your main plate," Forbes said. Did he see himself as a gourmet rolling back the clouds of local ignorance? I should have told him about the Di, where they've always treated me right. I held off eating, waving my fork over the pasta while this was going on. Finally we both dug in. "Do you think that you might be interested in what I've been talking about?"

"You still haven't said what you want," I said. "I'm always interested in making a living, Mr Forbes, but I also try to keep things simple. I'm afraid I have a conflict that will make it impossible for me to do any work for you for the moment. But if it will keep—"

"Conflict? What do you mean conflict?" Forbes's lower lip was distorting his face, lengthening out his upper lip and turning the end of his nose white.

"I'm involved in an investigation for your ex-wife."

"And that will be cleared up by Wednesday, you said."

"I said it might be. I've also got some other files in my office I have to do some work on. It isn't easy being a one-man band, Mr Forbes."

"But you accomplish prodigious miracles I've been told," he said with just the suggestion of a sneer.

"I don't know about that. I do know that I would find it hard to work for you without knowing in detail what it is you want."

"You want complete disclosure from me and you aren't committing yourself to zilch!"

"You've got both my ears across the table from you," I said. "I think the lunch just about pays for that. It also buys a measure of discretion. A PI who runs off at the mouth doesn't stay in business long."

"Okay, okay. Don't bother to rationalize. I'll come clean," he said. "Isn't that what they all say?"

"It's up to you. Tell me about it or don't. It's your dime."

"I'm being followed, Cooperman," he said in a voice that was hardly above a whisper. "I don't like it. There's a car that's always behind me. There are clicks on my telephone. There are people in hotel lobbies pretending to read newspapers who later turn up outside my office.

Once I noticed the first man, it started preying on my mind. Now I can see that there are relays of people watching, listening and following me. Damn it, Cooperman, I don't like it! I know I said that already but it's got me that rattled."

"Do you have any suspicions?"

"Oh, God! I don't want to open that can of worms here. Let's just say there are several possible sources."

"Does it have anything to do with last spring's stories about toxic wastes in fuel oil?"

"Well, that's a better bet than no bet at all," he said, removing a particularly stringy bit of beef from his mouth and placing it on his plate. He looked neither to the right or to the left afterwards, which gave me another glimpse of his social assurance. "The bedfellows in that deal were not of my choosing. It might be one of them. I don't know. What I want to know is: will you find out? I can't look around without seeing one of those pale faces and cheap suits."

"Well . . ." I knew that if I asked him if one of them was watching him at the moment and he indicated the old geezer with the white moustache or somebody hiding in the leafless bushes outside the window, I'd be hooked. In sifting for information, you always run the risk of getting in too far or too deeply. Having a look at one of the faces Forbes was afraid of would have made it difficult to walk out of the club digesting a good lunch but still my own man. "Well . . ."

"I'll pay top dollar, Cooperman. You won't regret this."

"Look, I could use the money. I won't lie to you," I said. "But it could complicate my life so that I wouldn't know where I was." Forbes was beginning to cloud over, as though a storm were coming up over the top of that continuous eyebrow. "I'll tell you something, Mr Forbes. I've discovered that I have a tendency to try to take the muddle out of my clients' affairs. When they come to me, you wouldn't believe it, the mess they're in. I'd like to help you too, but when I say I can't, that's what I mean. Now that's frank and honest as of this Friday afternoon. When next Wednesday comes and I'm cursing myself for talking to you like this, maybe I'll call you to say I've changed my mind. That's all I can do for you. In the meantime, if I see anybody following you and I can get a line on them, I'll let you know. As long as I'm not going to get my knees broken or come to a bad end in the harbour at Port Richmond." I watched his face when I mentioned Port Richmond but while it was growing angry, it didn't twig to my hint about Thursday night.

"They told me you'd be difficult!" Here he physically grabbed the passing waiter by the arm. "Joe, I want you to clean these places and bring coffee right away, please. We don't want dessert." He could have asked, but in his mood I decided not to press him. I looked slowly around the room to see if I could spot anybody out of place. I came up empty, and returning my eyes to Ross Forbes, I was glad to see that he was controlling his temper.

Chapter Twenty-One

The bill finally came and Forbes entered into a mild but firm argument with the waiter. I pretended that I was above such small disputes. Was this the way people got rich, questioning whether the rolls were included with the special or not? I'll never figure it out.

I left my cigarettes in my pocket, since I thought that Forbes, the spoiled brat, was going to get up and go once it was clear that he was not going to get his way with me. But before he could look at his watch and say "Well . . ." a face hovered to the right of my host. "Ross! Well, I shouldn't be surprised," he said. It was a youngish-looking middle-aged man with a mop of grey hair and a pointed nose. The impression of youth was abetted by the turtleneck shirt he was wearing under a light topcoat of non-animal origins. He looked like a man who was listening when the whisper went up around the swimming pool: "Plastics!"

"Harold, the brother-in-law," Ross explained to me, then completed the introduction giving a hurried, perhaps scanty, description of my present function in the head office of Phidias Manufacturing.

"Yes, I'd heard something about that. Tax people breathing down Teddie's *décolletage*, eh? Wouldn't mind a look myself. Into her books, I mean. Thought you had me there, eh, Ross?" Harold Grier's face looked as pained as his attempt at humour. I tried to place him. Grier was the brother of Forbes's present wife and connected by marriage with the man at City Hall who handled the toxic wastes contracts for the city. He also was the head man at Sangallo Restorations. I could now see why he was wearing that expression. The last time bodies were found in one of his restorations they dated from the War of 1812. Not so Alex Pásztory unfortunately.

"I wonder if I could have a minute, Ross? Hate to break up the party."

"You'll excuse me, Cooperman?" Forbes said with another trace of a sneer in his voice. What did he think I'd say? I didn't bother saying anything as a matter of record and Ross got up and went into the lobby outside the restaurant's front door. I took out my cigarette after all. Once lighted, it began tasting like an old butt I'd rescued from the ashtray of the car. I wasn't sorry to stub it out on the return of Grier and Forbes.

"We'll see you tonight, Harold," Forbes said. "And stop worrying about your friend from the Falls."

"He's *our* friend, Ross! Don't ever forget that. This is no time to distance yourself from reality. What time is this thing called for tonight? Six or six-thirty?" Grier tried to cover the visible panic of his remark about the Niagara Falls friend with the question about the wedding rehearsal. Ross looked like he was running out of patience. Not only had he bombed out with me, his business arrangements looked like they were in trouble. As far as Grier was concerned, from the look on his face, he seemed to be reacting badly to Ross's hands-off policy. This was not the moment for greater autonomy for the subsidiaries.

"It's called for six-fifteen, but I should think that six-thirty will see you all right."

"Good. You'd better hustle if you're going to see Paul."

"I'll look after it, Harold."

"Better hustle. No time to be wasted."

"I hear you. See you tonight." This last was a curt dismissal directed at an underling. You had to hand it to Forbes. He sure knew how to assume the right face for the moment. Only his temper got the better of him. He couldn't hide his displeasure. In his place that was a major liability. While I watched Harold Grier leave the restaurant, I wondered who the friend from the Falls might be. Paul was easy; Paul Renner from City Hall. Probably an attempt to cool out the authorities in their investigation of the fort murder. What did I know about Niagara Falls? Not much.

"Come on, Cooperman," said Forbes, wiping his mouth on his napkin although he hadn't eaten anything in nearly ten minutes. "I'll show you around. Do you know the club at all?"

"Only by repute. My father's a member. He haunts the card room."

"Oh, you're *that* Cooperman, are you? I think my father's lost a lot of money to him over the years. Gin rummy's the game, right?"

I nodded as we got up. I followed Forbes out of the dining-room. My father had often been a guest at the club during the years when I was growing up. He joined as soon as the restrictive membership practices of the past had been done away with. For a few years he was the man to beat in the card room. A gin rummy tournament was even set up and named in his honour. They called Pa *The Hammer* and the annual competition of that name was one of the indoor attractions of the long winter.

Forbes walked along the halls of the club, showing me racquet-ball courts and gyms, one full of women, accompanied by their babies, doing post-natal exercises. He was beginning a cook's tour of the facilities. Was this for my benefit, or was he working off the pique he had taken to his brother-in-law's urgent request to hustle downtown to

City Hall. With a skeletal running commentary, he led me room to room. "This room is dedicated to the cue and the ivory ball," he said. The light above the green baize tabletop seemed to conjure up the ghosts of elderly men with stiff white fronts and tepid drinks resting on the edges of the tables.

"Through here," he said, and we were again back in a central corridor, walking past a little man selling tickets for plump blue robes and towels. Forbes was greeted by name and the compliment was returned.

We went through a door and I was suddenly hit by that locker-room smell that took me back to high school. Even with fancy yearly membership fees and a stiff initiation fee, the locker-room was no rose garden. Men in the buff and semi-buff took no notice as we made our way through to the showers. Here I recognized a former member of a winning water-polo team standing on an old-fashioned scale getting his soaking-wet weight. From the showers we went on to the entrance to the pool area. My attention was caught by a sign on a door just next to the door leading to the pool:

PLEASE TAKE NO READING MATERIAL INTO THE SAUNA

I'd never seen such a clear bias against literacy in my life. I hoped that the rule was broken regularly.

Forbes pushed the door to the pool open for me and the scent of chlorinated water hit me along with the watery echo of happy voices. It was a large but not quite Olympic-sized pool. On one side the wall was made of glass doors which could be opened up in the summer. A life-guard was listening to a small stereo radio near the entrance from the women's side. Something familiar by Chopin, I think.

At the shallow end of the pool, a group of pre-schoolers were being instructed on water safety by a chubby woman with red hair peeking out from under her bathing-cap. She wore a blue Speedo swimsuit. All of the other lanes except the one closest to the solid wall were occupied by serious swimmers swimming serious lengths. You could tell just by looking at them that they 'had all been in the water for the last twenty to thirty minutes and that they'd still be at it half an hour from now.

"What do you think?" Forbes asked. Was he trying to sign me up?

"Glad you like it. My mother was on the committee that designed this place. She also helped to raise most of the money to pay for it. Dad is still Membership Chairman, I think." I nodded my approval of all this energy and Ross took it as encouragement to go on. "They spend most of their time here when they are in town. Do you want to go for a swim?"

"Not after eating. It'll give me a cramp."

"You're behind the times, Cooperman. Swimming's a great way to keep in shape. Look at my parents out there. Nearly one hundred and sixty years between them. And just look at them go!"

I had to follow Forbes's eyes to see which of the gliding bodies between the bobbing lane-markers had given him life. There was a swimmer in each of the five lanes. Except for size they all looked alike. They were all wearing goggles and white rubber caps. Murdo Forbes was the first to be spotted. His massive form wasn't easy to hide. He moved down the far lane like a pilot whale, his long arms moving up and down like flippers. At the far end, he climbed up a chrome ladder out of the pool, picked up a blue towel, and slipped into a matching blue terry-cloth robe and began walking in our direction.

"I meant that about going swimming, Cooperman. It's no big deal to get you a suit and robe." He meant it to be friendly, but his voice was already stiffening as the Commander drew closer.

"Thanks, Forbes. Maybe some other time. I should be getting back to your office. Unless my answer has made that deal come unstuck."

"You must think I'm a real son of a bitch, Cooperman, to say that. Well, you're right, but I'm not a small-minded son of a bitch. Maybe I still have an idea you'll see things my way." Here he turned and waved to the approaching figure. "Hello, Dad! I thought you'd have some lunch before your swim."

"Still checking up on me, Ross? I nibbled on some chocolate I always carry in my pocket while we were playing golf, if it's of any interest to you. I can't see why. I suppose you've been stuffing yourself with this fellow and charging it up to duty entertainment, eh? Who is this fellow? Do I know him?" The Commander looked at me as though I was a dubious piece of horseflesh that was ripe for the boneyard. "I've seen you around the office." He was actually addressing me. Did he think that the gift of speech extended all the way down to me, or did my presence at the club automatically put me in the social register?

"My name's Cooperman, Commander Forbes. Ben Cooperman. I was having lunch with your son as you've already guessed."

"'Guessed?' It doesn't take much guessing when this fellow has a meal. Wine with lunch! Unheard of in my day. I suppose that means no more work this afternoon. Given your usual time of arrival in the morning, Ross, I don't know why you bother. Well, as a man who has been collecting his old-age pension for fifteen years, I guess I shouldn't lecture you younger people. Just try to remember, Ross, you have a big weekend in store for you. Don't get yourself stewed when there's so much depending on you. You don't want to give the family another black eye." Ross didn't even try to correct his father's false judgment. In fact his lips were tighter together than usual.

"Ross," he said, as though talking to a lackey, "I want them to take the car around for a wash. Looks like something the cat dragged in. Take it to Jackson's. Those new people don't understand the Bentley. They've scratched it and can't get the tarnish off the bright work."

"I'll take care of it," Ross said through his teeth.

"Goodbye, Cooperbloom. I'm off to the sauna to work off some of that chocolate. At least I'll have the place to myself. The members are taking exception to my smoking cigars in there. Extraordinary, eh? Your mother's still got another twenty lengths to do, Ross. That makes the rest of her daily mile. You should get yourself involved more here at the club, boy. Put yourself back in shape." Ross made a sour face but didn't let his father see it. Murdo Forbes wasn't looking at him anyway, but the blast of advice kept coming, like it was carried in bulk and delivered in pipes. "I want to see you properly turned out tonight, Ross. Canon Nombril is an old friend. It may be just a rehearsal, but, damn it, it is a church, and I don't want you coming in half cut. Remember what I said."

The Commander went on in the same line for another few minutes. Poor Ross had to make up for the whole crew the Commander was used to tearing a strip off. Finally, he disappeared through the door into the men's changing area. Ross looked like he was glad to see the last of him. "You know, Cooperman, a week ago a little exchange like that would have been enough to make me head straight into the bar for the rest of the afternoon. Funny, isn't it? I think that now, by *not* doing the expected thing, I might disappoint him even more."

After I left Ross Forbes, I walked through to the card room looking for a trace of my own father and found it. He was sitting on the sideline watching a game. He said hello, like we ran into one another at the club twice a week. He then took me aside to tell me that The Hammer, that knocker of knockers, could no longer afford to play when they began at a dollar a line. I listened to him describe the high stakes of the contemporary gin rummy game and nodded sympathetically. Before I left, I told him that I hoped to see him and Ma next Friday night, that I wouldn't be over to the town house that evening.

"So, we'll see you next week. It's the same dinner no matter when you come. But I'll tell your mother. It isn't like we haven't already seen you this week. That friend of yours is a very interesting character. I didn't know there was so much to know about driving a truck. So many wheels to keep track of, it made my head spin."

"I called Ma to tell her I wouldn't be over for dinner tonight."

"Mmmm," he said watching the cards in the hand of the man in a cardigan.

"She didn't seem too disappointed I wasn't coming," I said.

"Mmmm," he said. "He should go down now," he added in a whisper to me. "He could do himself some good."

"She didn't even remember that I said I was coming over."

"She's just pulling your leg, Benny. That's all."

"I guess. I guess." Then he hit the top of his head a glancing blow with the flat of his hand and I knew the man in the cardigan had done something stupid.

Chapter Twenty-Two

St Mark's Church, at the corner of Collier and Chestnut, was officially known as St Mark's-in-the-Fields, but everybody in Grantham, including many who had never been inside, called it St Mark's-by-the-Greens from the fact that it overlooked the first tee and the last green of the Grantham Golf Club. It was a lowish, wide-shouldered stone church, built, according to Frank Bushmill, in the tradition of English country churches. There was a square tower with no steeple and a big wooden door that fitted snugly into a pointed Gothic arch in front. That much I knew on my own.

I was a little surprised to see the church again so soon; I had eaten my lunch practically in its shadow. Light was coming through the stained-glass windows making bright pointed shapes on the ground. I have to admit that churches make me nervous. Even when I was a kid singing in the Kiwanis Music Festival, the hammer-beamed roofs, the regimental flags, the plaques and memorials all made me feel peculiar. It was a different feeling from the one I got at the synagogue at the corner of Church and Calvin. That smelled of furniture polish. I could relate to that. But what was I supposed to do with the old tombstones preserved in the wall of the entrance: Sacred to the Memory of . . . To the Glory of God and in Grateful Memory of . . . whose unassuming worth, unaffected Piety and generous affection this humble monument . . .

"What are you thinking about? You're suddenly so quiet." Anna was wearing a blue-and-white-striped dress which went well with her long hair. I'd picked her up at Secord. She was looking wonderfully fresh after having taught all day. Maybe it was the touch of perfume. I'm a little slow on feminine subtleties.

"Churches make me feel very Jewish," I said. "How do they affect you?"

"I try to concentrate on the architecture. If it gets really bad, I hold my breath. Benny, this is just a little church. Nothing to be afraid of."

"I'm not frightened, Anna. I'm not soft in the head. It's just that I feel conspicuous."

"Well, then relax, Benny. You are conspicuous. But that has to do with your work and not your religion. After what you've told me, I'd feel like crawling into the baptismal font and not coming up for air."

"Thanks a lot!"

"Take a big breath and think of the dinner that comes after the rehearsal."

It was about six-thirty when we arrived. I held the heavy wooden door open for Anna and followed her into the cool interior. It was a church with a central aisle leading up to the altar, with hymn-posting boards on either side of the back wall looking like Mexican lottery numbers. Like a European car, it was one of those places that looks larger on the inside than you could possibly guess from the outside.

Most of the people taking part in Saturday's ceremony were already sitting in the first few rows of pews. Some of the men, having just come from the club, were dressed casually. The rest were still in their office clothes. Some of the women were dressed in a studied informality. Without looking, I could still guess some of the New York designer labels. An old gentleman in a cardigan and light grey slacks was shaking hands with some of the characters in the front benches. A blonde, with long hair tied in an old-fashioned pony-tail, caught sight of us as we came in and started up the aisle towards us.

"Anna, oh, Anna, I'm so glad you got here!" she said beaming a wonderful advertisement for her dentist. "I was beginning to wonder how I could go through with this without my maid of honour. Oh! What a relief! That makes the cast complete, I think, except for Daddy and Grandfather. But they are always late!" Sherry took my hand and introduced herself, then she grabbed Anna by both hands and held her at arm's length. For a moment they were both talking at once and I missed all of it. Sherry tended to talk in short enthusiastic bursts of energy, which was very attractive in her. It emphasized her youth. It made me glad to be with Anna, who could do that when necessary and for fun, but wasn't stuck with it as her only manner. It may not have been Sherry's either, but I make quick judgments in my work and most of them are inadequate or misleading. Maybe I should go to more weddings. Anna and Sherry were looking at me now, their heads together. Sherry smiled at me with her eyes and she mimed to me with an arched eyebrow what a find I had in Anna. I found myself grinning back at her without measuring my rights to be accepting any sort of compliment for my escorting Anna that night. This male/female thing is very complicated and I'm just beginning to find my way in it.

"I heard that you were out of town," Sherry said, turning to Anna again and giving her a hug. "But I'm so glad you're here. It's getting so that you can't believe anybody any more. I'll stick with the Farmer's Almanac."

"Where did you hear that Anna was away, Sherry?" I asked. I was thinking of my comment to the hoods outside the seafood restaurant in Port Richmond the night before.

"Oh, I don't know. Maybe it was Daddy. He's always trying to scare me. I really can't remember." For a moment, I thought she was about to remember, but it was quite a different idea popping into her head. "Benny, have you met Norman? You must meet my intended!" She was delighted to be showing him off. If I'd said I'd already had the pleasure, it would have been an unkind and unwanted frankness, so I kept my mouth shut.

Sherry called out, and the shortish, big-shouldered young man I'd seen in Ross Forbes's office came towards us. We traded knowing grins that covered the unspoken territory as we were re-introduced to one another. I looked Caine over carefully, making the most of this unexpected second opportunity. Like his fiancée, he was blond. In fact he seemed to be down-covered. At least he gave that impression. I'd be surprised if he spent a fortune on razor-blades. "I told you Anna wouldn't leave us in the lurch, dear. Here she is, and just in time too." I tried again to discover the source of the rumour that Anna would be away, and again I was disappointed. After more pleasant-ries, Sherry took Anna by the arm and dragged her down to the front to meet the bridesmaids. Norman Caine pulled his eyes off the departing figure of his bride-to-be reluc-tantly.

"Have you ever been through this sort of thing?" he asked me. I shook my head. From somewhere not far away I could hear a high, reedy voice saying, "Evelyn Alexandra Stagg's mother had been Josephine Mabel Deacon. Laura Evelyn Deacon never married . . ."

"Sherry's a wonderful girl," Caine said, whistling in the dark, or so it seemed to me. He was watching her with the other young women standing in the aisle before the altar. I nodded approval, noticing for the first time a thin spot under the blond hair of Caine's boyish round head. Down at the front of the church, talking to Biddy, who had just come over to the bridesmaids, Sherry was as animated and as bright as a bride should be and I said so to Norm Caine. Biddy, the Commander's wife, looked lively and young for her age as well.

"I'm damned nervous about this thing," Caine said. "We nearly funked it last week." He looked over to see if I was interested in hearing more. I was and showed it. "We almost ran off to try to find a simple civil way around all this." His gesture took in the far end of the church including the altar and choir. "But Sherry has always wanted a big white wedding. What's a mere man to do?" He put on a hang-dog look, but with his rosy cheeks he couldn't quite get away with it. The high woman's voice was coming over the pews again: "He was the first judge in the County of Renfrew. But the Metcalfs and the Heeses were all Deacons originally. Jane Louise Deacon married John Metcalf. The Dunlops come in there somewhere . . ."

"Are you going away on a trip afterwards?" I asked.

"Nobody's supposed to know. Sherry wants no pranks or visitors."

"My lips are sealed."

"We'll be away for a week. There's a nice warm beach and all of the tourists will be gone by this time. Our own deserted island." There was a slight noise at the entrance. I turned to see Ross Forbes coming in.

"Here comes the father of the bride," I said. The shoulders of his son-in-law-to-be fell with the news. Caine glanced behind him.

"I knew it couldn't last," he said. I felt honoured when he shared a knowing look with me. I didn't know to what I owed such intimacy.

"Haven't you two declared a truce until you and Sherry drive away picking rice out of your hair?"

"You're talking *theory*," he said with a pained expression. "*Practice* just walked in the door. For Sherry's sake I'm putting up with more than my share of abuse. I'm not even sure he'll give Sherry away tomorrow. He hasn't said a civil word to me for weeks."

"Ah," I thought, "you can't beat the first families at keeping the lid on tight and keeping up appearances."

"Hello, Cooperman," Forbes said flatly as he came down the aisle. "I won't ask how you got here. You turn up so many places nowadays. Could it have anything to do with my dear ex-wife?" I didn't answer. In a moment he had passed on down towards the front.

"Hates to share the spotlight," Caine said watching Forbes's back retreating. "We almost had to defy tradition and get the Commander to give the bride away. That would have been a major snub, seeing that Ross is still alive and kicking."

"You get top marks for keeping it out of the *Beacon*."

"Yeah, this town loves a feud like this. You haven't seen the Commander, by the way, have you? It's not like him to miss gloating at Ross's expense." I shrugged ignorance and let Caine pass on back to the main group at the front. I took a pew by myself near an assortment of men and women who were not themselves involved in the service. I spotted what might have been the father of the groom. He was a round little man, just over five feet tall, wearing an expression of limitless worry. Maybe he was paying for the dinner which was to follow the rehearsal. Teddie Forbes turned around and seemed to be counting the empty pews. She spotted me and gave me a friendly wave with her fingers. It seemed to say: What is either one of us doing here? It was fun trying to put names to the unfamiliar faces that occasionally turned and looked in this direction.

"People! Excuse me, people!" said the old man in the light cardigan. It was a melodious, clear voice that easily filled the nave of the church without any appearance of strain. He seemed to know exactly the right volume to pitch his voice at to be readily heard everywhere. "My name's James Nombril. I'm Canon Nombril from St Catharine of Jerusalem Cathedral. I'm one of those one 'n' canons, although they say that I sound off like a fourteen-inch gun at least once a week!" He paused here, acknowledged the laugh and went on. "I'm indebted to my friend Ronald Prine, the rector of St Mark's for letting me stand in the shadow of the Lion of St Mark tonight. I wouldn't think of putting Ron out of his pulpit, if it weren't for a promise I made many years ago to my old comrade in arms, Commander Murdo Forbes." Another friendly noise from the congregation. "Murdo?" he called. "Murdo? Where are you?" People began looking over their shoulders to see if the Commander was blushing properly. But, not finding him, they turned around to face the canon again and he continued. "Well, since he isn't here yet," the old man said in a sly stage whisper, "perhaps I can tell you about the time both Murdo and I nearly missed a convoy sailing from Halifax during the war." Canon Nombril was softening up his audience with great skill. He was being informal for a senior clergyman, but kept us reminded that he was standing below the altar in a place of worship. The large eagle on the pulpit's lectern cast a sombre shadow as Nombril went on with his anecdote, which ended: ". . . so you see we are *both* acquainted with lateness." Once he had collected his laugh, he could now be seen changing gears. He was moving to the business of the evening.

"If I may, I'd like to welcome you all here tonight, especially, if I may say it, those of you whom we seldom see. You may take that as a commercial message." Another laugh. The canon went on in his amusing but skillful way, asking those in the back to move closer to the front, and generally making a fuss over the young couple. He introduced the organist who had just seated himself in the choir. The young man sounded a chord to acknowledge the bobbing heads and expressions of approval. Again Canon Nombril changed gears.

"People, I want to see all ushers and bridesmaids moving back to the narthex." He then explained that he meant the foyer at the back of the church. I watched while he drilled the ushers in moving people into the pews down front, reserving the front two for the families of the wedding party. He showed the bridesmaids how to walk, admitting humorously that he was often surprised to see young women who lacked any notion of how to walk in long dresses. Anna shot me a look, which I pretended I didn't see. Canon Nombril took great pains in coaching the young flower girl, a pretty six-year-old, the daughter of Harold Grier, who sat next to Dr Gary Carswell. The doctor, I gathered, was going to stand up with the groom.

As a rehearsal it went very well. The only things omitted were the lines. I heard no prayers or exchanges of vows. We jumped from cue to cue. "People, the responses go in here and by now, Norman, you should be certain that Dr Carswell is holding the ring in his hand." Carswell amused everybody by flourishing the ring. "Very good, Doctor. We want to get the young couple off to a good start, don't we?" He went on to tell a story about a wedding in which the ring had been attached to a satin pillow by a stitch of thread. It took three minutes to separate the ring from the pillow. Meanwhile the bride had dissolved in tears.

By the time he finished with us, anyone who had been paying attention could have written a guide to the modern wedding. We knew who was to be seated on the right above the ribboned pew and who was to sit on the left below the ribboned pew. We knew that once Teddie was safely seated in the front pew on the left, the ceremony was about to begin in earnest. We knew who was to check boutonnières and transportation. Subtly, we were informed that this was the way these things were done. This was the standard, everything else a falling away from it. In addition, Canon Nombril wanted the ceremony to work the way a naval battle drill worked, with battle stations fully manned at zero hour or somebody was going to be on report. For a moment I thought he was going to get us to synchronize our watches. He didn't, but the pause before his "Any questions?" made up for it.

After the drill was concluded, with the procession and recessional worked out to the music, Canon Nombril huddled with the leading players in the chancel for another ten minutes. When they returned, beaming, as though some of life's secrets had already been opened to them, Canon Nombril thanked us for our kind attention. "I've been asked, people, by Mr Kenneth Caine, the father of our groom, to invite you all to break bread with us next door at the club in the General Brock Room, I believe." He explained that this was another of the traditions involved. Before we were able to get away, he asked us to go through the recessional one more time and to clear the church, beginning with the front pews first, just as we would on the great day itself. The organ struck up again, and the bride and groom led the way out of the church, with the rest of us following at a dignified distance the people in front. I've been in plays that had less time with the director than this wedding. I was amazed at the detail of the rehearsal. In me, at least, it awakened hunger.

Chapter Twenty-Three

I t was a short walk from St Mark's-by-the-Greens to the club. In fact, a well-worn path cut across the grass, avoiding the front parking lot, and ended at the side door. Three times Canon Nombril had referred to the club as being only an iron shot away from sanctity. He also allowed that St Mark's was the same distance from perdition. He said it with a generous grin, in case anyone might take him seriously. Anna was involved with the wedding party, so I had to content myself with walking along with Teddie. "I'll bet you're getting as big a kick out of this as I am, Benny," she said. "The only amusing thing is the sour look on Ross's face. You have to admit that's worth the price of admission."

"Teddie, tonight I'm just a camera. Lots of pictures, no judgments."

"Bull! You can't withhold making judgments any more than I can. We're both human, aren't we?"

"Maybe what I mean is I'm trying to be that fly on the wall you were talking about when we met two weeks ago. Have they been giving you a rough time?"

"No! That's just the trouble! Everybody's being so nice to me, it makes me nervous. They're treating me like the Queen Mother. You try it sometime."

"Thanks. So far I've been ignored by the people in the older generation. The bride and groom were civil, but that was because I was with Anna Abraham, who's an old friend of Sherry's. Ross thinks I'm with you."

"Let him. It'll do him good. Funny how I keep finding ways of making a man of my ex."

"I guess dinner's the next thing. Will that be a sit-down or a buffet?"

"We'll soon find out."

Ross Forbes walked by with Gary Carswell. Carswell looked back at us after Ross whispered something in his ear. The long line of the wedding rehearsal party moved into the club. I held the door for Teddie. We were in the wide corridor that led to the dining-room where I'd had lunch and to the other facilities the club had to offer. One of them, the General Brock Room, opened off to the left. People were pouring into the room like they hadn't eaten in a week. A small group was gathered around Biddy Forbes outside the dining-room. Biddy was giving orders in a firm voice.

"Try the house again, Sherry. He may have gone back there and fallen asleep."

"Norm's calling there, now, Mum-Mum. Please don't worry!"

"I'm not worried, child. I just want to know where he is. That's all." She looked rather frail standing there, but doughty, supported by her granddaughter. They made an interesting study, the two of them: both worried in their different ways. I was surprised that Sherry could withdraw from the drama of the wedding scenario to spare a moment for the older woman. Biddy, you could see, hated fuss. She was trying to get things moving again. Ross caught up with the front of the train again just as Caine returned from the phone.

"He's not at the house," he said. "Hasn't been seen since around eleven this morning."

"He isn't in your suite here at the club either," said Dr Carswell, who reluctantly added more unhelpful news to the collecting pile.

"Well, I saw him here at the club," Ross said. "He was boasting in the sauna that he was going to be the first of the wedding party to arrive at the church tonight."

"Ross, dear, we know where he *was*. It's where he *is* that's important," Biddy said.

"Well, that's only where I saw him. That was hours ago."

"We took a swim after our golf game," Biddy said to the assembled crowd, as though that would explain everything. "He left me in the pool. He wasn't in the pool when I left," she said rapidly, showing some confusion.

"Now, Mother, don't get excited. He'll turn up. I never saw him pass up a good roast of beef, have you?"

"Oh, everything's a joke to you, Ross!" the old lady scolded. "We might as well go in." She took a step towards the open double doors, then added quietly to Ross, "I'm sorry I was sharp with you, my dear. You can see I'm not myself. But I don't know why you've given up strong drink if you still intend to play the fool. Try to be more helpful. I need you to lean upon tonight. Indulge your old mother, there's a dear."

"I'm sorry, Mother."

"I know, I know. Just mollycoddle me a little, dear," she said. "He knows he should be here. It doesn't look right, especially with Norman's father here."

"Try not to get yourself worked up," Ross said, taking her arm. "You know what the doctor said."

Biddy gave Ross a peck on the cheek and patted the hand supporting her. Together they swept into the room to join the throng in the dining-room. As soon as he had escorted his mother to a chair, Ross came back in this direction.

"Gary," he called and Carswell turned. "Perhaps you could get some of the ushers to have a look around the club. He may be down in the card room." He said this last bit looking me straight in the eye. Did he think I was my father's keeper any more than he was his? I could almost see the Commander locked in a game of gin with my father. But Pa was rarely out at this time of day, and on a Friday night it was highly unlikely.

"Benny," Teddie said to me, tugging at my arm, "I forgot to tell you. I got notice this afternoon that there's going to be a meeting of the board of directors on Monday morning. Did you know about that?"

"No. They aren't wasting any time, are they?"

"What do you mean?"

"One, they are going to let Caine in at the upper level, and two, I think they may try to demote Ross."

Teddie mimed a surprised whistle, and rolled her lower lip into an expression of mock horror. "That will put the wind up them," she said.

"Will they get away with it? How many fans does Ross have left on the board? I can guess which way you and the Commander might vote."

"Benny! I never mix business and personal. Ross is a first-rate rat in his personal life, but he has his charms as a businessman. Apart from the little games he's been playing with the tax people on my behalf, I mean. But, you have to admit he had to be clever to figure that out."

"Teddie, I can never tell whose side you're on."

"That's the key to my fascination, Benny. Don't give me away."

While this was going on, Dr Carswell had pulled a few of the ushers from the General Brock Room, briefed them and sent them scampering through the club.

Inside the General Brock Room a buffet table of impressive length had been set up, and it stretched out in front of us burdened with good things. I counted three chef's bonnets and began to salivate at once. A huge lump of beef was being carved by expert hands. As the dark outer layer came off, the moist pink interior was laid bare. I moved into the line that was already forming and collected cutlery, a cloth napkin and a warmed plate. Teddie Forbes was right behind me.

"He really put them through it, didn't he?" she said.

"I should tell Ned Evans about him. He could direct some Shakespeare in Montecello Park this summer." Ned worked at being the local drama impresario when he wasn't drinking draft beer at the Harding House. "I guess directing people is how he got to be a canon, whatever a canon is."

"A canon's the rector of a cathedral, Benny. He takes over the parish chores so that the bishop can get on with bishopping."

The line was moving along more quickly than I thought it would. Soon Teddie was being served. I'd let her move ahead of me when I saw other women ahead of their escorts. She took a nice piece of rare meat with roast potatoes. When it was my turn, I asked for a slice from the outside as well as some medium-well-done from a part of the roast that hadn't been bothered much. I watched the white bonnet bob as the cook sliced off the pieces I wanted and carried them with his carving knife and fork to my plate. I told him which of the potatoes I craved and he gave them to me. I took the heaping plate from him and followed Teddie to a table. I could see that Anna was still conferring with Sherry and the other bridesmaids. Of course, Anna, as maid of honour, had special responsibilities. She was a little nervous about them, so I told her not to worry about me after we'd arrived. I was a little hurt to see that she'd taken me at my word.

No sooner had I placed my napkin in my lap and had started focusing on the feast ahead of me, when two of the young ushers came up to me. "Mr Cooperman?"

"That's right. What can I do for you?" I got a horrible feeling that started in my belly. My dinner was slipping through my fingers.

"Mr Burgess—he's the manager of the club—he'd like a word with you."

"But I'm—"

"It's important. There's been an accident," added the other usher. For a moment I thought I was going to get the old heave-ho for barging into a private party, but the word "accident" put another taste in my mouth.

"Accident?"

"You'd better come with us. Mr Burgess is just outside." The faces of my mother and father went through my head. Was this the introduction to a major family change? I saw my father slumped over the card table with a pair of aces and a pair of eights in his hand. I saw my mother . . . I squeezed my eyes shut and got to my feet. Reluctantly, and with a glance at my plate of roast beef and potatoes, I followed the ushers, feeling a little hot under the collar at the interruption. Unless it had something to do with me personally, I was just another guest here. My Red Cross first-aid training became obsolete with the triangular bandage. I was no doctor.

I didn't recognize Burgess at first. He looked like a lot of other dumpy dark-haired men that sweat a lot. He had done in his jacket. The shirt under it was wet through so that I could see the weave of his underwear top. There were beads of sweat standing on his upper lip as he took my hand. "Mr Cooperman, how are you? It's been at least five years since I saw you."

That's when I remembered him. Burgess was Jim Burgess, who ran the YMCA on Queen Street when I met him in 1985. His wife wanted an agreement for a trial separation and he'd grown suspicious. He wanted me to check out the missus before he divided up the assets. As I remembered, Burgess's instincts were dead on. His wife was seeing a schoolteacher on the side and helping him with the costumes for the grade six pageant. Among other things.

"How are you, Mr Burgess? Good to see you again."

"Oh, Mr Cooperman, this is a terrible thing. Just terrible." I was about to cluck my tongue in sympathy and read him my office hours, when he turned to the ushers and told them how well he knew me of old and what a wonderfully helpful fellow I was. There was no getting away from him. "As soon as I saw you come in tonight, I said to myself I was going to speak to you, never suspecting for a minute, of course . . ."

"Never suspecting what exactly?"

"Why this, naturally." I was being drawn away from the door of the dining-room and pulled along a pale green corridor. "In the year and a half that I've been here, Mr Cooperman, nothing like this has happened. He produced a large white handkerchief and began mopping his brow and neck. "Oh, we had accidents at the Y—I don't mean we had a perfect slate—but never anything like this."

"Like what?" I asked, trying to keep up with Burgess. "Give me a hint." Burgess kept up the pace as we came into the athletic section of the club, where men and women in shorts and sweatbands passed us carrying racquets and calmly going in the other direction. Whatever it was, the accident had not disrupted normal activities yet.

"It's just through here," he said, as though that was an answer. He led us through the door leading to the men's locker-room and shower. It looked like an old friend. I could see bodies in various stages of undress as we moved by the doorway, past the old-fashioned upright scale, then the automatic hot-air dryer and into the steaming shower room. The room was empty, but the grey tile walls were still dripping. From the shower room there was nowhere to go except through the door marked POOL or the door next to it. I recognized the notice that came down hard on reading in the sauna. One of the other ushers was posted outside this second door. As soon as he saw us, he stood aside, as the manager opened the door. I caught the room's hot breath on my face as I tried to make out what it was that Burgess wanted me to see.

The sauna was walled and shelved with golden planks of softwood. A series of benches rose upward from the front, a set of miniature bleachers leading up to the hottest part of the room. On the top shelf in the corner sat the Commander, wrapped in a blue Turkish towel. In spite of the wrapping, most of the Commander lay pink and exposed. I wondered for a moment what sort of trouble he could have got into that wouldn't allow him to leave the sauna. Moisture was still dripping from his face to the great folds of his body.

"What's going on?" I asked Murdo Forbes. "Can't we talk somewhere else?"

The Commander didn't move. The eyes that had at first seemed to be focused on me were bent on the middle distance. The stillness tugged at my throat. I looked around at Burgess, who was right behind me. "Will you please tell me what's going on?"

"But I thought they told you," he said. "Just look!"

I looked back up at the Commander. At his feet I saw discarded pages of a sodden newspaper with the newsprint turning almost green in the heat and under this light. Was that what he was complaining about? The newspaper? "Damn it, Mr Burgess, it's not up to me to enforce your by-laws."

"By-laws? I'm talking about the Commander."

"The Commander," I said in a whisper, "can buy and sell this club. I'd be careful if I were you."

"Mr Cooperman. You misunderstand. I think he's dead."

That knocked the air out of me. Could anything as round and rosy, so fat and hot, also be dead? I looked back up at him. He hadn't moved since the door to the sauna was opened. I climbed up the benches to the top of the bleachers where the Commander sat, leaning into a corner.

I felt his neck. It was warm and sweaty.

My first thought, if it can be called that, was that the old man was sleeping off a heavy meal or too much to drink. But I knew better. He had skipped lunch and hadn't had anything to drink. I was about to turn to Burgess with this information when I saw the blood, partly hidden by the towel and already looking dark and sticky. I could see it. I moved some of the newspaper and was immediately sorry. Great gouts of gore had landed on the duck-boards at his feet. In spite of the healthy, reddish look, in spite of the warmth of the body, it was plain that the Commander, Murdo Forbes, was dead.

Chapter Twenty-Four

As I waited for the cops to arrive, I thought of my plate of roast beef back in the General Brock Room. I was strangely able to think of it growing cold at the same time I was staring at the notice outside the sauna door. I couldn't see any reason for keeping the heat on in there, but I never liked to tamper with things at the scene of a crime if I can help it, especially when there are witnesses hanging around.

Burgess, the club manager, had gone to inform the police, when I convinced him that this was a formality that couldn't be overlooked. I sent one of the ushers, a twenty-five-year-old kid named Brant or Clint, back to the dining-room to make sure nobody left until the police said they could. He was a big kid, built like a football linebacker, and I knew that even Ross Forbes at his most bullish would think twice before crossing him. I checked my watch. Eight o'clock on the nose. It would be ten before even an optimist would predict we'd be clear of this mess. I was never that optimistic. Again I thought of the food.

It was my old friend and sometime antagonist Staff Sergeant Chris Savas who arrived to take charge of the investigation. Savas and I had run into one another on a few cases. I knew him to be a good cop. In spite of those cold, metallic eyes, he was honest and even imaginative for a heavy-duty policeman. He took in his information from the uniformed police already on the scene. He spoke for a few minutes to Burgess, whose arms moved in my direction, as though he was blaming me for not turning off the heat in the sauna. Savas looked over at me, but there was no sign in his face that we had eaten Greek food together or that he had shared a communal teabag in my mother's living-room. This was business, and if there was an advantage to be had from keeping everybody in an unbroken straight line, he intended to reap it. I didn't envy him the investigation into the death of a leading citizen. Wherever he walked there were toes to step on, and each of those little piggies came equipped with lawyers and access to the media. No wonder he didn't look like he was going to enjoy himself.

Savas strode into the General Brock Room and told everybody that the Commander was dead and that the circumstances were such that he had to ask them to submit to some questioning in order to determine the facts of the case. He thanked people for their cooperation before the first of the objections was raised. It was Dr Carswell.

"Sergeant, this is all very overwhelming. Wouldn't it be better to let some of the family leave? They've had a nasty shock, and I'm sure your questions can wait until morning."

"Gary's right," Caine put in. "We can attend you whenever you say in the morning at your office. I think that Mrs Forbes at least should be allowed to go home."

"Mrs Forbes?" Savas was looking at the widow, who was standing up very tall and straight for such a recent widow.

"I will answer your questions, Sergeant. I will do—and I beg the others to as well—whatever I can to clear up the death of my husband." I had told the usher to keep his mouth shut about what had happened in the men's sauna, but there was no surprise when Savas broke the news. They had known and had had a chance to get a handle on the information. Apart from a chalk-white face, Miss Biddy

was doing very well. Sherry, on the other hand, was
sobbing into Norm Caine's sweater. Was it the loss of her
grandfather or was it the inevitable postponement of their
wedding? I couldn't tell. Carswell moved in to talk in
whispers to Caine who then looked up from the blonde
head on his shoulder.

Savas conferred with Burgess and quickly began questioning the family and the inner circle, while the rest of us
sat, along with ushers, bridesmaids and the three chefs,
waiting. People in gym wear and others were ushered in
to find a place to sit as well. Anna separated herself from
the core of the wedding party and rejoined me at the edge
of the room. She took my hand but otherwise left me free
to keep my eyes open.

By the time he had talked to about twenty people, Savas
announced, through one of the uniformed men, that the
rest of us were excused. He wanted our names and ad-
dresses and phone numbers, but our presence was no
longer required. Anna grinned at me and we both headed
for the double doors that had been closed. It had just
passed ten forty-five, but there would still be a few places
open downtown where we could get a bite to eat. I didn't
get another look at any of the grieving family members as
we went out. I was glad of that. I didn't mind my job most
of the time, but when it came to a dead grandfather, father
and husband, I'd just as soon look the other way until the
funeral is over. Death demands privacy, even if murder
cries out for action. It was hard to do both at once.

The Di was closing up when we got there, so we went
on to one of the new restaurants that had opened up in the
former home of the Upper Canadian Bank on St Andrew
Street. They had moved into a new office tower across
from the market, and after several false starts, this restaurant with its little round tables and espresso machine
seemed to be thriving. Anna thought the music on the
stereo was a Bach Partita, and we settled in with the menu.

We were both starved. Neither one of us did much talking. We ordered coffee to start with and then a couple of sandwiches. I had a toasted cheese for a change; Anna went for crab on a kaiser roll.

"Do you think you know what happened?" Anna asked when she put down the coffee cup where the waiter could see it. He did and brought a prompt refill for both of us.

"Well, there was no sign of a gun or knife, so I guess he didn't do himself in."

"So, it was murder just like Jack Dowden and Alex Pásztory?"

"That's the way it looks, but right now I can't even say for sure that Jack and Alex were killed by the same person. I think they were killed for similar reasons, but I can't prove anything."

"You said in the car that you talked to the Commander this afternoon."

"Yeah. He didn't look like he was hiding from anyone. He wasn't on the run. No, I think we have one very surprised dead man in this case."

"What will you do now that the police are involved?"

"I guess I'll report to Irma Dowden and beg off. There's not much room to move with Savas running around on this end and Pete Staziak on the other. No, I think I've just found my excuse to get off this case. I can leave the scene with my honour intact."

"I felt sorry for Teddie Forbes in that room, Benny. Not a friend in the place. It was good of you to stay close to her." I looked at Anna to see if she was pulling my leg, but she wasn't. She was glad I'd kept an eye on her. What else could I do? Ross was nearly foaming at the mouth just seeing her.

"Yeah, Teddie can't wait to get back to Flagstaff. She doesn't like being here. What do you think Sherry and Caine will do? The wedding can't go ahead as planned, can it?"

"That's the first thing I thought of when I heard that the Commander was dead: 'I won't have to go through with this white-wedding charade.' Isn't that awful?"

"It's honest."

"Are you sorry that Sergeant Savas didn't consult with you about the Commander?"

"Oh, he can't do that on the first day. He'll find his moment when he's walked around the body a few times. This one's going to be a hard one to figure."

"Why do you say that?" I gave some bills to the waiter and he carried them to the cash register, one of the new kind with plastic covering everything. The place was empty except for us. We got up, and I tried to grab Anna's chair, but was too late. It fell over with the weight of her raincoat.

"For one thing the coroner's not going to be able to say when the Commander died. The heat from the sauna will screw up the usual calculations that have to do with bodies cooling after death. He told Ross and me that he hadn't eaten any lunch, so that will spoil the other way of fixing the time of death. Savas may get lucky, though. He may hear from somebody who was in the sauna at a known time and left the old man in there hale and hearty."

"Won't he automatically become the chief suspect?"

"Not unless he had an axe to grind. The Commander was heading from the pool to the sauna when I saw him and that was just after lunch. He was in there a long time."

"Well, at least you can eliminate all the female suspects. They wouldn't have been able to get past the fellow selling tickets for towels and robes into the men's locker room. So you can concentrate on the men. What about Ross? Do you think he did it?"

"He had a motive, all right. The old man was always meddling in the business, and it looks like he was trying to throw some or all of the action into Norm Caine's court."

"Could Caine be the guilty party, then?"

"Why would he kill the Commander, his chief ally in getting ahead in the business?"

"Maybe they had a falling out."

"Maybes don't fly, Anna. Savas will need something better than that." By now we had reached the street. Anna took my arm as we moved along to where I'd parked the car.

St Andrew Street looked dark and a little scary at that time of night, at least it did that night after what I'd seen at the club. The gentle curve of the store-fronts was a study in shadows and made the empty streets look like pictures by that American painter Anna liked, Edward Hopper, I think that's his name. The tunnel-like opening where Bixby's used to be looked like the entrance to hell or the Black Hole of Calcutta. While I was trying to sift through these sinister imaginings, I became aware that there was a car coming up behind us. Why was it hugging the sidewalk we were on when it had the whole breadth of the one-way street? Why was it slowing down? I didn't wait for an answer.

"C'mon!" I yelled and grabbed Anna's hand. We ran into Helliwell Lane and then turned right, under the fire escapes and dark windows, into Somerset Place. We blundered into the leanto that Apple Mary had set up. She began to yell as we came out on James, across from the Centre Theatre. Still holding on to Anna, I dragged her across James and into the alley, which followed the long unbroken line of the theatre's auditorium to the end and then bumped into the new warehouse behind Graham's bookstore. What I wouldn't give for a key to his back door, I thought. But I knew that the alley wasn't the kind that ended in a dead end, so we were quickly through the darkest part. We stopped in a doorway and listened in the shadows to the sounds above our heavy breathing. I could hear no footsteps, I could see no headlights.

"I'm putting you in a taxi," I told Anna.

"In a pig's eye, as you always say. You're not packing me off home the first time the game gets rough."

"It's not a game! These are the boys I was telling you about. Let me see you safe, then I can concentrate on this damned mess."

"I would prefer not to." She made it sound like a quotation. I certainly couldn't move her. After another minute we worked our way from Chestnut Street, through the bus terminal to Academy. From there it was a short sprint to my apartment. I left Anna standing behind a stout maple, while I surveyed the rest of the way to the front door. The street was quiet and there were no bogymen hiding on the landing watching me fish out my key.

Once inside, with the door locked and bolted, we began to find our courage again. I brought out a bottle of cognac and we both had a short sharp shot, just enough to restore perspective.

"You'd better call your pal Savas. He should know about this. And about the other night. Does he know about your drive out to Port Richmond?"

"Savas has his hands full tonight. The best thing we can do is give Savas a wide berth."

"Until morning."

"Sure. If you insist." Anna smiled at that and tried to relax. But I could see that she was shivering. I slipped her coat back over her shoulders and held her for a few minutes. That seemed to help.

"What I really need is a scalding hot bath," she said. "That's my defence against all known and unknown terrors."

"Help yourself," I said, suddenly aware of the limitations of my bachelor establishment. I found some fresh towels and a terry-cloth robe and handed them to her. She closed the door, and soon I heard the sound of running water. The apartment walls were looking at me as I sat there watching steam billow from the crack at the bottom of the door.

Later . . . But that's nobody's business.

Chapter Twenty-Five

I was having my morning coffee at the Diana Sweets and reading the Saturday *Globe and Mail*, when I felt an extra two hundred pounds on the bench I was sitting on. Staff Sergeant Chris Savas had joined me and the napkin dispenser. He carried his own coffee in a foam cup with a plastic lid. He didn't say anything. Before I even got my mouth open to tell him what he knew already—that he looked like he'd been up all night—Pete Staziak moved into the place opposite me. He carried no coffee of his own, but he too didn't look like a man who'd spent the night in the bosom of his family. I waved for the waitress. Savas surrendered his foam cup, and we ordered a new round to start afresh.

"Okay," I said. "I won't make any clever remarks about burning the midnight oil. I'll speak when spoken to."

"Damned right," said Pete, taking off his hat and giving us all a look at the red line around his head.

When the coffee arrived, Savas, at my elbow, took a sip and then turned to me. "What the hell do you think's going on? I'll be damned if I can figure it out." Such an admission from Chris was simply a ploy of some sort. He was too good a cop to be all that much at sea. It was meant to disarm me, to turn me into a cooperative witness. I shrugged. It seemed the best thing to do under the circumstances. Then Pete joined in:

"What cards are you holding face down, Benny? That's

222

really all we want to know."

"Just the name of my client. That's all I care about. The rest is yours or anybody else's. But remember, I only came into this thing a week ago last Tuesday."

Silently, Pete pulled out his wallet and handed Chris a five-dollar bill. "What's that all about?" I asked.

"Chris said you wouldn't volunteer the fact that there was bad blood between you and Ross Forbes. I said different, that's all."

"You didn't give me time, damn it! I didn't know you were putting money on me. Hey, and besides, Ross Forbes isn't in the morgue. It's his old man, who has never laid a glove on me."

"The point is, you aren't as freshly into this as you let on, Benny. That shows a lack of trust, a lack of openness—"

"Bull! I gotta mouthful of coffee and you just sat down, for crying out loud. What do you want, a printout of my comings and goings for the last ten years?" Chris leaned away from me. Either my breath was bad or I was making my point and he was not going to dispute it. He certainly wasn't going to return Pete's five. I ignored Chris for the moment and faced Pete. "How are you getting along on the other one?"

"Professional job. Very tidy," Pete said.

"Those pros took one of the Kinross drivers for a ride on Thursday night. I'd keep an eye on the house of Brian O'Mara who was within an ace of being accurately described as 'late of this parish.'"

"He didn't report anything."

"What do you expect? These guys always play deaf and dumb when it does them the least good. I know it happened because I was there."

"Damn!"

"They tried to get you too?" I nodded, and Chris gave Staziak a look.

"What's more, after we left the club last night, Anna and I went to that ex-bank restaurant at the corner to talk. When we left, a car was following us. We had to scuttle through back alleys to my place."

"What time was that?"

"After eleven-thirty. Maybe a quarter to twelve."

"What kind of car was it?" Pete was leaning towards me as though a lot was riding on my answer.

"Some kind of Ford, I think. I didn't wait around to get the registration." Pete looked at Chris and then at me:

"I was looking for you around then, Benny." He had taken on a sheepish look. "I didn't think you'd take me for a hoodlum with the mob."

"You son of a bitch!" I yelled, louder than I intended. Heads turned to see what was happening in our booth. I was getting hot where my tie was tied too tight. "You nearly scared Anna to death!"

"Sorry, Benny. Really, I had no idea!" He kept looking at Chris to help him out, but his partner let him stew. "Jeez, Benny. I only wanted to talk to you. Maybe I shouldda honked?"

"We woke up Apple Mary and ran four or five blocks!"

"Why don't you two continue this on your own time," Chris suggested. "I've got the jist of both your arguments. Just give it a rest." Chris looked at each of us and I bit my tongue.

"What's happening with the Pásztory investigation?" I asked Pete, hoping that it was an embarrassing question. "I didn't read in the *Beacon* that the body was found under Fort Mississauga in a hole with a few tons of poisonous waste."

"We don't want to scare the villains away, Benny. If they know we have the body, they must know where we found it."

"I don't see the advantage," I admitted.

"If we talk to somebody who knows more than has

appeared in the paper, then we know we're on to something. Crooks have a hard time keeping straight what they know and what they've read in the press."

"In that, crooks are like everybody else," I said. "But, I'll remember that. I can, by the way, give you a description of the three hoods who borrowed me and O'Mara from the Harding House on Thursday night."

"Is that where your consulting rooms are located these days?" Chris was beginning to sound like his old self.

"Why don't you go home and have a shower?" I asked. "It's one thing to be up all night, but another to look it. Chris, you look it."

"I will, I will, but first I want to know why you were having lunch with Ross Forbes yesterday at the Grantham Club?"

"Boy, you've had your little people out beating the bushes, haven't you?" Chris's eyes were not crinkling at the corners showing signs of laughter and humour. I changed tactics. "Nothing mysterious in my breaking bread with Forbes. He wanted me to do a job for him. Nothing to do with Kinross or Phidias. I turned him down."

"Why?"

"Conflict."

"You mean scruples, Benny?"

"I mean conflict of interests. I'm already working in that area, and Forbes is one of the people I've got my eye on."

"Well, you'll save expenses on him from now on."

"What do you mean?" Pete grinned at Savas and waited for him to enlighten me.

"I just had Forbes arrested," Chris said.

"Ross Forbes? For the murder of his father? You've got to be pulling my leg!"

"Let's not get technical. I'm telling you he's been arrested. Right now, as a matter of fact, he's cooling his heels in the lockup."

"Chris, you can't believe that he'd kill his old man. They've hated one another too long for it to end this way."

"Well, read the paper when it comes out. He was the last person to talk to the Commander. He even admits it. Says they had a little chat in the sauna in the afternoon. Of course the way he tells it, they were getting along better than ever. Benny, he was seen at the club, seen on his way to and coming from the sauna as he went through the changing room."

"You didn't book him for just being in the club at the same time, Chris. Now did you? Damn it, the old man was slow-roasted in that sauna for so long that the best bet you have of getting the time of death is by checking the date on the newspaper he was reading. All you know is that he was killed some time, maybe hours, before he was found.

"We've got the gun." That stopped me.

"Oh?"

"It came from the Commander's collection. Ross had access."

"Sure, and so did the rest of the family, I'll bet. Come on, Chris. Has he confessed or what?"

"No, he's stonewalling us, but he'll talk in the end."

"Why do you think he did it?"

"The old man was trying to bump him out of the family business. After the wedding, Norman Caine would become top dog at the next board meeting on Monday."

"You think he killed Pásztory too?"

"We're still working on that. We'll drop you a line if we link them up. Right now, according to Pete, Pásztory was snuffed by professionals from out of town."

"You're repeating yourself. I don't suppose you've ever heard about Jack Dowden?"

"Dowden? Doesn't ring any bells with me," said Savas, looking over at Pete who was dredging into his memory and almost but not quite remembering.

"Come on, Benny, this isn't a TV quiz show. There are no prizes for the right answer." I started to remind them and it was Pete who remembered the rest of the story. Between the two of us we filled Savas in.

"So, you're saying that this accident was maybe not an accident?"

"Chris, if you stand in front of me and I run you down with my Freightliner, I will pulverize your lower back and pelvic area. Dowden's chest was crushed. So, he was on his knees when he was hit. Witnesses have been paid off and have left town. Another one, O'Mara, was the object of a snatch on Thursday night. He told me that they saw nothing of the accident in spite of what they told the coroner."

"A minute ago you were going to bat for Ross Forbes. Now you're trying to stick two more bodies on him. What's going on?"

"I'm not saying Ross didn't do them all in. All I'm saying is that the picture is bigger than the one you were looking at in the club last night. It has to include Dowden and Pásztory. By the way, Pásztory was in Chet Bryant's office looking up the facts on the Dowden case. He read the coroner's report. Does that tie things more tightly together for you?"

"That ties Pásztory to Dowden. How does it put them closer to Ross Forbes? He was top dog at Phidias not Kinross. Maybe we should be talking to Norman Caine."

"I don't care whom you talk to—"

"You catch that 'whom,' Pete? Very pretty. That Anna of yours is sure a classy woman, Benny."

"I've been talking English all my life. Get off my back, Chris!" That came out a little more forcefully than I'd intended. I shot Pete a grin to show I was only fooling, and that reminded me of something. "Pete, Ross Forbes told me that he has noticed a tail on him. You know anything about that?" Pete rubbed the back of his neck, like he'd just got out of a car after a long trip. It gave him time to think of what he could afford to tell me.

"Look, Benny, without the charges from yesterday, Forbes has a full plate. There's an investigation going on into the improprieties that Alex Pásztory revealed last spring. As Chief Executive Officer of Phidias Manufacturing and former CEO of Kinross, there is a lot he's responsible for. There are people who want to know who he sees and whether he is buying any airline tickets, especially the one-way kind. That's about as far as I can go right now."

Chris acknowledged Pete's balance of candour and tact with a nod of his meaty head. "Whom did you think was following him, Benny?" he said. I ignored the "whom" which was aimed at my liver. From there on the conversation degenerated even further. I could see that Savas was proud of himself for pinning the Commander's death on Ross so quickly. I didn't blame him for that. Sometimes you can work for months without getting a break. He was lucky on this one and he knew it. The only other fact I learned from them was about the murder weapon:

"We found it in one of those big washing machines that do all those towels and robes at the club. Only one chamber fired, the rest all full. It was a thirty-two with a snub nose. Tidy little fellow. And it was registered to the dead man. How do you like them roses?"

"I give you top marks. Especially if you found a towel or robe with powder burns on it in the same machine. Since nobody heard the shot, the piece must have been wrapped up in a towel or something. But, then, you know all that."

"Sure," Chris said, with a glance at Pete.

"What about the slug that killed Pásztory, Pete? Was that another small-calibre piece?"

"It was a thirty-two all right, but—"

"But you haven't made a comparison." I shrugged and let out a full breath, just enough to give the impression that the boys in the lab were short-changing my pals.

"You don't buy Pete's theory that this was a professional job?" Chris asked.

"I'm not saying one thing nor the other. It doesn't hurt to check these things out. That's all I'm saying. Like, for instance, did you check out Paul Renner from City Hall or the other brother-in-law, Harold Grier? Where were they at sauna-time?"

"Grier's clean as far as we can tell, except for some shady friends. And Renner's not all that swift in the brain department."

"Yeah," Pete added, "if he had a cocaine habit, he's the sort of guy'd try to snort it off a bathroom mirror. You know what I mean?"

"How smart do you have to be to use a thirty-two?" I asked. That put an end temporarily to Pete's enjoying himself.

Chris finished his coffee with a flourish and shot Pete a grin I couldn't interpret. Maybe it had something to do with their having killed a quarter of an hour ribbing me about the cases. They enjoyed making me feel like I was a cop-shop groupie who liked having cops call him by his first name. I finished off the last of my cup—it was cold—and smiled back at them. They got up and slipped back into their coats. When they left me, I felt like I could use a shower, even though I'd started the day with one. As for Chris Savas, he was ready for another eight hours of work.

When the *Beacon* came out that afternoon, the murder of Commander Murdo Forbes and the arrest of his son were front-page items. What shocked me, however, was something that I don't think either Pete or Chris knew at the time they were talking to me in the Di. Old Mrs Forbes, Biddy, the widow of the Commander, had had a stroke on hearing that Ross had been detained at Niagara Regional Police Headquarters. She was in intensive care at the Grantham General.

I made a few calls and discovered that she was putting up a good fight, but that she was paralysed and had lost the ability to speak. I checked this out with my pal Dr Lou Gelner, who explained that with time, she could expect to get over most of her physical encumbrances. But with a woman her age, there was always a chance of a later and more severe stroke killing her. With that bit of uplift, I turned to the office dictionary and looked up the word Ross Forbes had used at lunch the day before: *lubricious*. It had been at the back of my mind since he'd said it about poor Martin Lyster. *Slippery, smooth, oily; lewd, wanton.* Hell, it sounded more like Forbes than it did Martin. I slammed the dictionary shut and went back to the apartment.

I killed the next half-hour or so looking over the book I'd brought away with me from Irma Dowden's house and the papers I'd taken from the basement files from Phidias's head office. The book helped add to my skinny background in this area, the papers added specific information. What held my attention was the dispatcher's log. It looked like any log that clocked cars and trucks in and out of a place. Then I noticed something odd:

NAME	IN	OUT
Dowden	6:00 A.M.	6:10 A.M.
O'Mara	7:00	11:00
Dowden	7:30	
Dr Carswell	7:40	7:50
Dr Carswell	8:15	11:00

There were other names listed too, but these were the most familiar ones. What I couldn't figure out was why did Carswell visit the yard twice. He stayed only ten minutes the first time, and the next time took him to the end of the police investigation by the look of it. I tucked the log in a corner of my head and left it there to see what the grey cells could do on their own.

That night, at seven, Anna and I went to the movies. There was a small repertory theatre that played old movies on St Andrew Street above the Woman's Bakery. Run by a part-time lecturer from Secord, it had its box office and aisles manned by his prize students. It was the sort of place where they made you feel like your fly was open if you asked for popcorn. The movie was *Great Expectations*. It was an old black-and-white post-war classic from England with a big scary scene in the first reel. Inevitably, after the show, we found ourselves at the Di, where they are soon going to start charging me rent. Anna asked:

"Well, how did you like it?"

"Great," I said. I might have confessed that I could have done without all that rowing on the Thames.

"You dozed off!"

"I was carried away by a daydream," I said. "I was wondering whether the English dumped toxic wastes into those bleak marshes where Pip lived."

"You were snoring, Benny. I had to shake you!" Anna was in a good mood. "I thought you liked it."

"I *did*. It didn't make me mad the way modern movies do."

"What makes you cross at them?" She was playing with me now, showing that gamine side of her her colleagues up at Secord knew nothing about. "Let's hear about it."

"I don't like movies where they wreck a dozen vintage cars in a police chase. And I get mad at the way people in movies never have trouble finding a parking space. Even here in Grantham I can drive around the block a dozen times and not see an empty space, but in the movies, even in New York, the hero always finds a spot right away. In my experience, the only time I get a parking space near a restaurant I'm heading for is when it's closed for Greek Easter or something."

"You don't really mean that?" She turned her head on the side, in order to see into my heart better. I could never argue decently with Anna sitting across from me. She had a way of exposing my illogical side. Without even trying, she could argue me into absurdity.

"Okay," I said. "I don't really believe it. Let's just say that such has been my experience. That's different."

Anna was looking particularly fetching to me as she sipped her coffee. She was wearing an old sweater over a pink button-down shirt. The way she did it, it didn't look preppy or fashionable. It wasn't what they call today a "look"; it was just Anna being comfortable, and watching me squirm. That was the first thing I noticed about her when I met her last year, a brattish quality that is always trying to see how much it can get away with. When she tried that one on, as she still did, she seemed about sixteen. She was now studying my face, like she wanted to sculpt it. She was making it all the more difficult for me to justify the position I'd taken. And she knew it.

"In my business," I said, trying to sound like sweet reason itself, "—and probably in yours—you learn to check the odds of some things turning out the way they do. If it works one way once, then there are odds for and against it working out that way next time."

"Are you saying that lightning doesn't strike in the same place twice?"

"Maybe I am."

"Maybe in legend and aphorism lightning doesn't strike twice, but in meteorology it happens all the time. The CN Tower in Toronto, the Empire State Building in New—"

"Okay, then let's stick to legend. Like that old movie on that poster in the lobby: *Mutiny on the Bounty*. What are the chances of a situation like that happening again?"

"You don't want to know the answer to that."

"Wrong example?"

"Uh-huh. Did you think Captain Bligh was going to

change his spots? Was it likely he was going to learn a lesson from the *Bounty*?" There was a nice glow in her cheeks now as she leaned towards me. I could smell her perfume, but I kept on listening. "People act according to the way they are. Bligh was a martinet. He thought he had to drive his men with fear to get an honest day's work out of them. The Admiralty said—in the movie—I haven't looked up the history—that it was an excess of zeal on the captain's part." Anna was really going now, and I loved to listen. "Well," she continued, "zeal was part of his character. It was excessive on the *Bounty* in the South Seas, on the *Nore* in the Thames Estuary and again still later in New South Wales in Australia. You must have seen that in your work, Benny?"

"Sure," I said. "Some people can hide their motives for a while, but it's what they do that comes out and damns them. It's no trick to talk like a saint. My job is to get under that to what they've done."

The talk went on and on while we had another refill of coffee, and I was getting a big kick out of it. In the back of my mind I was beginning to see the faces of all the strange characters I'd run into since Irma Dowden came to see me. There were no Pips or Miss Havishams, no Blighs or Fletcher Christians, but they were interesting in their own rights. I had to admit that I was having fun getting under their skins, trying to guess what made them tick. There was something Dickensian in the character of the Commander. Even in death, he was bigger than life.

"Oh, by the way, Benny," Anna said, after it became clear that my attention had been wandering, "did you know that Sherry Forbes and Norman Caine got married on schedule this afternoon?"

"What? I don't believe it! Nobody gets married with a grandfather dead and a grandmother in Intensive Care."

"To say nothing of the father of the bride in the calaboose," she added.

"Right. What kind of people are we dealing with?"

"All I know is that Canon Nombril performed the ceremony in a chapel at the cathedral with just two witnesses. So, at least it was as quiet as possible to still be legal."

"At least Sherry won't turn into a Miss Havisham. That's my first reaction. The second is, what are they going to do with the fancy white wedding they put into storage?"

"On that note, sir, you'd better drive me home." And I did that.

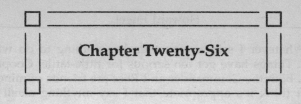

Chapter Twenty-Six

irst thing next morning, I looked up the residence of Dr Gary Carswell in the phonebook. It seemed reasonable that I might find him at home on a Sunday, so I drove around to 153 Hillcrest Avenue and found a large white stucco house with shutters and a lot of green grass to trim. I parked the car a few doors beyond the house and walked back. There I found the doctor delivering a green garbage bag full of leaves to the curbside. He was wearing a grey tracksuit with dark sweat stains under the arms. There was something ape-like in the hang of his big shoulders. The headband around his forehead looked wet. He appeared to have been working on his property for the last two hours at least.

"Dr Carswell? Good-morning!"

"Good mor—" He stopped and set his garbage bag down hard. "Now, look here, Cooperman, I've nothing more to say to you!"

"Not even good-morning? I remember you telling me to come back when I'd got myself organized. It was good advice. I was a little wet behind the ears when we last talked." I was doing my best to put him at his ease, but he looked as relaxed as a cat at the vet's. He needed the props of his office to give him dignity. The beard, which worked in his office, now looked like it was pasted on with spirit gum.

235

"Whatever I said to you then has nothing to do with now. Things have got too serious for tittle-tattle, Cooperman. Both the Commander and Ross are friends of mine. I don't think it's appropriate that I say anything at all to you."

"Well, you'll talk to the cops, then. That'll be just as good. I can't get rough with you. I can't work you over until your statement looks the way they want it to."

"And neither can they. This isn't 1939, Mr Cooperman. The third-degree is only found in cheap fiction. I know my rights and the authorities are aware of that."

"Good luck to you, Doctor. It's rare that you find people who still believe the system works. I hope they don't ask you why you visited the Kinross yard twice on the morning that Jack Dowden had his fatal accident. Lovely fall morning, isn't it?" I started walking back to my car.

"Dowden? What about Dowden? What has that got to do with Ross shooting the Commander? Now, you hold on a minute, Cooperman." He came after me, grabbed me by the arm. I looked at his hand and he took it away. "Come around to the backyard where you can sit down." I let him see indecision playing over my face for a moment or two, as though I wasn't overjoyed at the invitation. Together we walked along the high hedge that separated his place from the neighbour, who, I was told, ran the General Motors distributorship in Grantham.

It was a large green backyard, with an old-fashioned wire fence along the back property line, interrupted by a rusty gate that probably dated from the days when through it you could walk out into fields of open country. Now it was wired shut and you could see into at least a dozen large backyards. In the middle of the lawn, a white table with a faded umbrella formed the focus of attention. Near it were a set of matching chairs and a gas barbecue with its top covered in plastic wrap. We sat down. It was a comfortable setting, but neither of us was relaxed. I looked over the back of the white house and nodded my approval.

"Very nice here," I said. "You must be very comfortable, you and your family."

"And nothing's going to change that, Mr Cooperman. Nothing! I hope you know what you're messing in?"

"Dr Carswell, I have a client. I'm only assisting this client. If my investigations can also help the police in their work, which parallels mine, I'm obliged to cooperate. We have worked like this in the past. And you're right, I am trying my best to discover what I'm messing in. I was vague when I talked to you last time. I'm better informed this morning. For instance, the dispatcher's list of comings and goings at the Kinross yard shows that you came and went twice on the morning Jack died. I know you weren't asked about that at the inquest, but how would you answer that question if it came up again?"

"That's not likely, is it? What has it to do with Ross and the Commander?"

"We both know the answer to that one, Doctor."

"You think you know a great deal, but I wonder if you really do."

"Look, Dr Carswell, I'm not interested in playing guessing games or power games or button-button-who's-got-the-button? All I'm interested in finding out is what happened to Jack Dowden. Now, I think that what's happened to the Commander and to Alex Pásztory is all tied up with Jack's accident. I think that the Commander's death has changed things. And you know what things have been changed."

"You're not very frightening, you know, Mr Cooperman. I don't think you're going to strong-arm me into saying something I'll later regret."

"You're right, I'm no threat at all. And I'm no blackmailer, just in case you've heard otherwise. Maybe I can find out what I want to know from available sources. If

you think about it, there are a few of them, aren't there?
You know that being an accessory to a crime, Doctor, is a
very serious business, not one that the Ontario College of
Physicians and Surgeons takes lightly. I'm pretty sure you
did a lot of thinking since last Friday night, Doctor. I think
your only chance is to cooperate completely with the
authorities." He thought for a minute about that, pulling at
his lower lip and then working away at some bird-lime on
the table with a pocket knife.

"You may of course be right, Mr Cooperman. But I think
you'll agree that you are not by any stretch of the imagination 'the authorities.'"

"Hey, I'm with you! Whatever you do cuts no advantage for me either way. If I get a little gold star in heaven,
I'll be surprised. What I'm saying is that if you have ever
thought of telling what you know, this is the moment to
take it to Sergeant Savas. What with the murders and so
on, I don't think that a little cover-up going back eighteen
months is going to shock him into a major crack-down.
He's got bigger fish to fry. That's all I'm saying. Don't
forget that the police investigation of Jack Dowden's accident saw what you told them to see. Whether by collusion
or pressure or what you might call a blindness to all but
the expected, the cops bungled it. I don't think they'll want
that to get spread around. No, actually, I think your
position's not so bad, if you tell them what you know
today. Later on, who knows. This case changes from day
to day. If one of the others comes forward, O'Mara or
Teddy Puisans or Luigi—you know—they may not need
your help. That moves you over to the side of the room
where Caine and the others are standing. That's not where
you want to be, I'm guessing."

Some of the dried bird-shit came in my direction. I took
that as a good sign. Let him take it out on me and then call
Savas. I can take a little bird-shit.

"You see, Mr Cooperman, I've got a lot to lose. And there's the question of friendship. Norm Caine's been a good friend to me. I owe him a lot."

"Yeah, that's the dilemma of ethics, right? Who do I dump on: my friend or my fellow citizens? It's a big question, I admit. What can you do about it, look for the greater good? If you tell all to Savas, maybe Caine gets sent up for faking an accident, or worse. If you keep quiet and you get caught, you lose your licence, this place—which, by the way is a very nice little property—and you could do some time, maybe not in jail, but getting involved in worthy community projects of which the judge approves. I won't kid you, Dr Carswell, I'm glad I don't have to make that decision."

"Shut up for a minute, I'm trying to think."

"Sorry. I always talk too much. I'm sure your wife and family will back you up and stick with you. They won't let you down."

"Confound it, man, you've got me in a cleft stick!"

"Me? Doc, I haven't got you at all. I walk out of this nice yard, that's the last you see of me. You're the guy you have to worry about. Do you have the guts to stand by your friend and dump on the rest of the community? That's the question."

"Can I talk to you about this?"

"Well . . ."

"It'll be a relief to see what you think."

"I can't promise you any kind of protection. I'm not making a deal with you, Doctor. You understand that?" He bobbed his head up and down. I watched a line of sweat move down his cheekbone and drop to the hood of his sweatsuit. "At the same time, I can tell you I'm not going to make a bee-line to Sergeant Savas's office. In these matters, I generally keep my own counsel except where it involves my client."

"I don't know where to start."

"You were supposed to have breakfast with Norman Caine. You arrived at around seven-thirty."

"That's right. We met like that once a week to talk over what was going on in the yard. I told you I was a trouble-shooter for them on questions of pollution?" I nodded and kept my mouth shut. "When I got there, I could tell I was early, because Norm's car wasn't there yet, so I went into his office. I carry my own key. That's where I got my first surprise."

"He was there, right?"

"Yes! He was very upset. He told me I had to bring my car to the door and get him off the lot without being seen. I didn't ask him what was going on. It was just one of those times when you know that questions will destroy. I did what I was told and drove him through the gate as fast as I could. Norm was on the floor of the back seat.

"When I got down the road, I stopped to let him climb in front, and he started to talk. I couldn't make anything out at first. Then I understood. There'd been an accident at another location . . ."

"At the fort?" His eyes opened slightly at the word, then he continued scraping the table.

"You know about that?" I nodded. "Then you'll under-stand why Norm had to *move* the accident to the yard. We never kept illegal substances in the yard overnight. It seemed a harmless enough deception, Cooperman. I just helped to get Norm out of the yard. He'd already planted the body under the truck."

"I get it. Caine drove Jack's truck back from the fort at seven-forty according to the dispatcher's log. Why did you go back to the yard?"

"I had to make sure that Norm's absence was noted and to be the first medical man on the scene. I'd hardly got out of the car when the fuss started. Then there were the police and the inquest."

"Webster, the dispatcher, what did he know?"

"Only what I told him: that there'd been an accident and that it would be better for all of us if there were witnesses."

"So you stayed around to assist the cops until around eleven."

"I telephoned around and finally located Norm at the City Yard. He came right over. I don't know how we got away with it for so long, I honestly don't."

"Caine never gave you the details, later on, I mean?"

"I couldn't bring myself to talk about it and he never tried to explain."

"I see. I see." I couldn't think of any more questions for the doctor, not then anyway. He was looking pretty ragged. I didn't want to put him through any further cross-examination just then, not with his wife looking on from the screened-in porch. I thought I'd better leave him the ability to continue raking up the leaves after I left. Carswell walked with me to the street without adding anything to what he had already told me. What he was interested in was how it was all going to come out. Would he be charged? I told him that frankness was his only card at the moment and wished him luck. He shook my hand in a serious and unnecessary way. I felt like a Cub Scout. I got to the curb and caught him just as he was turning:

"What do you hear about the old lady? How is she?"

"I was over there first thing this morning. It's hard to tell. They've tried to make her comfortable, but she's very upset. The shock of it all, I guess. The fact that she's lasted through the night's a good sign, but it's still touch and go. I'm surprised you're interested, Mr Cooperman."

"She seemed like a woman of spirit on Friday night. I'm sorry it's ended like this."

"Yes, the arrest of Ross was more than she could bear. Well . . ." He made a helpless gesture and I found a sad smile.

I walked to where I'd left the Olds and got in. By the time I drove by the house, Carswell's wife had arrived on the lawn and was talking earnestly to her husband.

Chapter Twenty-Seven

Monday came, and with it a keen sense that I had to talk to Norman Caine, who, I was guessing, packed his plans to wander the long, warm beaches of a special island, along with the big wedding cake, the long dresses and the flower girl. If he was still in town, he was probably at a hotel with his bride. In Grantham, there is only one hotel that beckons to special family events among the well-to-do: the Stephenson House, which is partly owned by a friend named Linda Kiriakis. I telephoned the front desk.

"Stephenson House. Good-morning."

"Good-morning. Is that you Stavros?"

"No, it's Renos. Who is speaking please?"

"Renos, it's Benny Cooperman. I was just checking up on the newly-weds. I hope that they haven't been bothered over the weekend." I was using a voice that pulses with concern and worry. I hadn't lost the gift.

"They've had a quiet time, Mr Cooperman. Nobody goes in. Nobody goes out. Like it should be with newly-weds, right? Your friend Bill Palmer from the paper wanted to know if they were staying here. I had my orders, so I told him they weren't expected. Stavros took up breakfast half an hour ago."

"Well, you might get some out-of-town papers now that the weekend's over. I hope you can manage the security."

"Don't worry, Mr Cooperman. Slowly, slowly, we are getting our security in apple-pie order. Okay, I gotta get the other phone."

"Just checking, Renos. I'll be talking to you. Goodbye."

I hated to do it, but I couldn't think of a shorter way. I drove over to the hotel, parked myself in the lobby and moved about from the coffee shop to the bar and back to the lobby again. It's what a private investigator does best: wait. I waited through the rest of the morning and into the afternoon.

I was doing a crossword puzzle in an out-of-town paper, when I caught sight of my quarry heading for the tobacconist like a man possessed. He bought four packs of my brand and a pack of menthols. He was learning about married life and had a way to go. I let him pocket his change and get a cigarette alight before walking over to him. It looked like his first smoke in some time.

"Mr Caine, congratulations on your marriage!"

"Oh," he said looking back to see who had recognized him behind a pair of sunglasses, "it's you. Thanks a lot. It's not what we'd planned, but it's just as legal. Nice running into you."

"It wasn't a coincidence, Mr Caine. I've been waiting for you. I think we'd better have a talk. Ross Forbes is in custody. I think we should talk before they let him out." Caine grinned at me, but it was without warmth.

"Why would I want to talk to you at all, Mister . . . Cooperman, isn't it?"

"I think you know my name. Let's try to be as honest as we can with one another, starting with the little things. Like Sherry knowing that Anna was going to be out of town and would miss being part of the wedding party. That must have put a crimp in her plans when she thought she'd have to get another maid of honour. But you'd just heard the news from someone who heard it from me: one of those hoods who picked O'Mara and me up at the

Harding House last Thursday night. I didn't want them bothering Anna, so I made that up. But they reported back to you. That's how I know you tried to— Hell, it was more than an attempt! You *did* effectively snatch both O'Mara and me and take us to Port Richmond. Were you planning to leave us at the bottom of the harbour?"

"Cooperman, I haven't got time for this. I've got to get back. I don't want to waste my breath answering these groundless complaints."

"Have it your way, Caine. I've already talked to some of the others. You may end up in the prisoner's dock alone, if the others are prepared to give evidence on the other side."

"You're bluffing!"

"Maybe I am, but you won't find out standing in the draught. I suggest we sit down someplace."

"I've got to get back." His eyes moved in the direction of the elevator.

"On Thursday you were willing to risk prison to talk to me. That's putting the most harmless construction on that episode. Now you haven't got ten minutes." I tried on a rather theatrical laugh and turned away.

"Look, Cooperman, I guess we can talk in the bar for a minute. I'll have to make a phonecall, that's all." He walked over to a house phone and picked it up. I backed away, leaving him lots of room for explanations. It took longer than I thought it would, then he was standing looking at me again. He still resembled a big teddy bear. He was very good at disguising his well-known ambition. "You still want to talk?" he asked. We both started making our way into the bar.

The bar at the Stephenson House on a slack Monday afternoon was not a hive of activity. The bartender was polishing glasses while conferring with the solitary waiter over the Friday stock closings in the business section of the *Globe and Mail*. There were no customers. As soon as we came in, the paper disappeared behind the bar and the waiter came smiling in our direction. Caine ordered a Campari and soda. The waiter nodded as though this was a normal drink instead of something almost unheard of in any of the other water holes in and around Grantham. The Stephenson House was an echo of the outside world in the centre of rye-and-water drinkers. Actually, I took mine with ginger ale, when I took it at all. By the time the waiter returned with our drinks, I was breathing the smoke of a Player's at the dark panelling of the wall, waiting for Caine to break the ice and knowing that he was waiting for me to do the same thing.

He looked sallow under a fine fuzz of neglect on his chin. He looked like a senior executive, junior grade, on a holiday. If he'd worn shorts, I wouldn't have been surprised. "Okay," he said, slightly more breathlessly than I was expecting, "let's talk." The word "talk" seemed to stab between the radar whorls emanating from both of us. He sat up straight in his chair, like I was going to strap him down and play electrician.

"You can assume for a start," I said, smoothly, I hoped, "that I know a good deal. That will save time."

"You're working for Dowden's widow. That's no secret any more." I let that fly over my head without comment. So what if he knows. If he was using this as ammunition against me, he didn't have much. He was bluffing at least as much as I was. I had to remember that. "I don't think you know as much as you let on, Mr Cooperman."

"I see you're a poker player. That's good. Let's start with Dowden's death. How much do I know there? I know you faked the accident. You got Carswell to help you get away once you put the body under the truck. Yes, I know he wasn't killed on the Kinross property. You took him there in his own truck. Hell, without even spreading the mess to Niagara-on-the-Lake, I can get you into a lot of trouble."

"You're not even a policeman, Cooperman. What is this, some kind of shakedown?"

"That would simplify things, wouldn't it? Just another palm held out regularly. The trouble is, I'm not in the blackmail business. And whether I do anything or not, you know you're in a lot of trouble. The Commander's death has pulled the tower you've been building down about your ears. Take the oil drums buried at the fort to begin with. We both know they don't contain oil. A couple of years ago you might have got away with it; now anybody who can read knows what PCBs and dioxins are."

"I think I can stonewall you, Cooperman. Anything you say against me goes double for Ross Forbes. He's got more to gain in this than I have. And he's the one they've arrested. Your friends downtown won't like having to let Ross go when you bring me in. And who says you can make your accusations stick?"

"What about Alex Pásztory? Are you going to claim that as a misdemeanour?"

"You can't touch me with Pásztory!" He said this loudly enough for me to form some hope that I might be able to move him with something else. He tried to distance himself from Pásztory, like Pásztory was the only dirty thing we were talking about. Why was this special? Why was he presenting the fact that he had nothing to do with Pásztory's death as the one clean thing in his life?

"Everybody knows there was bad blood between you ever since he began writing those articles in the paper last spring. It would have been very inconvenient for him to have passed on to the cops what he found at the fort. I think Pásztory's got a long reach, Caine."

"Sherry and I were watching a play at the Shaw Festival theatre that Thursday, Cooperman. I was seen by hundreds of people."

"You seem to know more about this than has appeared in the paper, Caine. As far as I know no time of death has been reported. Wouldn't it be funny if it turns out to be the exact time you were watching the play? But then you know, it's hard to establish the time of death as precisely as they do in books and on television. Your alibi may not have been worth the price of admission."

Caine realized that he'd fumbled now and his face was getting rosy with anger. That was good for me. An angry man is careless, and God knows I needed every scrap of carelessness I could find.

"What do you want, Cooperman? What's the bottom line for you?"

All of the questions in the back of my mind began coming out at once. To Caine, I must have looked like a hooked carp. I tried to organize myself, impose some order and chronology on the confused and cloudy past. First, I thought, I should get back to Dowden. It began with Dowden. Begin there.

"I want to know what happened to Dowden at the fort that morning."

"You don't want much, do you?"

"I think it will all come out anyway. If you tell me now, it won't look so bad on your record later on."

"You say that so smugly. Like we weren't talking about lives. My life, for instance!" I couldn't tell whether this was the cut-off point or a preamble to further confidences. I was betting heavily on the latter.

"Come on, let's get it over with. Dowden was killed at the fort. I've seen the dispatcher's log. I know that Carswell came and went *before* he arrived for your breakfast meeting. Earlier, Dowden came in and drove his truck to the fort. What happened at the fort?"

"You talked to Carswell?"

"Forget Carswell, damn it! He'll break in half if the cops raise their voices at him. He'll dump you if he has to save himself. You can depend on that. And don't forget O'Mara. The cops are watching his house, so you won't have another chance to reinforce his silence. Once O'Mara talks, you're cooked."

Caine's eyes moved around the room, looking for an answer that wasn't written on any of the empty tables. "The medical evidence, Norm. It never would stand up to a serious police investigation. Come on! I thought you were a realist. The game's over. There's no sense to the cover-up any more." Caine glanced up at me from the floor where his eyes had become fixed for the last few moments.

"Okay," he said. "It happened at the fort! But what does that prove? It was still an accident wherever it happened. It was just more convenient not to have the cops wandering around the fort just then. The tunnels had just been started, but it wouldn't take a smart cop long to see that it didn't have anything to do with the archaeological dig."

"There had to be more than that. Dowden was crushed in the chest area, that's not consistent with injuries received standing up or walking away from the truck. He was on his knees. Were you behind the wheel?"

"I'm not saying anything else about that. You're right as far as you went. I hope that makes you happy."

"You think I enjoy this, Mr Caine? I can think of lots of things I'd rather be doing. So, let's just try to get through this as painlessly as possible. Who else was out at the fort and saw the accident?"

"Just—nobody. Nobody saw it but me. So you'll have to take my word. I hope you don't think that's intended to be funny."

"It'll have to do for now; I can't prove you're lying. But I know you're covering up for somebody. If they lay a murder charge against you, Mr Caine, we'll see how loyal you're prepared to be. I suggest that it stops just this side of formal charge of murder."

"I say the police can make just as good a case against Ross. I already told you that."

"But with you, Caine, they get extras. They get Kinross. You're the chief executive officer. They'll say you made all the decisions about the planting and dumping of toxic waste. They'll be able to draw a line that leads from Dowden and his knowing too much to Norman Caine. They'll draw another line, this time running from Pásztory to Norman Caine. Dr Carswell told you I came to see him. That put you on your guard. After more than a year, Jack Dowden was coming back to haunt you. Then Carswell saw me talking to Alex Pásztory. That was breathing too close. I was lighting a match and looking down a gas-filled barrel and you were in there.

"O'Mara will talk, you know. We can get the other witnesses to come back to tell the truth. Carswell is scared. Unreliable."

"They only know about the yard. They can't talk about what happened at the fort. So where's your case?"

"The cops aren't greedy, Caine. If they can get you for intimidating witnesses, failing to report an accident, leaving the scene of an accident, giving false information. Oh, if they want, they can cut very deeply into the early years of your marriage."

"Christ, Cooperman! Shut up, damn you!"

"Sore spot, eh? Sorry. I was forgetting that you are on your honeymoon."

"Look, I'm an ambitious kind of guy, right? I want to get ahead. And I've damn well done it! I've got Kinross and the holding company right in the palm of my hand. I've got the votes I need to get on the board of directors and—"

"You're forgetting that the death of the Commander spoils those chances. At least you didn't have a reason for killing him. You're right there. The cops won't have too much trouble bringing Ross to court on the evidence they have already. And as for the business, do you think that the city will renew its contract with Kinross after all this?"

"Who else is there?"

"I'll bet the Environment Front people will have the answer to that one. And of course the city doesn't have to worry. All blame will be attached to Kinross. That's in the contract. So Paul Renner in the Sanitation Department can officially say you are beneath contempt, but never quite look you in the eye while saying it. Your bringing him into it won't help, because legally they're in the clear and the dioxins and PCBs are all on your head."

"You've really been through this, Cooperman. I apologize. You work for your money. It's not all bashing around in the petunias with my esteemed father-in-law."

"That's not an answer."

"Damn it all Cooperman, what do you want me to say? That Environment Front is doing a grand job? That we in business are grateful for their interest? That's all bull. I'm in business to stay in business. That's the bottom line for me. Those people are trying to put me out of work, put my whole payroll out on the street. And damn it, I'm not doing anything new! Everybody's doing what we are. So why am I the only villain? And as for the people who get so excited about a few buried drums of chemicals and go into orbit at the loss of the rain forests down in South America, tell them they're going to have to give up their plastic bags and spray cans and packaging. You'll see those bleeding hearts turn to stone! Oh, you can count on that."

"What about the kids you and Sherry plan to have? Don't they mean anything?"

"Come on, Cooperman! Join the real world! I want to give them the best that I can, and that means position and the money to keep it up. They'll be long gone before your beloved ozone layer disappears."

"So you're abandoning your grandchildren and their children? If you don't see them, they don't count. Is that it?"

"Look, Cooperman, we could go on like this, back and forth all day, and I still wouldn't be convinced. From my office, the world is a rough place. You show you're soft and you're gone by Thursday! Every fraction of a cent I can pare from expenses is not only legitimate but the difference between sinking or floating. If I clean up Kinross, the city will enter into a deal with Millgate-Falkner or one of the others. They don't care what we do with the rubbish; they don't want to know about it. Everybody has a bottom line. I didn't invent it."

"Why did you pick O'Mara and me up?"

"That wasn't exactly my idea. I've got partners."

"Partners? Oh, not with Kinross but with Sangallo Restorations?"

"Yeah. We didn't have much choice there."

"That would be my old friend, Anthony Horne Pritchett. Well, well. There aren't many pies he hasn't a finger in. What was it he had in mind?"

"He was just going to scare you. He has a boat in the harbour down at Port Richmond. I don't know. He said he wasn't going to do away with you in case your records showed that you were working on our street. That would be bad for both of us, Pritchett and me."

"So, if he was all that concerned about me and O'Mara, both potential witnesses in a case against you, why did he ice Pásztory, who could have given him just as much trouble?"

"How should I know? Do you think Pritchett phones me and keeps me informed? He's always been a monolith. There are no handholds on him. I pass that along for nothing."

"Yeah, I always found him lubricious in my dealings with him in the past." I was glad that I could work that word in. Maybe it was the rye giving me courage.

"The cops think that Pásztory was finished by a professional. What's your opinion?"

"Look, Cooperman, opinions are chicken-shit. They won't buy paper to wrap fish in."

"I haven't taken your little billet-doux to the cops yet. They might take it seriously," I said. He looked at his watch, like I was boring him. "Go placidly amid the noise and haste," I quoted. "Do you think they'll buy that as Pritchett's style, Mr Caine?"

"Shove it, Cooperman!"

"Doesn't sound like him, does it? I never did get the pronunciation of *Desiderata* right. My tongue keeps tripping over the Latin. Or is it Greek?"

"Okay, you've had your little joke. Now get off my back."

"Remarkable things they're doing with lasers these days in Toronto at the Forensic Centre. They can find fingerprints just about everywhere. There are a lot of tricks they can do with a bit of paper like the one we're talking about."

"Don't push too hard, Cooperman. I've already told you plenty. The note? You say it's a threat. I say it's calligraphy. You won't ride far on that whatever the forensic people say."

"Still no comment on Pásztory?"

"I'm expected upstairs. I can't waste any more time shooting the breeze with you." Were we running out of gas in our conversation or was he avoiding that particular question? My money was on the latter. The latter is always a good bet. That's why I'm still working for a living.

Norman Caine finished his Campari in a gulp, which didn't look right with that kind of drink, and then he was on his feet. "Before you go, Mr Caine, will you tell me this: Is there still a dimension in this I haven't discovered yet? I'm only asking."

"In a word, yes. Good-afternoon, Mr Cooperman." And he walked out of the bar towards the elevator and pushed the button.

Chapter Twenty-Eight

I walked out of the hotel trying to recall where I'd left the car. Parked in front of the door was a black limousine with its back door open and a heavy-set man sitting in the back seat. While I was wondering which local moneybags looked like a hood from a Warner Brothers gangster movie, a voice in my ear brought me back to earth:

"Mr Cooperman?" The voice belonged to a beanpole wearing a brown leather jerkin and cavalry twills. He was smiling like I was an old friend. I tried to place him as I admitted that I was indeed the man he was looking for. As soon as I said that, he caught me under the arm and scooped me into the car. It took less than a second, it seemed. He got in after me and no sooner was the door slammed shut than the car took off with a lurch. I hadn't seen the driver in the front seat.

"Hey! I don't want a ride!"

"Don't worry, it's not far," said the big fellow to my left. Somehow, that didn't assure me. The car had turned down Yates Street. It was still going at the speed limit or faster. I could feel my back pressing into the car seat.

"But I brought my car with me to the hotel! Let me out, I'll be right back." This seemed to strike them as funny, although nobody used it as a moment to crack wise at my expense. When I looked out the windows again, I was lost. I knew we were somewhere west of Ontario Street, but I couldn't say exactly where. "Look, you guys, I know your boss. I just got through talking to him. You better check with him about this." It was as if they were deaf, all three of them. I tried to gauge whether I'd be able to get over the beanpole's knees to reach the door. I'd have to wait for a traffic light. That was the trouble with a town this size; I couldn't remember a single light this side of Ontario Street. I kept thinking how stupid I'd been to walk out of the hotel without taking even simple precautions. I could have used the side door, or come out the back way through the kitchen. Damn it, give me a chance to replay the scene!

The car turned sharp left just as I could glimpse Montecello park under the trees. We were behind an apartment building, heading down a ramp with a metal door at the bottom. The driver pointed a black box at the windshield and the grey metal door began to slide open. Without altering its speed, the car moved smoothly under the opening door without scratching the roof. The car looped around the underground garage while the driver looked for a free space. That was a good sign; it seemed to mean parlay of some kind and not summary execution. The car came to a stop with the same lurch that it had started up with. I felt it in my neck.

"Okay, here we are," said the beanpole as he got out. I would have tried to run, but I could feel the breath of the big fellow on my neck. We had come to a stop beside an elevator door. The driver had already summoned the car by the time we caught up to him. The driver was a short man with blond hair and a full set of exploded blood vessels on the end of his nose. He was wrapped in a cheap raincoat that smelled mouldy when he stood beside me. The beanpole pressed the button marked "PH" and up we went. There was a chance that a stop at the main floor might save me; but we shot past it. Residents wouldn't be visiting back and forth, so I couldn't hope for a stop before we reached PH. When the car stopped and the doors opened, the shortish guy got out and pointed the way. The other two were right behind me. The leader rang the bell and we all waited. In about twenty seconds, the slowest third of a minute I've ever known, the door of the penthouse opened and pressure on my shoulder invited me to step in.

The man who opened the door had a sallowness that was almost green. He was wearing a dirty Irish sweater. "Glad you could come," he said, as though I didn't know about irony for God's sake.

"Okay," I said, shaking off my friends from the car, "this has gone far enough! I want to talk to whoever's in charge!" I was buttressed by the kind of anger that goes with the idea of selling your life as dearly as possible. I was going to make a lovely fuss before I was finished.

"That would be me," said a familiar voice. I looked up from the adam's apple of the green-faced acting-butler into the face of my friend and neighbour Frank Bushmill.

"Frank! What are you doing here?"

"Such as it is, Benny, this is my home. And you are right welcome."

"What? I don't get it." I was led, still confused, from the hall, relieved of my coat, into a large front room which was full of people talking and drinking. "What the hell's going on here?" I said to Frank as I recognized faces in the crowd. There was Bill Palmer from the *Beacon*. There were Anna and her picture-collecting father. Anna was sitting in a big overstuffed chair next to Eric Mailer, my friend from Secord, fresh from his herbarium and old newspapers. Pia Morley, a woman I once suspected of killing a few people, gave me a peck on the cheek. I repeated my question to her and was ignored. Talk continued uninterrupted. Glasses clinked and bottles were lifted. I wasn't even the guest of honour. Nobody even looked at me. In the middle of the room was an enlarged photograph of my friend Martin

Lyster. Then, of course, it hit me. How stupid of me not to guess. Like that writer fellow in *The Third Man* played by Joseph Cotton, I'd been kidnapped all right, but not to be bumped off. I'd been snatched so that I wouldn't miss the wake for poor Martin! I wasn't going to die after all. I wasn't going to have to take as many of them as I could with me.

"Here, Benny, take this glass. There's plonk enough in this room, but I've got some of the real stuff left in the kitchen."

In the movie, Joseph Cotton ended up on a platform facing a room full of earnest Austrian readers thirsty for fresh blood asking questions like: "And where would you put Mister James Joyce?" I felt my knees beginning to desert me for the kitchen where the real stuff was hidden. Frank was talking at me again.

"Let go of me, will you," meaning my grip on his arm that was spilling some of the real stuff on his broadloom. I couldn't get over it. The wake was for Martin. It wasn't my funeral. I emptied the glass in my hand without tasting anything. Frank looked on, marvelling. He'd never seen me drink anything so fast in all the years he'd known me. Including water.

"I didn't bring any snuff, Frank," I said, when I got my breath again. "What's a wake without snuff?"

"Ah, there's no lack of it, Benny. Rest assured. Wally Lamb has some, for one." I looked across the room now that I had a name to go with the familiar face. Lamb was a local painter. The room was full of semi-strangers. We'd all been pals of Martin's, but we hardly knew one another at all, unless those factors that tend to throw people together in a small town surfaced. For instance, I recognized a couple of professors from Secord. I didn't know their names. One was telling the other about a happy working sabbatical in Texas. When he finished, the other began telling a long story about interviewing the head of the Greek Orthodox Church at a dinner in Istanbul. A third learned head, this one with a red beard, moved into the group and began asking questions about movies on videotape.

I was going mad, of course. It was all in my imagination. Wasn't it? Wasn't I being taken for a ride by Tony Pritchett's boys? This couldn't be a real wake for Martin Lyster. Maybe I'd passed out. Maybe this was all I was going to get of my life passing before my eyes as I slowly bled to death in a ditch. It was the pressure of Anna's hand on my arm that brought me back to the world of acid rain, skinheads and unleaded gas.

"Are you all right?" she asked. "You look like you've had a shock."

"I'm fine," I said and she could read the lie on my face.

"Here, drink a little of this Irish whiskey. Frank has a private supply in the kitchen." She handed me the glass and I killed most of it. The three professors had stopped whirling around in my head. Now they were just three friends of the departed Martin and not figures from a personal allegory. I thought that perhaps I should sit down. It seemed like a good idea. But before I could move, a grey cat skipped between my legs and disappeared in the curtains. He was followed a second or two later by another, this time a greyish tabby with an orange nose. At the same time, a song was beginning in another part of the room. Bill Palmer was leading, with the painter Wally Lamb chiming in with his arm around Bill's shoulders.

> They say there's a troopship just leaving Bombay,
> Bound for Old Blighty shore,
> Heavily laden with time expired men . . .

"That's right," said Frank Bushmill, "let's give 'em a song! 'Bless 'em All'" Frank wasn't my idea of a sing-song kind of person, nor do I think he thought of himself that way, but here he was joining in with his own version of the lyrics. Even Jonah Abraham added his voice. I found a chair and sank into it, feeling a little more weight than I thought I was carrying. Was the drink getting to me? Couldn't be. Shock would have carried off the sting of twice what I'd had. Anna came over to me again. She was lovely as ever. She had a way of surprising me with sides of her that I'd never seen before. She was wearing a long pearly linen jacket over a skirt with a floral print. Under the jacket was a shirt that buttoned up the front, but she was only partly buttoned, as though it was a crime against nature to button the rest of the way.

"Any better?"

"Sitting works better than standing up. I took your drink, I guess. Is the real stuff in short supply?"

"Don't worry. I'll get us both one when you want it." She sat down on the arm of my chair and we watched the wake in progress for a few minutes without talking.

In the middle of the room a song had ended. Now Bill Palmer, who must have been among the earliest arrivals at Frank's apartment by the look and sound of him, began reciting a mock epic of some kind. With his right hand thrust into his jacket and with a Napoleonic intensity, he declaimed something like the following:

> I lost my arm at the Battle of the Marne,
> I lost my leg in the Navy,
> I lost my biscuit in the soup
> And I lost my spoon in the gravy!

The verse was so bad, they made him say it again, this time those close to him recited along with him, lengthening out the syllables *Nay-vee* and *gray-vee* with delight. They went through it a third time and we all joined in.

This time the last words in each line were exaggerated even more. The words *Nayyy-veee* and *grayyyy-veee* stuck in my head.

Pia Morley came over to us. She was holding a glass of soda water, by the look of it. She looked terrific in a simple dress that probably cost the earth in Toronto or New York. I asked her how she was after making appropriate introductions.

"Me? Hell, Benny, haven't you heard? I'm a momma. A real downright, up-all-night momma. And my kid's the baby from hell. He's six months old and chewing the paint off his windowsill. If he can't get into the New York Marathon in a few months, he's going to be very frustrated. You want pictures? I got pictures." She dipped into a large leather bag and pulled out several pictures of a baby with most of Pia's own features but the smile of his father, Sid Geller. I didn't have to ask about the paternity. I went through the pictures a second time, with Pia adding comments from the arm of the chair. The names of baby playthings filled the room. I heard Anna ask about Jolly-Jumpers and Kanga-rock-eroos. I felt the walls closing in on me and I wanted to get out of there.

Chapter Twenty-Nine

When I left the wake, it was nearly eight o'clock. Anna had gone with her father back to the house on the hill. Pia Morley had gone home to her husband and son. I walked back to the Stephenson House to pick up my car. It was a chilly night with the moon in its first quarter, scudding about the back-lit clouds like a picture in a Mother Goose book. I walked around the car once to make sure I couldn't see any wires attached to it that didn't belong there. I was getting jumpy and I didn't care if it showed.

I think we'd done well by Martin's memory. I think it was a party he would have enjoyed, snuff or no snuff. I had had rather too much to drink at the beginning, but I mellowed towards the end when everybody began telling his favourite Martin stories. Since many of my fellow wakers knew Martin through the book trade, a lot of the detail went over my head. What was "foxing," for instance? I asked Anna, who stayed close to me until she had to leave.

"You know those liver-spots that old books get, Benny?" She gave me a warm kiss goodbye, which Jonah, standing by, accepted as the lot of every father with a grown daughter. It goes with the territory, whether you're a millionaire or a pauper.

I turned off Ontario Street into Church, still thinking of the wake and Martin and the Blue Jays training camp down in Florida and losing my arm at the Battle o the Marne and losing my leg in the *Nay-vee*. I wa thinking of the cunning way Anna's shirt buttoned, when saw a familiar shape getting out of a car. I slowed th Olds to a walk. It was Fred McAuliffe from the office. I sli into the parking space behind him and turned off th ignition.

"Mr McAuliffe!" I called out, as soon as I'd achieved th sidewalk. Fred turned around and came slowly over t me. He was dressed with a little more care than I'd seer before. These were his best clothes I was willing to bet things he had been saving to wear at Sherry's wedding las Saturday.

"Why, hello, there, Mr Cooperman. Glad to see you. Ar you coming in?"

"'Coming in?' 'Coming in' where?" McAuliffe smiled a my apparently dumb question and looked over at the bi house on the corner.

"Why, to the Forbes's, I mean. Didn't you recognize th house?" I examined the scalloped tile shingles on th turret and the round porch and conservatory to one side all illuminated by a streetlight. "This is where they al grew up," McAuliffe said.

"Ah, right. I remember it from the picture of the Gran tham Hunt, now that you mention it. It looks a littl different at night and without the horses." Fred smile politely. "Don't tell me they are entertaining tonight? shouldn't have thought there'd be anybody home. Ross i in jail, Mrs Forbes is in the hospital and Sherry's on he honeymoon."

"You're forgetting the people from out of town. And o course you might not know yet that Mr Ross was release late this afternoon."

"They didn't have enough to lay a charge, I guess Enough to arrest him, but not enough to make it stick." nodded my head, recalling the conversation I'd had wit

Chris Savas. "Have you been summoned by the family, Mr McAuliffe?"

"Please, outside the office 'Fred' will do," he said. "In answer to your question, no. There was no general muster or call to assemble. Concerned friends pay calls at times like this. That's all."

"I don't think I qualify there," I said. "I hardly knew the Commander. I'd be wrong to intrude now."

"Nonsense, Benny—if I may call you Benny—I'm sure you'll be welcome. You did have lunch with Mr Ross quite recently, didn't you? I'm sure you'll be welcome."

"Well, if you think I won't stand out like a styrofoam cup with a silver tea service, I'd be happy to go in with you."

Together we walked up the walk and climbed the curved front steps, where the door swung open without our knocking.

"Good-evening, Mr McAuliffe" said the man on the other side. "It's good of you to come."

"Good-evening, Edward. This is Mr Cooperman who is working with me at the office."

"You are very welcome, Mr Cooperman. Most of the people are in the upstairs sitting-room, Mr McAuliffe. It's a little less formal than downstairs, don't you think?" We climbed the stairs. I counted the shining brass rods holding the carpet runner in place as it cascaded down the curving staircase. As we reached the top, the sound of voices could be heard. We made our way in dignified silence to the sitting-room.

While my introduction into Frank Bushmill's apartment and the wake for Martin Lyster had been unusual, it was still a million miles more relaxed than the sitting-room in the late Murdo Forbes's house. Both men and women, many of them middle-aged or older, were standing and sitting in the large, high-ceilinged room. While no one was formally dressed, the feeling was one of formality, and in spite of a fire in the grate, I felt an icy draught reaching for the small of my back. The most dominating feature in the room was the Commander himself glowering down at us from his portrait above the fireplace. His bulk and his presence had been captured by the painter. It was quite like him to dominate his own funeral assembly. It wasn't cheerful enough to be a wake. I didn't get the feeling that we were here to celebrate the life of the departed. I wasn't going to hear stories about good old Murdo. Nobody was going to sing "Bless 'em All" or recite memorable lines about losing my leg in the *Nay-vee*, even though there were a few present who could give an account of themselves at the Battle of the Marne, by the look of them.

"Let me get you something to drink, Benny," said McAuliffe. He moved away from me before I could open my mouth. At my side he was a bigger comfort to me than ten drinks. I searched the room for a familiar face. My first survey turned up nothing, but panning back to where I started, I did a little better. There was Dr Carswell with his wife talking to Harold Grier and his wife. Were the women sisters? I tried to remember. No. Grier was married to Carswell's sister. Carswell's wife must come from somewhere in the general population. That possibility raised my spirits marginally. Then I caught the eye of Ross Forbes, who was looking over the stooped shoulders of a voluble elderly man with his back to me. In that setting, Forbes was a friend and I grinned foolishly at him, and immediately regretted it. Two weeks ago Forbes was the man who'd bloodied my nose; today he was a familiar quarter in a mess of strange foreign money. As soon as he could free himself, he came across the room. I tried to read what I could from his face.

"I'm sorry for your trouble, Mr Forbes," I said as he shook my hand. "If you want me out of here, I'll understand."

"I can't blame this on you, Cooperman. No matter how much I might want to."

"I didn't think the police would hold you. I'm glad I was right," I said.

"I'm still their best bet. I have no illusions that it's all over. I've been warned not to stray from town. They're doing their best to put me away for good. Would you like a drink?"

"Frank McAuliffe's getting me one, thanks." Forbes wasn't holding a glass and I mentioned it.

"Circumstances are not helping me to stay away from the booze, Mr Cooperman. For instance, did you know that Teddie is engaged to that lawyer of hers? That was the big news when I got home."

"Tim Colling and Teddie?"

"Yes. They'll make a lovely couple. I picked a bad time to go on the wagon."

"You didn't try by yourself this time. I'm guessing, but it seems to me you're getting help."

"I suppose I won't be able to keep it a secret," he said. "Yes, I've gone underground, become anonymous. I'm Ross F., Cooperman. Funny, it's the last thing I told my father. I've been pretty shy about mentioning it. Everybody's ashamed of something." We traded more small talk and then he was off to refill a glass for a tall woman with shoulder-length grey hair.

"You've been talking to Mr Ross?" McAuliffe said, handing me a cocktail glass with a shot of rye in the bottom. We touched glasses and exchanged suitably sombre smiles. "How did he seem to you?"

"He's tough," I said, "tougher than I thought." Fred was watching Forbes move in and out of groups across the room. He seemed to approve. "Fred, I wonder if you remember hinting to me that there was more to the stories about Ross and the firm's involvement with toxic fuels than ever appeared in the newspapers. I wonder, now that the Commander is dead, whether you are any freer to talk about it?"

"It was wrong of me to have mentioned that at all." I steered Fred into a book-lined corner where we were not so conspicuous.

"Were you trying to say that it was the Commander who had acted improperly and not Ross? Was Ross covering up for his father and taking the blame on himself?"

"Oh, more than blame, Benny!" McAuliffe was looking up at the oil painting of the old man frowning down at his family and friends. "There have been formal charges. And more will be made when the present provincial inquiry is made public." McAuliffe shook his head. "The Commander was not keeping up with the changes in business, you know. He came from an old free-wheeling school where there were few rules and no supervision. Mr Ross tried to make him see that times had changed. But Murdo always knew better. He knew people in the federal cabinet, he had friends in the provincial government. He wined and dined judges and senators. He was used to having his own way."

"This came out in the book of minutes you removed from the boardroom?"

"Why yes, but I put it back later. It didn't seem right to alter history. I couldn't sleep until I put the pages back."

"You're an honest man, Fred."

"Yes. You know, I've been hearing that all my life. It haunts me. Well, it's too late to change now, I suppose. Too late to start dealing in old books and maps. I'd have liked to run a little second-hand bookstore. Isn't that funny? That's a little joke I've only shared with Miss Biddy."

"How is she?"

"I just left her. Not much change, I'm afraid. She can't talk or move. It's terrible. She was trying to will me to understand her moaning. It was very upsetting. The poor woman can't speak. What a horrible thing for a literate and sensitive woman."

"I hope she rallies, Fred. I know you're very fond of her."

"For more years than I care to remember," he said, turning away from me. I didn't try to follow him.

I looked up at the portrait, shifting my haunches so that highlight moved from the large disapproving face. Here was a face that might have been valanced with whiskers from the last century. Unsmiling, it judged all of us. Had the Commander ever known a moment's doubt? Only Biddy would know that and she was unlikely to tell us.

"Getting acquainted with the Commander, are you?" It was Ross again. Some of the tension of the times was showing on his face. What would the painter see there? Nothing to hang on a panelled wall above a fireplace.

"I was also looking at some of your books," I lied. "Your mother's collection?"

"About half, I'd say. The rest are mine. Does that surprise you?" he asked.

"I have a low opinion of businessmen, is that what you want me to say? To be honest I shouldn't have thought that books would mean a lot to a man like Norman Caine."

"Cooperman, book people aren't the doers and moulders any more. The game has moved on from books."

"To people like Caine? To the bottom-line people?"

"It's too late for books, Cooperman. They were a good idea, but they didn't work."

"I'm still working my way through the Russian writers, Mr Forbes, slowly. Maybe I'll never finish. I've got a friend who's always pointing me in the direction of new books. Seems to me there are a lot of questions and answers out there, if I don't lose my library card. Maybe your printout doesn't include all the available data. Maybe you need a reinterpretation. Maybe there's something going on that your computer isn't fast enough to catch?"

"Every year they keep coming out with a new generation of computer, Cooperman. In the end, they'll get it right."

"And in the meantime?" Forbes pulled the corner of his mouth higher. It could almost pass for a smile. Not one of his usual cynical inverted scowls, but an honest beginner's smile. Five out of ten.

"Mr Forbes, to change the subject if I may . . ."

"Be my guest."

"You told me a few minutes ago that you'd joined AA." The scowl was back. "You hinted as much the other day at lunch."

"So?"

"And you told the Commander in the sauna? Is that right?"

"Sure, I told him. So what?"

"This is important: Who else knew?" Forbes looked at me and then began to scan the faces in the sitting-room.

"There was no one else," he said at last. "I planned not to tell anyone. Then I mustered courage to tell Dad before the wedding. Thought it might make a difference. Things haven't been—"

"Never mind about that. Who else did you tell? Did your wife know? Or your old drinking pals?"

"I didn't tell anybody else. I'm sure."

"Why did you tell me, then? I'm nobody special to you. In fact we aren't even friends. You don't like me really. Why did you tell me?"

"I wasn't trying to build an alibi, if that's what you mean. I told Dad because he and it were on my mind. And you're the sort of ingratiating son of a bitch who gets people to say more than they mean to say."

"I wasn't asking about your boozing."

"Well," he was twisting his mouth again, "maybe I thought it might get back to Teddie through you. Hell, I don't know why I told you!"

"Who else knew you'd stopped drinking?"

"Damn it, Cooperman, I told you. Nobody except me, you and dad. Unless you count the people down at AA. But they don't talk about things like that to outsiders. Why is this so important? Am I going to get an answer?" He was doing his best to glower down at me like his father. By my guess it would take him another eighty years.

"Not right now, but you will. I promise." I left him standing in the alcove with the books and made myself free of the staircase and then the front door. Edward had my coat ready for me seconds before I hit the bottom step.

Chapter Thirty

After the upper-class wake on Church Street, I went back to the one still going on in Frank Bushmill's apartment. I felt a need to touch the earth. There were still enough people there to keep Martin Lyster's memory green. Bill Palmer from the *Beacon*, for instance, was still in good form. I was surprised to see Chris Savas sitting in a corner. I knew that he'd known Martin, but I didn't know he'd known him well. When I went over to where he was sitting, he explained:

"Martin got me the books I needed to get my stripes, Benny. A cop has to be educated these days and Martin got me through it."

After the drink ran out, Chris and I went looking for Anna up at her father's house on the escarpment. She was surprised to see us again, since she'd said good-night to me less than three hours earlier. Jonah Abraham, Anna's father, was both surprised and amused at our late visit and insisted on pouring a round of drinks and showing us a new painting by Wally Lamb he'd just purchased for his collection. "Old Wally hasn't lost his touch," I said, looking at a platter of beautifully rendered green apples.

Anna had changed from the linen jacket and flowered skirt to a sweater and dark green cords. When we finished our drinks, she kissed Jonah affectionately and the three of us got into my Olds.

"Anna, don't let these fellows keep you up all night," Jonah called from the front door. "Remember you've got school in the morning." The effect of this was to turn Anna into a thumb-sucking teenager as we drove out from under the *porte-cochère*. Jonah quickly went back into the house as we made for the highway.

It had been some time since I'd ended an evening at Lije Swift's place outside St David's on the road to Queenston. Savas had introduced me to it maybe ten years ago and I'd been back a few times, but not for the last year at least. Lije, which was short for Elijah, used to run a boat above Niagara Falls packed with illegal Canadian booze during Prohibition. He now owned a roadhouse that ignored all federal, provincial and local laws regarding strong drink and licensed hours. I don't know whether he paid off the authorities or whether they left him alone as a kind of living human monument to a colourful bygone age. Whatever the reason, Lije carefully screened his customers through a slot in the door before welcoming them out of the night. He was known as the provider of good food as well as teller of bootlegging tales from along the Niagara. Since the last time I was at Lije's place, his son and daughter had taken charge of the practical management, leaving Lije, who was getting on in years, free to bother the customers with his stories.

The place was about half-full. I recognized a few of our most distinguished citizens sitting at some of the tables, which Don and Maggy attended to. Lije insisted on looking after Chris, Anna and me, himself. He plied us with illicit drink while Savas went to make a phonecall. He never served booze in teapots. Lije was used to living dangerously. After the drinks he brought a large platter of hors d'oeuvres to the table. It was plain that this was going to be a memorable night. About twenty after twelve, Pete Staziak walked into the room. He'd just come off duty in town and had taken all of the short cuts to get there. More baked beet salad, tapénade and chorizo in cider were brought to the table. In Lije's short arms, the platter looked huge.

"You both missed the best part of the wake," Chris said, looking at Anna and me, after Pete had settled in. "Frank Bushmill recited a very funny piece about sucking-stones. You should have heard it."

"That's right, Chris, rub it in," Pete said, chewing on a piece of celery filled with Stilton. "Remember I had to miss the whole show trying to make sense of a couple of murders."

"I had a few questions to ask Ross Forbes," I said, "so I visited the wake going on up at his house."

"Bet nobody sat on the floor there," Anna said.

"I got a few important answers, though."

"When do you think you'll begin to see the light, Benny?" Chris asked. "Before or after the provincial inquiry into toxic dumping and tainted fuels nails your friend Ross Forbes to a permanent address in a minimum security institution?"

"I'm beginning to see light, Chris. A glimmer. Maybe more. Nothing that would do any of us any good in court, but I don't think this case is going in that direction?"

"What kind of murder case doesn't go to court, Benny?"

"The unsolved ones," Anna suggested.

"Political ones?" said Pete, answering his own question.

At that moment, Lije was back with a great silver platter with roast duck on it along with a rosy garnish of red cabbage. Chris began to carve and we passed our plates to his end of the table. Anna helped him by dishing out the vegetables. I added gravy. Pete just sat there with his knife and fork already in hand. When we had all been served and Chris had added his comments to the rest of the ones we larded on Lije about the food, we settled down to serious eating. I discovered that I was hungrier than I'd felt; I even ate the slices of orange that had bedizened the golden roast duck. For a full twenty minutes we made table talk and laughed at Pete's jokes. These weren't all that funny, but the wine helped. There's hardly a joke that wine doesn't make better. Then Chris looked across at me and asked:

"Are you serious about talking about this thing, Benny?"

"Chris, it's not talk yet, just thinking out loud."

"We'll buy it," Pete said.

"At least we'll listen," said Anna, who hadn't had as much to drink as Pete.

"I can't believe that you think you've done it again," said Chris, chomping on a wing.

"If you've done it, you took a lot longer than in the other cases we worked on. You used to wrap these things up in under a week. Maybe you're losing your touch?" Pete was digging more stuffing from the bird's cavity and carrying it to his twice-emptied plate. He looked from one face to another to find agreement. Figuratively, I kept my mouth shut, while I went on eating. There would be time to talk when coffee came.

Then it came and they were all sitting back looking at me. Three or four herds of angels flew by and they were still looking at me.

"Honestly, I'm stuck. I don't know where to start." I took a sip of Lije's famous coffee to see if I could find inspiration there. When I came up for air, things were still in a tangle in my head. "Let me try to sort through this," I said. I took a deep breath and started in. "We know that Kinross Disposals has been getting rid of toxic wastes for industry in and around Grantham. It has also been doing the same service on a contract from the city. Last spring, Alex Pásztory nearly blew the lid off part of their operation when he wrote those pieces in the *Beacon* that were also printed in the *Globe*. That was the tainted-fuel selling and tax-evasion aspect of the much bigger story that has come to light at Fort Mississauga. Here at the fort, they are dumping terrible things directly into the lake and they are burying drums of other nasty stuff under the earthworks of the old fort.

"Now, Kinross isn't alone in this. Sangallo is in charge of the restoration work at the fort. They have also buried a few tons of poisonous garbage under a floral clock on the Niagara Parkway. Both of these companies have cooperated in this illegal activity. The responsibility for this rests with Harold Grier and Norman Caine, the CEOs of the two companies. In the background, Sangallo has Anthony Horne Pritchett and his mob lurking and giving professional advice. But remember, for Pritchett, Sangallo is a way to clean up his dirty money. He's not interested in turning it into another of his rackets."

"How's that?" asked Pete.

"As a semi-legal business, Sangallo has its uses for Pritchett. He doesn't want it to become another of the string of shady clubs, tourist towers, gambling rooms and other vice-related games he controls in the Falls. The cleaner Sangallo stays, the happier Pritchett counts his money. That's why I couldn't get past your conviction, Pete, that Pásztory had been taken out by a pro. Pritchett's the closest professional, and I could never make it dance in time."

Chris and Pete both turned towards the other. Chris spoke first. "Benny, we just found out this morning that the slug that killed Pásztory was fired from the gun that killed the Commander."

"Yeah, it kinda smothered my theory, eh?"

"Well, it makes me feel better about what I was going to say," I said, feeling like the last pieces were fitting together.

"Benny, you took us over a lot of this ground before. We know about Kinross, but have never been able to make a charge stick. They've got a bunch of lawyers working right around the clock. They make it hard."

"Working around the floral clock. Can't you see it?" Pete said looking rather rosy and sinking down in his chair.

"We've got three deaths to deal with: Jack Dowden's, well over a year ago—remember we talked about him at the Di?—Alex Pásztory's a week ago last Thursday and the Commander's last Friday night. Let's look at them in reverse order. Chris, you think that Ross Forbes killed his old man. And you've got some solid reasons: He was at the club, saw and talked to his father, admits they talked in the sauna. He and the senior Forbes had long been at one another's throats. No love lost, right? This feud was particularly bitter right now because the old man threatened to oust Ross from his CEO position at Phidias at the scheduled board meeting on Monday—that's right, it would have been today. With Caine married to Sherry Forbes, the Commander could argue that Caine was the new blood the firm needed. So, Ross is your favourite suspect. He looks like the guilty man."

"Benny, on TV and in the movies the suspect that looks guilty is always innocent. But in real life, the guy holding the smoking gun is usually the guy who fired it. Please, save us from some elaborate scheme designed to incriminate Ross Forbes."

"Yeah, Forbes looks guilty because he is," Staziak added, just in case I'd missed the thread of Chris's argument. Soon he had returned to working on his back teeth with a toothpick. He was a little hard to hear.

"Chris, I'm not saying there *wasn't* premeditation, but I don't think it was of the elaborate variety. And speaking of smoking guns, I forgot to say that the gun that killed Murdo Forbes came from the family collection and Ross had access to it. Does that cover your arguments, Chris?" Savas nodded slowly over the rim of his coffee.

"Well, Chris, I was in the club that afternoon. So was Harold Grier, his brother-in-law, so were my father and a couple of dozen others. When the wedding rehearsal started, just about everybody in town who was related to or knew the Commander was within striking distance of the sauna. Okay? So, let's eliminate opportunity. With the time of death so vague, we've got an army of people who could have done the old boy in."

"You can cross the females off your list of suspects, Benny. The Commander was killed on the men's side. The murderer had to pass the man handing out the towels, robes and whatnot. That cuts out half your suspects. They wouldn't be able to pass the physical." Chris smiled and Pete laughed out loud. Anna gave me her consciousness-raised eyebrow as I waited, feeling a little school-teacher-ish, for quiet.

"Let's look more closely at Ross's motive. He wanted a second chance to make good as CEO at Phidias. (Everybody says that his first try lacked energy and bite.) He wanted to see Caine penned in at Kinross and to keep out of his way at the City Centre. I saw a bit of this when Caine tried to have me thrown out of Phidias and Forbes protected me. He needed to win all the battles he could with Caine. He knew that he couldn't stop Caine marrying Sherry. How could killing the old man stop the wedding? It couldn't. It could only slow things up at best. Not worth a human life, wouldn't you say?

"What do we know about the confrontation in the sauna? No physical signs of a struggle. According to Ross they just talked. He told his father that he'd just joined Alcoholics Anonymous."

"*Ross Forbes* in AA?" Anna said. "I don't believe it! It's like saying your father's given up gin rummy and your mother's sold her precious television set."

"Nevertheless, that's what he told Murdo Forbes. Ross also told me that besides his father, I was the only other person—apart from fellow AA members—who knew about it." Eyebrows across the table were raised at the news. The two cops knew it wasn't proof of anything, but it was a good story.

"Now, suppose someone did have that information. Suppose there was somebody who knew Ross had given up the bottle. That would mean, at the very least, that that person spoke to the Commander *after* Ross left his father in the sauna. Such a person would replace Ross as our leading suspect. Right?"

"Keep talking. Sounds reasonable. Since the Commander never left the sauna alive, then we know the murderer had to get the information right there in the men's sauna. Who was he?"

"Well, Chris, first of all I have to attack your assumption that the murderer has to be male."

"What is this, quibble time? Of course he has to be male!"

"Chris, you were right when you said that a woman couldn't get into the men's locker room because she couldn't get past the guard who checked on everybody going in and out. If she did manage to get by him, she'd cause a major sensation when she went through the changing-room and showers." Here, as I might have guessed, Pete smiled again and Anna refused to encourage him. She bit down hard on a green onion for his benefit and glanced back at me. I went back to my narrative to see how it would come out.

"No, a woman couldn't get into the sauna in the usual way, but she could if she came from the pool."

"What?" They had all stopped playing with their coffee spoons and wine glasses.

"The sauna's just inside the door from the pool."

"Now hold on! You're saying—"

"Wearing a robe and a bathing-cap, and maybe goggles, a woman might just slip through the door without raising a fuss. The lifeguard isn't particularly watching the comings and goings from the pool area. I understand that the women's changing-area is a mirror-image of the men's side. So, if she knew where the women's sauna was located, she could have hatched a plan to kill Murdo Forbes in the men's."

"Benny, a woman can't just walk into the men's sauna," Pete said with finality. This was a crack that was going to break up his idea of the universe.

"Pete, the afternoon Ross took me to lunch, we looked into the pool. He pointed out his parents and it took me a few moments to recognize Murdo from the other swimmers. I never did pick out Biddy. Remember that these are serious long-distance swimmers. They wear identical goggles and bathing caps. In that rig and wearing one of those blue terry-cloth robes, there's no particular visible difference between the sexes."

"Two things," Chris said holding up an appropriate number of fingers. "One, you are still talking premeditation, right?"

"Sure. You don't carry a gun into the pool without some plan to use it."

"Two, I think I know where you are heading, Benny, and I won't buy it for a minute!"

"She had access to the Commander's gun collection."

"You're saying that the old lady killed her own husband! That's crazy! She's not even in the picture, Benny. Why are you pulling our legs?"

"Damn it, Chris! I don't like this any more than you do! Just hear me out, okay? Of course she loved Murdo; of course she didn't want to kill him; of course she isn't our usual idea of a murderer; but, she was a woman at the end of her tether. Murdo was about to cut Ross out of the family business. She knew that on Monday morning, when the board met, Caine would oust Ross with the Commander's blessing. I'm sure she tried to move the old man to a less drastic course of action and failed. You say she was a good wife, I say she was also a good mother, according to her lights. That's why she took that last desperate step to ensure that Ross would get his second chance to make good in the business. There's something else and I'll come to that in a minute."

"You think that Mrs Forbes could have managed all that, Benny?" Pete asked. "A nice old lady like that?"

"Remember, Pete, that Biddy's a tall and rather stringy woman. I'm not saying that Anna, here, could get away with it."

"Is that a compliment or a slam?" Anna said. "That's all I want to know."

"How did she know that Murdo would be alone in the sauna?" Chris asked.

"Murdo's cigars. He smoked everywhere, even in the sauna. The men in the locker room gave him a wide berth. He ignored all of the NO SMOKING signs, with a certain evil glee, I suspect."

"So, she knew what she was doing all along. A very cool villain."

"Until you began to suspect Ross, Chris. She hadn't figured on that. That spoiled everything. You arrested the very person she'd set out to protect. And now, he wasn't just out of a job, he was facing a trial and prison. No wonder she had a stroke. She planned a tidy swift kill and executed it perfectly. Then you spoiled things by locking up her son. I'll bet, if she hadn't been felled by the stroke, that she would have come forward and told you everything. When I saw a friend of hers earlier, he said that in the hospital she was desperately trying to tell him something. She's frustrated and unhappy because of the way she's left things. And she can't do anything about it."

"Well, I'll be damned!" said Chris.

"Me too," added Anna and Pete in unison. After a minute Anna turned to glare at me. "Benny, why does it have to be Biddy? I'm still sceptical. I mean, it sounds like a good story, but what makes it more than a story? What makes you so sure?"

"It has to be Biddy, Anna, because she knew that Ross was on the wagon. She knew he was in AA. She could only have learned that from Murdo just before she shot him."

"You mean to say that they had a little family talk before she pulled the gun?"

"No, I'm suggesting that as soon as he saw her, the Commander announced his son's latest idiocy triumphantly. He always took pleasure in Ross's failings and here was another, from his point of view, that topped most of them. The old man had resented Ross trying to clean up the mess he'd made of the business these last few years. He was angry at Ross's shouldering the blame for a lot of illegal things he'd been doing. To him that was the way business should be carried on. It was the way everybody did it not so long ago. Ross's attempt to take the blame lined him up with the enemy in the old man's eyes. The last thing he wanted from his son was to be interfered with. To the Commander, it looked like he was being undermined by everybody, Ross included. This stuff will come out when the provincial inquiry is published."

"I'll still be damned, but it does sound like the Commander," Anna said. Both Chris and Pete nodded slowly in agreement. I called out to see if Lije could find us more coffee.

Chapter Thirty-One

We were now sipping liqueurs and *cappuccinos* in an empty dining-room. I hadn't noticed when the other customers had left. We'd been sitting in a cloud of our own smoke for so long that the rest of the room vanished into a blur. Maybe it was the wine and the food. Anyway, Lije Swift didn't look like he was anxious to start putting the chairs on the tables, so we relaxed and kept on talking. And least some of us kept on talking.

"Benny, you said that Biddy had another reason for killing her husband besides Ross. What was it and was it less—what shall I say?—noble than her other motive?"

"You tell me, Anna, when I've finished."

"It'll be light soon, Benny. Maybe you can skip the side-issues, just hew straight to the meat."

"I'll try, I'll try. Let's see. Pásztory was shot with the same piece that killed the Commander. In fact the gun came from his own collection. Our premier suspect, then, has to be Biddy Forbes, since we have her on the other killing. But when I look at it, it just doesn't make sense. Biddy was interested in Ross's future with Phidias, but not really concerned about the daily workings of any of the companies. Maybe she was in the past; I'm talking about right now. I don't think she cared much one way or the other, just as long as there was a place for Ross at the top.

"Pete, you thought that Pásztory was killed by professionals, by out-of-towners brought in for the job, a typical

contract hit. Well, I told you I don't buy any serious
involvement by Pritchett. He wanted Sangallo, where he
was a silent partner, to stay as honest as an illegal toxic
dumper can. He left the tough stuff to Harold Grier and
Norman Caine. They could play as rough as the game
required. If the mob did a job on Pásztory, you wouldn't
have found him at the fort. He would have been dumped
on the railway tracks somewhere, or pushed over Niagara
Falls. Leaving him at the fort was a rash, dumb idea. It
meant if we found the toxic dump, we found Pásztory; if
we found Pásztory, we found the dump as a bonus.

"I told you before about Jack Dowden's death and how I
think it happened at the fort and not at the Kinross yard.
Since we talked, I've got more backing for this. Both Caine
and Carswell were part of a cover-up. They moved the site
of Jack's death to the yard and manufactured the required
witnesses. Brian O'Mara will tell the truth about what he
saw now. And I suspect that if you compare the dirt on the
back of Dowden's work clothes you'll find that it matches
the parging or pargeting on the wall of the fort."

"Parging? Pargeting? Cooperman, where do you get
pargeting?" Savas was always questioning my words. If
he'd never heard a word, he doubted that I had. It was
grossly unfair. I looked at him leaning back lubriciously in
his chair while I explained what pargeting was. I repeated
what McAuliffe told me, making the gestures he'd made
with his pipe with my unlit cigarette. Then I told them
what Dr Roppa had told me in Toronto about how his
archaeological dig was quite separate from what Sangallo
was doing at the fort.

"So, do you think the same person killed both Dowden
and Pásztory?" Anna asked, leaning into the table and
hunching her shoulders.

"Yes, I do."

"Okay, Benny, pargeting aside, who killed Dowden and
Pásztory?"

"Yeah," echoed Pete, "enough with the suspense already."

"Don't be condescending, Sergeant," said Anna. "But I'm sure we are all dying to know."

"When I had my one and only talk with Alex Pásztory, he told me, just before he spotted Dr Carswell sitting near us, that he was off to meet with the AV. I was certain he meant the AV at Kinross."

"The AV? What's that? I've never heard of an AV."

"Well, when he said it I was sure it must be one of those business terms like CEO and GNP and CIO. You know, an acronym well known by people in the business. So, I didn't say anything at the time, but I looked it up in my dictionary later. I couldn't figure out what connection any of this had with the Authorized Version. I had to admit that AV was a dead end. Then, earlier tonight, I heard some friends reciting an old rhyme. I don't know where it came from, but listening to it I heard the word 'navy' as 'AV.' That put me on track again. Maybe Pásztory didn't say that he was going to meet with the AV. Maybe he said he was going to meet with the *navy*."

"The navy?" said Anna. "He must have meant the Commander. He was a hero in the RCN during the Second World War! But, I don't get it."

"Neither did I at first. Why would Pásztory be getting in touch with the Commander? Murdo Forbes certainly knew who Alex was after those articles he wrote in the paper last spring. Murdo was still chairman of the board at Phidias. Maybe Pásztory wanted to confront the man at the top. We now know that Ross had been doing his best to cover up for the Commander's part in the illegal dirty work going on at Sangallo and Kinross. Maybe Pásztory believed that Ross was the chief villain, the Forbes with the toxins on his conscience. Pásztory could have tried to show Murdo what was going on behind his back while he and Biddy were away in Fort Lauderdale."

"Wasn't the Commander out of town when Pásztory died?"

"He'd just got back but was keeping a low profile, until the arrival of guests for the wedding made it impossible to stay in hiding. He and Biddy had been living at the club since their return from the south."

"Benny, you're not saying that Murdo Forbes killed Jack Dowden and Alex Pásztory, are you? That would be too ironic!" Anna was looking at me earnestly. Her cheeks were quite flushed with the excitement of what she was participating in. I had to break the connection and focus on some neutral object, Pete Staziak, who repeated the jist of Anna's question.

"Well, all I can tell you is this: Dr Roppa, the archaeologist told me that he met the Commander at the fort on the morning that Jack died. We know that Caine was covering up for somebody. What better candidate than the man who had been lobbying the board to take him on? Caine was the fair-haired boy in the Commander's eyes, and the Commander was Caine's best hope for a foot on the ladder to success. Is it taking a big leap to say that Caine would look out for the Commander? In the case of Dowden, Caine only had to move the body to a new and potentially less threatening location and to arrange for witnesses. It was the second death that involved the hiding of a body."

"Can you place the Commander anywhere near the fort on the day Pásztory was killed?" Chris asked.

"The people running a Bed and Breakfast in Niagara-on-the-Lake say a Bentley that matches the description of the Commander's car was parked in front of their place on the afternoon Pásztory was murdered."

"Where exactly is that?"

"Four short blocks away from the fort. I'll give you the names."

"Wouldn't there have been a lot of drivers and working

men on the site at the time of both killings, Benny," asked Staziak.

"Dowden was killed very early in the morning. If it was witnessed only by Caine, I'd call that luck, dumb luck. The second killing took place at a time arranged by the Commander, who knew where and when they wouldn't be disturbed. He was getting more calculating, becoming better at it."

Savas took a deep breath and finished the cognac in his glass. "It's not a suit of nettles, Benny. You haven't really wrapped up the Commander in his guilt. What else do you have?"

"Pásztory was shot with the Commander's own gun. We knew that but weren't taking it into account since the Commander's dead too. And that brings me, Anna, to the other reason for Biddy shooting her husband. He was getting out of hand. He had always been a businessman of the old school, more a robber baron than an enlightened bureaucrat. Dowden got in the way, so he knocked him to his knees and rammed his own truck into him. Pásztory threatened to blow the lid off everything, so he was given a short, sharp shot right in the heart. Not just a lucky shot, Pete," I said facing Staziak. "Remember the Commander had military training. So had Biddy, now that I think of it."

For a few moments we just sat looking from one face to another. There didn't seem to be anything more to say. The cognac was gone from Savas's glass, so I gave him some of mine. I put down the cigarette I'd been waving around unlit for the last hour. The ashtray nearest me was almost empty.

"This isn't very satisfying, Benny. Who gets the handcuffs? Biddy Forbes? I don't think that's likely."

"Chris, I'll let you dance around that question. It goes beyond the scope of my jurisdiction."

"Hell, Benny," Pete reminded me, "you don't have any jurisdiction!"

"I feel sorry for Biddy Forbes," Anna said.

"She was in a tight corner."

"Still. They'd been married for nearly fifty years."

Savas turned to Anna, grinning. "That's a better argument for it than Benny gave!" he said, jerking his thumb in my direction.

"There's just one more thing: how did you know that Dowden was killed at the fort and not in the Kinross yard?"

"It's a question of pods and seeds, Pete. Are you familiar with a plant called Dame's Rocket, also known as *Hesperis matronalis*?" And that's when they started clobbering me. All three of them.

Chapter Thirty-Two

I t was nearly noon when I climbed out of bed. The first thing I noticed was the stale smell of dead cigarettes. I was growing sensitive to the state of my health. My infatuation with smoke was fading. I was going to have to face it, but I put it off until I could look at myself with clean teeth and a shaved face.

After a leisurely breakfast at the Di, I drove over Western Hill and parked outside Irma Dowden's little house. Behind one of the houses of a neighbour, somebody was burning leaves, which was against the law but smelled nice in the wind.

Ralph, the dog, met me at the front door. He hadn't grown any friendlier since our first meeting just two weeks ago. Irma's small face appeared a few feet above the dog's.

"Oh, it's you, is it. I was wondering when I'd hear from you. Get down, Ralph! Let him be! You better come in, Mr Cooperman, I mean—what was it—Benny?"

"That'll do nicely," I said, making my way once again into the simple living-room with the picture of Jack and his Freightliner on the mantlepiece. We both sat down, before Irma jumped up and headed to the kitchen. Again she offered either tea or coffee. She was still bluffing about the coffee, I think, but I'll never know, since I opted for tea. After talking with our voices shouting from kitchen to living-room through the empty dining-room, I decided to join Irma at the back of the house. Soon we were sitting at the antique green table drinking tea. I told her what I'd found out and what had happened since I'd seen her last. When I finally finished giving her the short version, she looked into her cup sadly.

"You've done a lot of work in two weeks, Benny, and I know I should be thankful. I am in a way. But, in another, it still won't bring him back, will it?"

"Would it have been better if there was somebody going to jail?" She shook her head.

"I don't think so. I was never out for blood, you know. I was never out to get people. It was just that damn company, Kinross. I was thinking that Kinross was different than people, but it turns out that it's this fellow Caine and all those others."

"I guess it doesn't help when the murderer is a stroke victim in her upper seventies."

"I might go see her in the hospital. She must feel terrible not being able to communicate and all. I'm not doing anything this afternoon. I could just drop in for a few minutes around three o'clock." She caught me smiling. "What's the matter with that?" she asked.

"I was just thinking that three o'clock was the time of your appointment to see me back at the beginning of the month. You were ready to take on the world that afternoon. You'd already been to other investigators. Now, it looks like a provincial inquiry, which was already underway when you came to see me, will put an end to the way Kinross and the other companies have been ignoring the law. Maybe we'll get better laws after this. We need them."

"I hope so, I hope so, but it still won't do me any good. I'm not getting the lift, Benny, that I hoped you'd provide. All I can think of is those poor people and that terrible, mad old man."

"That's why Biddy killed him."

"She put a stop to him, that's what she did. Funny the law can't touch her for it, isn't it?"

"It wouldn't enhance the image of the law. It would bring it into disrespect, detract from its majesty and authority. And we can't have that, now can we?"

"Well, I guess it's all too late now anyway. It's all dead and buried. Would you like to have another cup of tea?"

"Why not?"

Howard Engel

THE RANSOM GAME

Benny Cooperman is slowly going crazy. It's winter in Grantham, Ontario, and he has nothing better to do than watch the frost creeping in under his door. Nothing, that is, until stunning Muriel Falkirk, girlfriend of Johnny Rosa, the key conspirator in the kidnapping of a beautiful heiress, enters his office.

It's been ten years since the sensational kidnapping, and Johnny's served his time. But now he's skipped parole—or been murdered—and Muriel wants to know where he is. A lot of other people do too, most of them interested in the unrecovered half-million-dollar ransom. Benny joins *The Ransom Game*, in this witty and intriguing thriller, only to discover that nobody plays by the rules.

"Engel has come up with a labyrinthine plot that will satisfy even Ross Macdonald fans."
Publishers Weekly

Howard Engel

A CITY CALLED JULY

There are all kinds of propositions you can't refuse. For gumshoe Benny Cooperman it's being asked by the Rabbi and the President of Grantham's synagogue to try to find a missing lawyer who has absconded with the life savings of half of the Jewish community. Benny knows he'll never see a dime out of it, but what can you do? It's summer in the city—and it's going to be a hot one.

"Engel has achieved the top echelons of mystery fiction. Benny's growing experience as a detective can get you hooked on the series."

Saturday Night

"Engel has an entertainingly strong sense of where he stands in the traditions of detective fiction. Cooperman may soon be as well-known as [Holmes and Marlowe]. On this showing, he deserves to be."

Kingston Whig-Standard

"In the American private-eye genre, the Canadian investigator Benny Cooperman has been creating a ripple or two since his first appearance . . . *A City Called July* is a nice piece of detective work."

New York Times Book Review

"Engel is a careful craftsman of plots and *A City Called July* sparkles with fresh turns, false leads, murders and trenchant observations of life along Lake Ontario."

Hamilton Spectator

Howard Engel

A VICTIM MUST BE FOUND

In his sixth important case, Grantham's own Benny Cooperman finds himself mixed up in the art world. More out of water a fish can't get. After all, Benny only heard of Picasso last year and now he's hot on the trail of some missing paintings by Wallace Lamb—a trail that leads him to the people who buy, trade and sometimes steal pictures in the bosom of Grantham's elite. The sleuth soon learns that art can lead to murder—Benny's own client is found dead and the shoes peeking under the curtains at the scene of the crime belong to Benny!

"Benny is as scruffily charming as ever . . . A delightful, original creation."

The Gazette (Montreal)

"Another winner. . . ."

Publisher's Weekly

"The Engel/Cooperman wit remains in top form, the characters continue to be interestingly odd and well drawn and the convoluted plot is worth puzzling out."

Sun (Vancouver)

"First-class entertainment, stylishly written, the work of an original, distinctive, and distinctively Canadian talent."

Julian Symons

"One of the best of the series."

The Globe and Mail